It's PAMELA Rigby Actually

CJ Morrow

Tamarillas Press

Cover image: ©Mohammed Hassan, Pixabay.com
Cover design: © CJ Morrow

ISBN: 978-1-913807-00-9

For my husband...

Other books by CJ MORROW

Romantic Comedy:
Sooo Not Looking For a Man
We Can work it Out
Little Mishaps and Big Surprises
Mermaid Hair and I Don't Care
Blame it on the Onesie
A Onesie is not just for Christmas

Psychological Thriller:
Never Leaves Me

Fantasy:
The Finder
The Illusionist
The Sister

One

'Pamela Rigby to checkout number four, please. Pamela Rigby, checkout four.' There's an irritated urgency in the voice that annoys me.

As I wipe the earth from my hands before beginning the march to the checkouts, I wonder what it is this time.

'Pamela, over here,' Derek calls as I arrive. Derek always sits on checkout number four; he insists on it. He's been at Jolliffe's Garden Centre for most of the twenty years I have and you'd think there'd be a level of camaraderie between us, instead there is antipathy.

'Yes?' I reply to Derek at the same time nodding and smiling at the customer waiting patiently at the till, the same customer I have just spent ten minutes with, helping him choose a nice potted arrangement for his mother's birthday. It had to be something simple and easy to look after, requiring little more than watering as she's in a care home and no one has time for anything which requires elaborate care. I'd stuffed an extra primula in it for him, one I'd saved from the compost pile.

'This pot has an extra plant in it,' Derek says making a whistling sound on the last word. 'Customer says you did it but you haven't repriced it.' He gives me his look, his special "now sort that out" look.

'It's fine, there's no extra charge.' I smile at the customer, a man near my own age. We'd had a nice chat, he'd told me about his mother, how they're struggling with her advancing dementia and depression. She used to love gardening, he said, and he hoped the plants might cheer her up.

'Yes, but it's got an extra plant.' Derek narrows his eyes at me. He cannot cope with anything slightly out of the ordinary. Even the slightest deviation from the norm, and Derek knows what every plant arrangement should look like, throws him.

'It's fine, Derek, just put it through.'

'Well I need *your* authorisation code,' he says.

'Fine.' I lean over him as he scans the price again and I flash my staff card – what he calls my authorisation code – at the till scanner.

'Thank you, Pa-me-la.' He's taunting me with the way he says, almost sings, my name.

'You're welcome, Derek.' I walk away at the same time exchanging knowing looks with the customer.

Derek has never actually forgiven me for refusing his offer of a drink-date when he first joined Jolliffe's. I was thirty-one then, very much in my youthful prime. Derek was fortyish, but I don't think he'd ever had a prime. His hair was long and lank then and still is now, the only difference is that now it's iron-grey and there is a significant bald patch in the middle.

He's one of those men who has his hair cut once a year and lets it grow the rest of the time. It's usually

January when he comes in with a short pudding basin style, by December it's flowing around his shoulders. We're in early January now and he hasn't yet made it to the cupboard where he keeps his pudding basin.

He thought, because we were both older and single, or *solder* as he put it, that I'd jump at his offer. Oddly, I didn't and I didn't consider myself *solder* either. I was on the tills then too, number three, or if I could manage it, number one, as far from Derek as possible. Jolliffe's had been busy then, far busier than it is these days. It used to be the biggest independent garden centre in England, now it's fighting for its life against the big chains, constantly refusing takeover offers. We all know it's only a matter of time before it is bought out, something Derek lives in fear of. If I'm honest, so do I. Don't we all fear the unknown?

Just as I'm turning the corner, just a microsecond before I'm out of earshot I hear the familiar tones of a tune that has followed me around my entire life. Derek is humming The Beatles' "Eleanor Rigby". I'd once been stupid enough to confide in him, that was just before I turned down his drink-date offer.

♫♫♫

Okay, let's get the elephant in the room out in the open right now. My name. It's Pamela Rigby, not Eleanor. I know, I know. The song is already in your head, isn't it? Lennon and McCartney could certainly write a catchy tune.

It's been the bane of my life. Right from the start. It's followed me wherever I've gone and, sadly, it's become a self-fulfilling prophecy. I have my dad to thank for that. It was his idea, he loved The Beatles, and especially that song. My mum, unusually for her, didn't object or argue. I was named Eleanor Pamela Rigby. As I've said, that's not the name I go by now, but it was to begin with.

I was five when I rebelled. Sitting at the tea table, my brother, Keith humming it softly to annoy me, smirked when I scowled. It's the kind of song that, once heard, cannot be forgotten. And it's sad; poor old Eleanor ends up all on her own, having little or no life and no one to miss her when she dies. Alone.

'Eleanor,' my mum said. 'Eat up, we're waiting for you.'

'I don't want to be Eleanor anymore.'

Keith, ten years my senior and so superior, muttered, 'God's sake,' under his breath, it was low enough for neither of my parents to hear him.

'Pig face,' I screeched; at that age I hadn't learnt the art of slyness.

He rolled his eyes and grinned.

'Eleanor, really. Apologise.' My mum sat waiting for me to say sorry while my father just stared at me.

My brother narrowed his eyes and waited for the apology, even the three spots he had on his chin, their heads ready to burst, seemed to mock me.

'No. I. Won't.' I pushed my plate away and hurled myself down from the table. I ran up to my room and flung myself on the bed; at five I was a drama queen. No one followed me, which was lucky because this was the mid-seventies and the concept of the naughty step hadn't quite reached our part of Wiltshire, and I'd be far more likely to receive a slap on the leg than five minutes sitting on my own to contemplate my misbehaviour.

No one came and enough time passed that I started

to play with my dolls and not care about my family. Then I heard shuffling outside my door followed by the faint notes so familiar to me, my brother humming the song, my song, "Eleanor Rigby". Looking back through all those years I know now that I shouldn't have responded, that not reacting would have been the best way to treat my brother's taunting and driven him mad too, but at five, I didn't know any better. I jumped up, yanked open the door and threw my doll at him. It hit him fair and square on the lips before dropping to the floor.

We both stared at the blood on the back of his hand after he'd wiped it across his face.

'M-u-u-m,' he yelled. 'I'm bleeding.'

This brought both our parents hurtling up the stairs where the usually non-communicative Keith managed to give a detailed, and much exaggerated account of how I'd beaten him around the head repeatedly with my doll. He did, of course, omit the part where he'd taunted me. I duly received the slapped leg that had been coming since teatime and Keith was taken to hospital by our dad, where he had two – just two – stitches.

The scar followed him into adulthood, but mainly because he picked it, along with his spots, until it became infected.

I wanted to change my name, officially, by deed poll but I never did. My parents never agreed, especially my father. My mum cried and said my dad was so hurt and upset that he couldn't bring himself to talk about it. So in their house I was Eleanor, everywhere else I was Pamela. I am Pamela. Or Pam. I never wanted to be Eleanor, alone and forgotten.

Funny that.

♫♫♫

I'm back in my safe haven, far away from Derek and his till number four, far away from almost everyone, sorting through the pot arrangements that have come in from abroad – what has the world come to? We used to make all our own arrangements, using plants we'd grown in our own greenhouses, it was lovely then. So many men, exclusively men, worked in the greenhouses and out in the planting beds, tending the seeds, repotting, planting out. It was amazing. Jolliffe's was so old fashioned and anchored in the past, and I loved it. But even then it was changing, growing land had already been sold off by the time I joined Jolliffe's. Houses were built on that land and when the people who live there come in to buy their bedding plants and garden furniture it makes me smile, most of them haven't a clue what used to be grown in their gardens.

I was on the tills to start off with but I wanted to be outside, feeling the earth between my fingers, nurturing plants, potting up. One of the men retired and I applied for his position, there was some opposition, which seemed ridiculous then, and would be even more so now, but eventually I was promoted to the position of Plants Woman. Sadly, my lovely new job title only lasted six months, before major changes occurred and everyone, whether nurturing plants, stacking shelves or sitting on the tills, became a Customer Service Assistant. At least I still get to tend the plants, not sit on a till. Not much has changed since, except there is just me and two other men working with the plants and I'm the youngest and fittest of the three of us, which says a lot about Jolliffe's staff retention.

'Pam, how's it going?' Tim Jolliffe's pleasant face

pops up in front of mine. I always think of him as Young Tim because he was only sixteen when he started here working evenings and weekends, Jolliffe's liked its family members to start at the bottom then, not so sure about how it works now. He's thirty-five, or six, now but, to be honest, he looks older. He runs the place along with his older sister, Cherry, but we don't see much of her, she's not the sort to get dirt under her nails. Even when she was younger, when old Mr Jolliffe, who'd inherited from *his* father, ran the place, Cherry only ever went on the tills though she was already safely tucked away in the office by the time I joined.

'Great, Tim,' I say, giving him a smile, because he's a nice lad, well man now, I suppose.

'Getting excited? When do you go?'

'Last day today, then I'm off tomorrow.'

'I hope it's everything you've dreamed of. See you later, Pam.' He's wandering off, doing the rounds like he does most afternoons, glad of a break from Cherry and the superheated office, and keen to get out in the air and among the workers.

'Me too,' I say to his retreating back, but I'm really talking to myself, because I hope it is everything I've dreamed of, and more.

I've never been on holiday before, not even with my family. My dad would take two weeks off work in the summer and we'd *go out for days*. It was what a lot of people did then, cheaper than a proper holiday and easier than making the effort to book anything beforehand. Going out for days meant one trip to Bristol Zoo and one trip to Bournemouth during the entire two weeks. We'd be crammed into the back of my dad's car; I'd be squabbling with Keith and my mum would try to slap us into better behaviour by squeezing her hand between the gap in the front seats and flapping it blindly about. Keith was good at avoiding the slaps, me, then, not so.

I've never been on holiday as an adult either, circumstances always prevented it, and, if I'm honest, it never really occurred to me. Holidays were for other people, people with families and friends to go with.

But three years ago, I decided that had to change. I decided I had to get myself out there, live my life before it was too late. I've just turned fifty, fifty, how did that happen? I've been nowhere, I've done nothing, and, crucially I have no one. Not now.

Three years ago, Keith died.

He was fifty-seven and he hadn't really done much either, or not much that I knew about. At eighteen he'd escaped to university in Manchester and never come back. He liked us to think he had a secret, exciting life up there, away from our prying eyes, but judging from what I saw after he died, he didn't. There was no wife, no children, no obvious friends to miss him. As next of kin it was my duty to sort out his affairs after his death; with both our parents dead there wasn't anyone else. He lived in a small, rented flat, he worked for a tiny company that had something to do with computers, I don't know what. His life looked as small as mine.

Mercifully, he'd had a massive heart attack at work. If it had happened at home would anyone have missed him? He and I spoke rarely on the phone, half a dozen times a year, maybe. The calls, either me to him, or him to me, were irregular. I wouldn't have noticed his absence until I called him, and I don't know when that would have been. I've often imagined him rotting in his flat, no one noticing until the smell leaked out and alerted his neighbours. That could happen to me too.

All the lonely people.

Four people came to his funeral, which cost the entirety of his savings which I accessed before I told the bank he had died. How else would I have paid for it? Four people, including me. The other three worked with him and they seemed as lonely and odd as he was. It's no secret we never really got on; too much water under the bridge, sibling rivalry and all that came with it. Keith had never really forgiven me for arriving unexpectedly when he was ten. My parents hadn't anticipated another child so long after their first; my dad was older than I am now, my mum my age, it had been a shocker all round.

Even though we weren't close Keith's death affected me, made me realise how small my life was.

So now I'm going on an adventure and I'm both excited and terrified.

Two

It's taken me since Keith's death to save up the money. It's almost five-thousand pounds. I know that might not seem a massive amount to some, but to me, it's enormous. You see, much as I love the garden centre, the wages aren't high and by the time I've paid my rent and bills, there's not much left. So this holiday is a big, big deal.

I still don't know if I'm doing the right thing.

It's a cruise, four weeks around the Caribbean. I've had to save holiday from last year to be able to take the time off. Although Tim was very good about it, Cherry was a bit sniffy; she insisted I didn't use my entire year's allocation up in January just in case something cropped up later. By cropped up later she meant that I might need a sick day and she'd rather I use my holiday for that. She's a hard one, is Cherry.

Anyway, one way or another, it's happening and I'm going.

At first, I thought I'd travel alone, I'm quite self-contained, I live on my own, I don't need people and I imagined I'd meet others like me on board. But then I saw the price if I wanted my own room – almost the same price as a couple would pay. I couldn't afford that. But then someone at work suggested I check out some internet forum about singles holidays and find someone to go with. I delayed doing it for weeks then I thought, what the hell, I don't have to commit to anything.

That's how I found Fiona Federer, her surname like the tennis player, but they're not related. She emphasised this to me several times in our online conversations. Unlike me, Fiona is a seasoned traveller. She's done this holidaying with a stranger thing before and says it was very successful. And she's cruised a lot.

When I asked about her previous partner, she said the silly woman had remarried so wasn't available any longer. She said that we could partner up again if we get on and hoped that *I* wouldn't go off and remarry. I told her I'd never been married and didn't anticipate doing so in the future. Ha, chance would be a fine thing. She asked me if I was a lesbian. I briefly considered saying that I was because that would make me more interesting, wouldn't it? But, when I didn't reply straightaway, Fiona pressed me for an answer and said she didn't really hold with lesbianism so she needed to know. I admitted I wasn't, although, surely I'd have said that anyway, now that I knew she didn't approve.

We've spoken on the phone a few times since then. Fiona sounds very cultured. She asked about my job, I told her what I did and I could tell that she deliberately kept her tone level when she told me how interesting that sounded. It's not, and we both know it. But I like it. She's a civil servant, apparently, though she wouldn't go into detail about it. She's a widow, ten years now. She's a mother and a grandmother, although she doesn't see her family as much as she'd like to because they live in Canada. She's lucky enough to spend Christmas with them every year although she didn't go this Christmas because she wanted to cruise the Caribbean in January and she only has so much leave from work, don't you know? She called it leave too, in Jolliffe's we call it holiday whether you go away, or not.

She asked how tall I was, which I thought was odd. I told her five-three on a good day with no shoes on. She said that was okay. I'm not sure what she meant by that so I asked her and she said she was only tiny herself and didn't really want to be dwarfed by an Amazonian woman. Right, good, that's okay then.

I hope Fiona likes me. I hope we get on.

Fiona is saving me money, not just by sharing a room with me – Fiona says I must get used to calling it a cabin – but she also managed to sort out some good travel insurance, we're on the same policy because that works out cheaper. I have to admit I hadn't thought about insurance but when we came to book it was obvious that the booking wouldn't be accepted without insurance. Good job Fiona knows these things.

♫♫♫

We've arranged to meet in the departure area in the Mayflower Terminal building in Southampton. Fiona was a bit put out when I told her I was travelling by coach – it was included in the cost, so why wouldn't I? She says she always has a driver. I'm not sure if that means a chauffeur, a taxi or a friend, she didn't elaborate. She also said that if it hadn't been such a big detour, they would have picked me up on the way as she's coming from London and almost passing my house, but not almost enough, apparently. I told her I was quite happy with the coach which picks up at our local superstore, only a five-minute walk from me.

I hadn't factored in the suitcases.

♫♫♫

I arrive at the superstore car park hot and sweaty; this is not a good way to start my lovely holiday. I have two wheelie cases, they're large but very stable. I also have two bags which sit on top of the wheelie cases. They all match. They're not mine. Of course I don't have suitcases, I've never needed them. These are rather lovely and belong to Cherry, yes Cherry who made a fuss about me taking holiday brought them in one day and told me I could borrow them. She also told me not to scratch them or dent them. Before she lent me these I was just going to get some second hand ones from the charity shop, you see them in there all the time, then it wouldn't matter how they were treated. I'm paranoid now.

As I approach the bus stop I can see the coach already there. Surely, I'm not late. I sweat a little more as I quicken my pace. A sea of faces stare out at me as I get closer, almost running now, the cases pulling on my arms; my handbag, which I have across my body is slapping against my hip.

The driver, having a sneaky cigarette by the front corner of the coach, sees me approach and smiles before stubbing out his cigarette with his foot.

'Don't worry, you're not late,' he says. 'Those go in here.' He points to the cavernous storage areas beneath the coach and takes a case and top bag from me. He's quick, and evidently expert at separating them and slinging them into the coach's underbelly. I stand and watch, feeling useless but grateful as he takes the second set from me. Another hurl, a slam, and they're out of sight.

I've bitten my tongue and not told him to be careful, but his actions have made me anxious and I worry about any damage that might have been done to Cherry's luggage. I wish I'd gone with the charity shop ones now.

'Ticket?' the driver asks, with a wink. I know it's not that sort of wink, not for me.

'Oh yes.' I yank at my handbag which has twisted itself round so it's now sitting on my left buttock. Finally, I find my coach ticket and hand it to him. A quick glance, and he ticks me off a list he pulls from his pocket. Then hands the ticket back to me.

'Let's get going then.' He tells me where to sit and I climb on. I'm at the back and by the time I reach my seat I'm tugging at my coat to get it off before I die from heat exhaustion, in January! I can feel sweat gathering along my hairline; so much for that blow dry I got up extra early to give myself. I don't usually bother, for work I just scrape it all back into a ponytail.

Once in the seat I make an effort to calm down. I'm here now. Cases in the boot – or whatever it's called on a coach – and I'm on my way. Caribbean, here I come.

♫♫♫

It takes us a couple of hours and two more stops before we arrive in Southampton. We haven't even got off the coach before the porters arrive to start taking the luggage away. I scuttle, well, push, my way to the exit to retrieve my small cases as one has my computer tablet in it and the other has toiletries which I don't think will stand being hurled around. I just manage to grab them off a porter's trolley before they disappear.

I hurry along to the departure area because Fiona has already messaged me to tell me I'm late – as though I have any control over what time the coach arrives.

I look around me hoping I'll be able to spot Fiona. Now, I realise that we didn't exchange photos, bit silly that.

'Pamela?' a voice says from behind me. I turn and see a short woman, with old lady curly hair, carrying a gaudy bag made from carpet.

'Fiona?' I'm sure she said she was a similar age to me, but suddenly I feel young, and tall.

'That's correct. Pleased to meet you.' Fiona extends her hand. It seems very formal to me, but what the hell.

'Nice to meet you in person too.' I offer my best smile, the one I hope she'll warm too.

'Quite. Shall we continue on up? Are you going to manage the escalator or would you prefer the lift?' She casts an eye over my two bags.

'Escalator's fine,' I say, with another smile.

'Follow me.' She marches off and I scuttle along behind her, up an escalator and into a short queue. 'Have your ticket and passport ready,' Fiona whispers as though it's a secret. I rummage in the outside pocket of my handbag until I find them. We're given a red card with the letter A on it and told to take a seat.

There are hundreds of us sitting and waiting, all with a coloured card.

'I hope they're efficient today,' Fiona says, with a frown. 'Sometimes they are and sometimes they aren't.'

'Oh. Okay.' I spy a little tea and coffee kiosk in the corner, there are cakes too. I haven't eaten or drunk anything since breakfast and that was hours ago.

'Would you like a coffee?' I stand up and start to pull my purse from my bag.

'No. No. Don't buy one from there, you can have copious quantities of coffee once you're on the ship and you won't have to pay for them either.' She pulls at my sleeve and I find myself sitting back down.

'Oh. Okay.' I really wanted that coffee. And a cake.

An hour later and *Red A* has still not been called. My mouth is dry and my stomach has started to rumble. The kiosk in the corner is doing a roaring trade and I feel annoyed with myself for letting Fiona dissuade me. I stand up again.

'I'm just going to get some water,' I say. Surely she can't object to that.

'Oh, yes please.' She offers me a thin smile. 'Since you're going anyway,' she adds.

I return with the waters just as our letter is called. Fiona doesn't even take her drink from me, but fusses around collecting her carpet bag and the scarf she has taken off.

'Come along,' she says, sounding like a cheery scoutmaster.

'I'll just drink this.' I flop down into my seat and sip my water. I'm tired and another few minutes won't make any difference.

Fiona raises one annoyed eyebrow and stands in front of me, her eyes following my every move and her foot tapping lightly on the carpet. Finally, I finish my water and then I start on hers. She doesn't say a word, but I hear a little snort escape her nose. Oh dear, this isn't going well.

Feeling harassed, I don't finish the second water, but gather up my bags and trot along behind her to join the queue. We're quickly pointed to an empty desk and begin to have our documents processed. We each register our credit cards to settle our onboard extra spend. I've only recently acquired a credit card, especially for this holiday, I've never really needed or bothered having one before.

It's all rather exciting. Even going through the metal scanner and hand baggage X-ray is novel and exciting for me.

'This is so tedious,' Fiona says as we put our shoes and coats back on before heading towards the ship. 'I'm desperate for a nice cup of tea.'

Or coffee, I think, but don't say anything. I'm hardly flush but I would have treated her if she objects so much to paying for a drink.

Oh well.

On board we're greeted by a waiter with a tray of champagne. I take one but Fiona frowns at me. I'm about to put it back when I stop myself. Hey, this is my holiday and I don't have to do what Fiona wants.

'I'd rather have a cup of tea,' she says, frowning again. 'In my cabin.'

For a moment I hesitate, the champagne flute hasn't reached my lips yet, so I could put it down and follow Fiona. I could. But no. I take a sip which is not especially easy since I'm balancing one of my bags with that hand too.

'Why don't you go on ahead and I'll catch you up when I'm done,' I say with a big smile.

Fiona looks at me for a moment too long then nods. 'Okay, but don't forget there'll be a sail away party later and we have to do muster stations before then.'

'Don't worry,' I reply, wondering what the hell mustard stations are. I take another sip and decide I really don't care; I'm on holiday and I'm going to enjoy myself.

I finish my champagne and look around for somewhere to put it. A waiter appears and takes my glass, then another appears with another tray of champagne. Oh well, it would be rude not to, wouldn't it? Then there are more drinks and music and I've dumped my two bags under a table and I'm really rather enjoying myself. I'm chatting away to a couple from Scotland who have told me this is their twenty-fifth cruise and their tenth time around the Caribbean and their fourth time on this ship. I tell them I'm a complete novice and they become so excited for me you'd think it was their first time too.

Yep, I'm on holiday and I'm bloody well loving it and we've hardly started.

An announcement from the bridge suddenly stops proceedings, apparently all the passengers are on board and we're preparing to sail but first we have to undergo mustard stations. We've to assemble when the alarm goes off.

'Better get back to the cabins and dump all our stuff in readiness,' says the female half of the Scottish couple. 'Will we see you at the sail away party?' she asks as they, and everyone else, suddenly scamper away.

'Oh yes,' I answer enthusiastically. I don't know where and when it is but I will be there.

Sighing, I grab my bags, check my cabin number and set off to find Fiona and her cup of tea.

Three

'At last. I was getting worried. Where have you been?' Fiona looks annoyed with me.

'At the welcome drinks thing. You knew that.' I don't tell her that I've been longer than expected because I got lost finding the cabin. She doesn't need to know that.

'It's muster stations,' she says, the irritated tone in her voice barely masked by panic.

'Yes, I know.' So it's *muster* stations. 'Just need to use the loo. In here, is it?' I pull on a little door, not so little, because like all the doors on this ship that I've come across so far, it weighs a tonne. Once inside the bathroom I smile when I see a bath with shower over, a sink with twin wall mirror cabinets and the highest toilet I've ever encountered. I launch myself onto it. I wonder how Fiona will cope with this, she's so much shorter than me. I giggle to myself as I imagine her taking a run and jump to get on it.

'Everything all right in there?' Fiona's muffled voice calls through the door.

'Yes. Just washing my hands.'

'Well hurry up. We need to go.'

'I haven't heard the alarm thing yet.' I assume I'd hear it in the bathroom, after all, if there was a real emergency, surely everywhere would be covered. 'I'm ready,' I say as I step out of the bathroom and almost bump into Fiona.

'We need to go now before the alarm starts. Then we can get a decent seat. Fortunately, we no longer need to take our life jackets, unlike in the past, it was such a nuisance. Come on.' Fiona urges me out of the door and we're soon marching down the corridor towards our muster station. I haven't even had time to see the rest of the cabin or even put my bags down properly, I've just dumped them on the bathroom floor.

We're in the front row of the theatre, that's our muster station, the theatre. I had imagined some windswept spot on deck, so this is a comfortable bonus. There are about a dozen other people. Suddenly the alarm and the announcement to proceed to muster stations is blasted through the ship.

'Why did we need to be so early?' I ask as Fiona scans the horizon. 'Are you looking for someone?'

'No, no. This ship has had a refit since I was last on it. They've changed the seat colours.'

'Right. So why did we need to be so early?'

'It's just better. And good practice. And we've got excellent seats, haven't we?'

I nod slowly. I can't be bothered to argue with that. My early start, no food all day and the champagne are catching up with me and I feel very tired. I close my eyes and lean back in my seat. I'm so very comfortable.

I definitely doze off; I don't know for how long but I'm suddenly aware of Fiona nudging me in the ribs.

'You need to pay attention,' she says. 'This could

save your life.'

I blink myself awake and watch as a crew member on the stage demonstrates how to put a life jacket on – it's florescent and bulky. All around the theatre other crew members do the same. There's a lot of Velcro ripping going on.

'It's so much better since they stopped making us do it. Imagine all these old people fumbling with all that orange polystyrene.'

I glance around; most of the other passengers don't look any older than me and Fiona.

After we've listened to a recorded message from the captain about our safety, he wishes us a good holiday and reminds us to go to the sail away party. More alcohol. I just hope there's some food.

'I'm starving,' I say as we leave the theatre.

'Yes, I expect you are. I had a little bite to eat while you were imbibing.'

'Imbibing?'

'Drinking. Alcohol,' she says with a slight tone of distaste.

'I think I need a bite to eat too, before this sail away party.'

'There's not really time, you need to get your unpacking done.' She urges me up the stairs, along with everyone else, and back to our cabin.

Once inside I retrieve my bags from the bathroom before checking out the rest of our cabin, the place that will be my home – our home – for the next month.

A pair of twin beds fill half the space and they're only about six inches apart. I hope Fiona doesn't object to my snoring. I hope she doesn't snore too loudly herself. I snigger to myself at the thought.

'Something funny?'

'What? No. I'm a bit lightheaded from lack of food.'

'Mmm,' she says, managing to make it sound like the judgement it is.

I drop my bags onto the luggage mat on the bed and start to unpack, looking round for somewhere to put my tablet and its charger.

'In a drawer,' Fiona offers. 'This one here would be best.' She pulls open a drawer in a unit that could double as a dressing table or a desk.

'Thanks,' I say as I drop it in.

I carry on unpacking my bags with Fiona offering helpful suggestions as to where my things should go. She's taken the left-hand side cabinet in the bathroom and allocated me the right. Which is fine, except mine is smaller than hers as it has the shaver socket in it. Oh well.

'Have you seen my suitcases?' I ask. 'Or have they not arrived yet?'

'Oh yes. They're out on the balcony.'

I glance over, past the sofa and TV and out onto the balcony where it looks as though it's about to rain and there they are.

'Why did you put them out there?'

'They were cluttering the place up. Trip hazard,' she adds, as though that makes it all right. 'I'll help you get them in now you're here to unpack.'

Together we struggle with my cases until they are back in the cabin. I don't know how Fiona managed to get them over the balcony door step on her own although I could probably have got them in without her help, she was more of a hindrance really.

'This is your wardrobe space,' she says, throwing open a door. 'And these are your drawers, plus your bedside table too.'

'Thanks,' I say as, under her scrutiny, I put my clothes away. 'All my clothes are freezing,' I add pointedly.

'Well it is January.'

'Not that one,' Fiona screeches as I yank open a drawer filled with large, wrapped packets. She slams the drawer shut and I pretend that I didn't see that it was full of incontinence pads.

When I'm finally done, and I'm amazed at how everything has fitted in, Fiona instructs me to push the cases under my bed, which I do.

'Where can I put my passport and money?' I ask, not wanting to carry either around in my handbag all the time.

'Oh yes, in the safe. It's here, in my wardrobe.' She opens the door and shows me a tiny safe with numbered buttons on it. 'If you give me your bits and bobs I'll pop them in.'

I pull the relevant *bits and bobs* from my bag and hand them over. Fiona stands in front of the safe, punches in numbers and opens the door.

'What's the number?' I ask, not unreasonably.

'It's secret.'

'Not from me. I'm in this room too.'

'Cabin,' she corrects as she flicks through my passport. 'Eleanor Rigby?' she says, reading the incriminating thing with a little smirk on her face.

'I go by Pamela, or Pam,' I snap, my response automatic.

'Of course.' She pushes it inside the safe, closes the door and locks it, without me seeing the number.

'What's the number?' I try again.

'I'd rather not say. It's my own personal number that I use for everything.'

'So what happens if I need to get inside it?'

'I'll do it for you.' She smiles but somehow it doesn't look like a nice smile.

'We could change the number to something else, something that we both know,' I offer.

'It's fine. It won't be a problem. Shall we go?'

'Do you think I've got time to get something to eat?' I ask, giving up on the safe nonsense. For now.

Fiona glances at her watch. 'No,' she says. 'We need to get to the sail away party. You'll need a coat. And don't forget your voucher for a free drink. I do love the sail away from Southampton, they usually have a band playing.'

'What voucher?'

'It's in the welcome pack.' She points towards the desk and for the first time I notice an array of leaflets and envelopes, one of which is addressed to me.

♫♫♫

I'm in the queue to get my free drink when the music starts playing down on the quay. I'm glad I've taken Fiona's advice and put my coat on because it is freezing on deck at the back of the ship, even though there are a lot of bodies here to warm us up. I pick up my champagne, better not to mix drinks, I think, and make my way towards the rails so I can look down at the band – a ten-piece brass band, dressed in peaked caps and heavy, dark overcoats to keep out the cold.

'Lovely, isn't it?' Fiona says as they launch into a selection of Beatles hits. 'I wonder if they'll play your song?' she asks. Do I detect a hint of malice there? I choose to ignore her question and move away.

'Hello,' says a Scottish voice, and a beaming face

pops up in front of me.

'Hello,' I say warmly, as though I'm greeting the oldest of friends.

'Isn't this fun? Love these sail away parties. Wait until we get to the Caribbean, it'll be hot and we'll sail away into the sunset.' She raises her glass and clinks it with mine.

'Hello?' Fiona's voice comes from behind.

'Hello dear. It's Pam's first cruise.'

'I know. We're travelling companions. I'm Fiona.' Another handshake.

'I'm Shona, and this… oh, where is he? Anyway, he's Jockie, my husband.' Shona waves her arm around, knocks back her drink then looks towards the bar. 'I need to find Jockie,' she says, laughing. 'I need more fizz. Coming?'

'No, we need to get changed for dinner, we're on first sitting,' Fiona answers for me.

'Us too. Might see you there. It's very casual tonight. I won't be bothering to change.' She laughs as she drifts away, having spotted Jockie at the bar.

Fiona doesn't say anything but I can feel her disapproval and I'm not even sure why. Inwardly, I tell myself not to be so mean, maybe Fiona just has that kind of demeanour: miserable. Maybe she's tired and grouchy. Or maybe, like me, she's hungry. No, it can't be that because she had a bite to eat earlier when I was imbibing.

♫♫♫

Fiona has made me put on smart trousers and a silk top, she even compliments me on my taste when she sees the top. If she knew it had come from a charity shop, she might not be so nice about it.

I feel overdressed when we enter the dining room; I was wearing jeggings and a cosy jumper and that's pretty much what everyone else is wearing.

'Standards,' whispers Fiona when she sees my face. 'Important, I always say.'

We're taken to our table, a table for two, the table we will sit at every night for the entirety of the cruise. Fiona arranged this as she has so many aspects of this cruise because she's a seasoned cruiser.

I'm not sure that I want to spend quite so much time with her and her alone, in our room and at dinner every night. I glance around the vast dining room looking for a friendly face.

'Pam, Pam,' shouts Shona from the next table, a table of eight, although not everyone is there yet. That looks like fun.

I hear a soft groan of displeasure from Fiona.

'Hi,' I wave back. 'Fancy seeing you here.'

Shona laughs, Jockie waves and Fiona forces a brief smile onto her face.

Dinner is lovely and I eat all five courses even if we hardly speak. I've also ordered myself a bottle of white wine – I am on my holidays after all. I offered Fiona a glass but she mumbled something about keeping it simple and not complicating who pays for what. I was only offering her a drink! I have the rest of the bottle put away for another night.

'We'll have to watch ourselves,' Fiona says. 'We can't eat like that every night or our clothes won't fit us by the end of the cruise.' She laughs an odd effected laugh. I can't help but think that her announcement is purely for my benefit as she's hardly eaten anything, just pushed it around the plate.

'First meal I've had since breakfast,' I say, trying not to sound irritated.' I eat what I like, always have. I'm neither fat nor thin. I have a physical job that sees me humping large plant pots around, sacks of compost and even bags of stones, so I never worry about what I eat because I burn it off. I may be fifty but I'm not fat and flabby yet.

'Come and join us, come and join us for coffee,' Shona calls over from their table.

'Oh yes,' I say, standing up. I can't wait to get over there.

'Must we?' mutters Fiona.

I'm beginning to wonder if coming on this holiday, sharing a room, sorry cabin, and generally potentially spending so much time alone with Fiona, is a good idea.

Four

We spend a jolly ten minutes having coffee with Shona and Jockie and the other two couples on their table before the waiters tactfully suggest we leave because they need to set the table for the next sitting.

'We're off to the theatre, are you coming?' Shona asks. 'There's always a fun show on the first night.'

'Oh yes,' I say sounding as enthusiastic as I feel. I'm going to go to everything, experience everything, that's why I came.

'Oh, well, it's a bit late…' Fiona mumbles to herself but Jockie hears her, as do I. It isn't even 8.30pm yet.

'Come along, lassie,' he says, putting his arm around her shoulders, which makes her flinch. 'You're on holiday. Enjoy yourself.'

Fiona nods and smiles and allows herself to be corralled towards the theatre, although we don't get our front row seats like we did for the muster stations.

We sit through forty minutes of entertainment, dancing, singing, introductions to the entertainments team. It's all very jolly and certainly beats watching TV on my own which is what I do most nights at home.

'Did you enjoy that, ladies?' Jockie asks as we file out

at the end of the performance.

'It was a fun watch,' I say. 'I don't know how they do that with the ship moving and everything.'

'It's still calm,' Jockie says, laughing. 'We're still in the English Channel, wait until we hit the Bay of Biscay and see how they manage then.' He chuckles away to himself.

'Very well, usually,' Shona says, nudging Jockie in the ribs. 'Are you good at sea, Pam?'

'I don't know yet, but I've brought plenty of seasick tablets with me.' Six boxes to be precise; I'm not taking any chances.

'Good plan,' Shona says. 'We're off to the top bar now, care to join us?'

Fiona looks shattered, so I say no thanks for both of us. I'd love to go, but there's plenty of time, I don't have to do everything on the first day.

Back in our cabin we find the beds turned down, a little chocolate each and the ship's newsletter spread out on my bed. I grab it. It's tomorrow's and lists a whole day of activities. I sit down on the sofa and go through each entry at the same time scoffing my little chocolate. There's so much to choose from.

'Oh, would you like a look?' I ask Fiona when I realise I have hogged it for ten minutes or more and she's staring at me.

'No thank you. I read it earlier.'

'Oh?' I'm confused.

'It was in the welcome pack.' She shrugs before disappearing into the bathroom.

While she's gone, I hunt out this welcome pack she knows all about and look through it.

'Now I know when all the formal nights are,' I say to her when she returns.

'Yes, they do usually list them. They'll put them in the newsletter anyway.'

'Have you eaten your chocolate?' she asks, knowing full well that I have because she sat and watched me.

'Yes. Greedy me.' I laugh.

'Only I usually save them up for my visits to the grandchildren.' She gives me a thin little smile.

'Oh, right. Well I don't have any grandchildren.' And surely she doesn't intend saving up little chocolates for a whole year, it's January and she told me she only sees them at Christmas.

She doesn't answer but yawns, a bit too obviously for me.

I take my cue and use the bathroom too, when I come back she's tucked up in bed, the main lights are out, the only light left on is my bedside light. Fiona's eyes are closed, but I don't think she's actually asleep. Sorry, Fiona, but *I'm* not going to bed at ten pm. I hunt through my things until I find the brochure with all the excursions listed in it. I've already marked a few, even booked a couple before I left home, which I've paid for with my onboard spend, so they haven't actually cost me anything.

'Oh, by the way,' she says, confirming my suspicions that she wasn't asleep. 'I've taken this bed because it's nearest the bathroom and I do tend to get up in the night.'

'Okay.' That's fine by me. If I need to get up in the night, I'll just have further to walk. I'm sure I can manage.

'You don't need to book lots of trips, you know. They are expensive and often you can find your own way about.'

'Right. Okay.'

'When we stop in Madeira I thought we'd just get the shuttle bus into Funchal and have a little wander.'

'Oh, right. Um. I've booked a trip there. I'm doing that toboggan thing.'

'Oh. Well, good luck with that then. I hear it's terrifying.'

'Looks really good in the brochure,' I say, wondering why I need to justify myself to her.

'I'm sure you'll enjoy it then.' She turns over, her back to me. 'Goodnight.'

♫♫♫

I'm woken by a shadow looming over me. I open my eyes and for a moment or two wonder where I am. Oh yes, I'm on holiday, cruising. Hurray!

'Morning,' the shadow says.

'Hello, Fiona. Err, what time is it?' Now my eyes are focussing I can see her face better.

'Ten to eight. I find it's better to go for an early breakfast. I've finished in the bathroom, shower's all yours.' She smiles but doesn't move away.

'Right,' I say but make no attempt to get up.

'That's if you're having breakfast.'

'Yes, I will.'

'Then you need to get up.'

I weigh up my options, do I tell her to bugger off and leave me alone? Is now the time to have *the conversation*, because one thing's for sure, we are going to have to have that conversation as it's become increasingly obvious to me in a very short time that Fiona thinks she's the boss of me.

'Okay.' I throw back the covers and stand up as Fiona gives me a genuine smile and steps aside. I turn back to make my bed.

'Oh no, don't do that,' she says. 'You'll cause offence. It's his job.'

'Whose?'

'The cabin steward.'

♫♫♫

'I thought we'd go to the formal dining room today, so much nicer to be served than participate in the bun fight that sometimes ensues in the buffet,' Fiona says, as we leave our cabin.

'Whatever.' I really don't care, I'm not even that hungry after last night's five course binge.

Fiona gives me a slight frown. She probably thinks I'm too old to say *whatever* in that tone but I work with a wide range of ages and hear it all the time from the sulky Saturday kids who come and go with the frequency of the seasons.

We're served from a menu and I struggle to find anything I really want to eat, just as well I'm not starving. It's actually quite convenient to be up this early as I've already earmarked my next activity and it starts at 10am.

'I'm going to check out the watercolour class, well the intro to it,' I tell Fiona, as she tucks into her third cup of coffee. I've noticed she doesn't have a big appetite, but she does love her coffee. And tea.

'Oh. Really?' Disapproval then.

'Yes. I quite fancy having a go. Used to be good at art at school.' I laugh because, let's face it, school is a long, long time ago. 'In fact, I took my art O level early, and my English.' I don't know why I'm telling her this, why I feel the need to justify myself.

'Oh,' she says. 'But you didn't pursue either as a career?'

'No, stuff got in the way.' I'm not going to tell her about the stuff that got in the way, I don't think we're ever going to be *that* friendly, no matter how much time we spend together.

'Well, don't be surprised if they want you to buy art equipment, paints and the like. It can be very expensive.'

'Oh, I'm relying on it, I have nothing. Do you fancy coming with me?' I really hope she doesn't.

'Oh, no, thank you. I might go to the coffee morning.' This is followed by a tight-lipped smile.

Now it's my turn to frown. 'Oh, I didn't see that.' I pull the folded ship's newsletter from my pocket and open it out on the table. 'Ah, this one, the singles coffee morning?'

'Yes,' Fiona hisses under her breath. 'It's good to meet like-minded people.'

'Absolutely.'

'Also, could you not fold that up like that, it's supposed to be for both of us to read, if it's stuffed into your pocket how will I know what's going on?'

'Yes, sorry, I didn't think.' I smooth it out and pass it over to her.

'I don't need it now,' she says, before taking another swig of coffee, so I fold it again and stuff it back in my pocket.

♫♫♫

As Fiona predicted I am able to buy watercolour supplies at the intro session, which is great, even if she doesn't think so. The first lesson starts tomorrow and

33

I'm really looking forward to it. On my way back I stop by Reception and see that they have spare copies of the ship's newsletter, I take one for Fiona.

Back in our cabin I lay hers out on her bed, now pristine after the cabin steward has been in. I love this, though I find it quite hard to just get out of bed and not make it. But then, I suppose if a customer came into Jolliffe's and started tidying up the plants and pots, I would take offence too.

Fiona comes into the cabin looking quite jolly, her cheeks are rosy and there's what looks like a grin on her face, I think.

'Hi,' I say. 'Did you have a good time at the coffee morning?'

'Oh yes. Very good.' She giggles again before nipping into the bathroom. I think she might have been drinking more than just coffee.

When she comes back I wait for her to ask about the watercolour session, but she doesn't, instead suggesting that we go to a talk on our next port, which is starting in the theatre shortly. I agree. Why not?

'Oh,' she says, picking up the pristine newsletter. 'The cabin steward brought another one.'

'No, I got that from Reception, for you.'

'Oh. Thank you.' The tone of her voice suggests she really doesn't want to thank me.

'I've got my watercolour kit,' I say as we head out again. 'Really looking forward to starting the lessons tomorrow.'

'Good,' Fiona says, but I don't think she means it. 'It's a formal night tonight. I do so enjoy those. It'll be quite novel for you.' I think she's patronising me.

'Not really,' I lie. 'We have formal dinners for our Christmas events at work.' I glance at her. 'Every year, for years,' I add.

'Oh, good.'

In reality I've been to one formal event, where the men wore dinner jackets and the women wore glittery frocks, but even then it was held in the sports hall of our local leisure centre. Sadly, no matter how much they dressed it up with dark drapes and balloons, it still had a slight odour of sweaty trainers about it and there was no disguising the court lines painted onto the floor.

But Fiona doesn't need to know that.

♫♫♫

So, the pattern of our first few days is set, I go to watercolour class, where I learn how to apply a colour wash to the paper then paint over it, and Fiona goes to the single people's coffee morning, where they definitely drink more than just coffee. Sometimes we go to talks in the theatre together and we always dine together in the evening, although we tend to breakfast separately. I'm a cereal girl and happy to grab something quickly from the buffet; I'd rather stay in bed a bit longer. Fiona likes to be waited on.

The formal night is lovely, I wear a dress I bought from eBay and Fiona even compliments me on it. She wears black because, as she says, you can't go wrong with black. I agree with her but I actually think she looks a bit crow-like, especially with her skinny little legs dangling from beneath her puffy dress which covers her skinny little body. But each to their own.

On day four we arrive at Madeira, it's cloudy when we arrive and there's a heavy drizzle, but it's warm, so much warmer than home. I pull out my trusty cagoule and look forward to my trip.

'Well,' Fiona says, sounding rather smug, 'I wouldn't want to be dangling in a cable car or sliding down a hill in this weather. It'll be super skiddy.'

'Thanks for that,' I say as I leave her to her wandering and go and find my tour guide.

Five

The view from the cable car is obscured by cloud, which is a curse *and* a blessing.

There's enough of a breeze to make the cable car swing a little and I'm starting to feel queasy – shame I didn't bring some of my travel-sick tablets with me. As the car chugs its way up the hill towards the toboggan terminus, I take an occasional glance down through the clouds. I really didn't think I had vertigo until now; I don't think I like heights. So, while it's a shame I can't see much below me, it's also a relief.

It's an even bigger relief when we reach the top and I'm able to clamber out.

'Pam, Pam,' trills a voice and I recognise the jolly tones of Shona.

'Hello,' I call back, waving.

Shona comes over with Jockie following behind her.

'Are you on your own? Not got your little friend with you?'

'No, she's stayed down in Funchal. She didn't fancy this.'

'No? Well, why don't you come with us, they have

some sleds that are big enough for three. Save you rattling around on your own or going down with strangers. We've done this before, haven't we, Jockie? You'll scream all the way down but it's still fun.'

'Oh, it is,' Jockie says, while grimacing behind Shona's back.

We pile into a wicker sledge, wedge our backsides onto the flowery, padded seat and prepare ourselves. The pushers, two men in white trousers and shirts, and wearing straw boaters, introduce themselves. I don't catch their names because I'm mesmerized by the shiny tarmac beneath us and the knowledge of how high we've come up in the cable car and how far down we need to go – on wet tarmac.

They start off slowly, pulling us along the flat with ropes until the road starts to slope down and they start to run before skipping behind us and jumping on the back. They then alternate between riding and running along pushing us. It reminds me of dodgems at a fair, except this is far more frightening.

As we approach the first bend Shona starts to scream. I see Jockie pat her knee but it doesn't reassure her, in fact her screaming gets louder.

Then I realise it's not just Shona screaming, it's me too.

The bends in the road are sharp and sudden and we slide from one side of the sledge to the other. It's frightening, terrifying, but also exhilarating.

We come to a juddering halt. I'm both sorry and relieved it's over. I'm also glad I've got thick knickers and a long tunic on over my trousers. Maybe I need to borrow some of Fiona's incontinence pads.

'Told you,' Shona says as we clamber out. 'Scary fun.'

'Yes, yes. I think so. Only I think I might have left my stomach up at that first bend.' I'm not joking.

'I think we need a quick pick me up,' Jockie says as he puts his arms around my and Shona's shoulders and steers us towards a bar.

I definitely need a stiff drink because my heart is pounding – not sure whether it's fear or excitement – and my knees are shaking.

A few hours later we saunter back to the ship, happy and giggly.

'See you later at the sail away party,' Shona calls as I head off towards my cabin.

'Oh definitely.' I'd quite forgotten there would be another one, though no free drink this time.

Fiona is already back in our cabin when I enter. She's lying on the bed, a wet flannel across her forehead.

'Hi,' I say, flopping down onto the sofa and kicking off my shoes. 'Did you have a good day.'

'I did, I did, but I think I spent too long in the sun. I have a bit of a headache.'

'Oh, sorry to hear that. Have you taken anything?'

'No, no.'

'If you need any tablets, I've got the full range, ibuprofen, paracetamol. I might even have a rogue tramadol or two from when I had a bad back last year.'

'Oh no, no. I don't hold with drugs. I've put some lavender oil on my temples, that'll do the trick.'

'Okay, well the offer's still there if you change your mind. I'm just going to have a quick shower before I go to the sail away party.'

I disappear into the bathroom and when I come out Fiona is sitting up and looking quite peaky, which is quite a feat given how red her nose and chin are –

sunburn, I presume.

'Lavender working yet,' I say, trying not to sound sceptical.

'Starting to,' she says, before shuddering and shivering.

'Sunstroke, that looks like. You should take something.' I start going through my drawers until I find my bag of pills and potions.

'I'll be fine,' she says, lying back down and at the same time putting her hand up to refuse my offer.

'I assume you're not coming to the sail away.'

'No, no. I've been to hundreds and there'll be plenty more.'

No need to brag about how many cruises you've been on, even indirectly, I think.

'But come back for me for dinner, I don't want to miss that.'

'Okay. Look, I'll leave the ibuprofen on the side in case you change your mind. But only take one, these pink bombs are mighty strong. They're good for inflammation though, so would help with your sunburn. See you later.'

I skip off down the corridor and head for the back of the ship where the sail away party is taking place.

Shona and Jockie are already at the bar when I arrive. I squeeze in next to them and order myself a drink, cider this time, as I'm quite thirsty. I really don't need another massive hit of alcohol to enjoy myself, given how much we've sipped all afternoon.

'It's best of British today,' Shona says, pointing at the Union Jack bunting spread around the deck. 'It'll be *Land of Hope and Glory* and all the rest of it,' she says, while Jockie rolls his eyes.

Soon we're being given little flags, although Jockie

pulls his own from his pocket.

'Flag of Scotland,' he tells me, as he waves his blue and white flag around with gusto. Now it's Shona's turn to roll her eyes.

The entertainments team jump up on the side of the pool – their improvised stage – and the music starts. Jockie is correct, it's all patriotic stuff and I join in as much as everyone else. Maybe it's the combined effects of the warmth and the alcohol but I'm singing along and clapping as though my life depends on it.

It's fun, I'm enjoying myself, I'm on the best holiday I've ever had. The only holiday I've ever had.

'I wonder if they ever fall in?' I shout to Shona.

She laughs and nods. 'I'm sure they do sometimes, or get thrown in.'

We finish off, as predicted with *Land of Hope and Glory*, then the team say farewell and the disco starts.

🎵🎵🎵

Fiona's asleep when I go back to the room to get ready for dinner, fortunately it's a casual night so I don't really need to change, just freshen up my face and hair a little. I let her sleep on and start to rummage through the welcome pack, I still haven't read everything in it. I notice a voucher for the spa; I could get my nails done.

I've never really bothered with manicures before because they'd be a waste of money with my job, but I'm on here for a month so I'd get the value from it. On impulse I pick up the phone and book myself an appointment. They've even managed to squeeze me in tomorrow at 11.15am. I'll go straight from watercolour class to the spa. Excellent.

Fiona lets out a long snore, followed by a loud fart.

She wouldn't be happy if she knew she'd done that.

'Fiona,' I call over. 'Do you want to go for dinner?'

She doesn't respond. Then I notice that she's clutching the *pink bomb* pack I left her. I prize it from her hand and study the strip. She's definitely taken one but I think she might have taken two, despite me telling her not to.

'Fiona.' I shake her shoulder. She snores in response.

Oh God, have I overdosed her? I told her to only take one, especially given her minute size. I once took two myself when I had a cold and I slept for twelve hours, probably the best night's sleep I've ever had. What should I do? I shake her again, but she doesn't respond. On the plus side her sunburn doesn't look so ruddy.

'Fiona.'

She farts again.

At least she's alive. If she's farting and snoring, she's definitely not dead.

I take her shoes off for her and drag her duvet from under her and lay it loosely on top of her. Will she be too hot? Should I undress her? No, that's a step too far.

Maybe she'll wake up soon.

I pop into the bathroom but when I return, she's still unconscious. Of course she is. I adjust the air con so she won't overheat under the duvet, stuff the remaining pink bombs into the farthest reaches of my drawer, grab my handbag, put the Do Not Disturb sign on the door and skip off for dinner.

'No Fiona tonight,' Shona asks when I approach my table.

'No, she's tired.' Well, it's not a lie, is it?

'Come and sit with us.' Shona waves me over and I don't need telling twice.

'But what if these people show up?'

'Ah,' Jockie says, leaning in. 'They won't. We found out earlier that they never actually got on the ship. Some emergency prevented them. Hope they're okay, but their loss is your gain. You can sit with us permanently.'

'Oh, that's great.' I've watched this table every night enjoying themselves, laughing and joking while Fiona and I sit with our poker faces.

I sit down and am soon introduced to the other two couples.

'Let's have a bottle of bubbles to celebrate,' Shona says as Jockie pulls out his cruise card to get the attention of the wine waiter.

In the end we have two bottles; I buy one with what's left of my on board spend, the rest I've used to book as many excursions and trips as I can. I want to see as much as possible on all these lovely Caribbean islands.

I've had a great night and when we've finished and everyone troops off to the theatre to watch a singer, I go too. Why wouldn't I? I do feel a little guilty about Fiona sleeping off my drugs, but she's an adult, she should have listened to what I said.

I hope she's okay.

She'll be fine.

Even so, after the theatre I don't go up to the top bar to carry on drinking, I make my excuses and head back to my cabin.

I let myself in and close the door quietly behind me, well as quietly as you can when the door feels as though it weighs twice the weight of the average person. I put the light on and go straight to check on Fiona.

She's not there, which means she's woken up.

Which is good and bad. At least she's not dead. But she's probably going to be annoyed that I didn't wake her for dinner. She's probably off roaming the ship now, looking for me and hoping for dinner.

Oh well.

I put the TV on, slump down on the sofa and start flicking through the channels. There's really nothing I fancy, so I flick it off again. I could always go and join Shona and Jockie and our new tablemates – I wonder what Fiona's going to think about that – up in the top bar.

Yep, that's what I'll do. And, I'll leave a note for Fiona so that she knows where to find us if she comes back to the cabin.

Just use the loo first.

I attempt to open the bathroom door, but I can't, it won't give. It's locked from the inside.

I hope Fiona hasn't drowned in the bath. They'll do a post mortem and know that she's overdosed on ibuprofen.

I yank the door again and call her name.

A little whimper comes from the other side of the door.

'Fiona? Are you okay?'

'No,' comes a pathetic voice. 'Get help.'

'Okay,' I call, wondering what sort of help she needs. 'I'll get the door open first. Don't worry, soon be back.'

I dash out of the cabin and hunt up and down the corridor for a crew member. Finally, I find a cabin steward, not ours, but maybe he can help.

When I tell him that my roommate is stuck in the bathroom, I can see him suppressing a smile. We head back to my cabin and he pulls a tool from one of his pockets, inserts it in the bathroom lock from the outside and the door springs open.

'Thank you so much,' I say, hoping that he'll go now, because Fiona won't want him to see her floating around in the bath in all her glory.

But he doesn't go, does he? Oh no.

'Fiona?' I call as I push the door open slowly – well, she could be slumped against it, those pink bombs are powerful.

She whimpers just as we see her.

The good thing is she's fully dressed. Not, actually, in the clothes she had on earlier, but in full *formal night* gear, including high heel shoes and glittery black tights.

It's the shoes and the tights I see first, surrounded by immense folds of black dress that make her legs look more sticklike than ever. They're poking up from the small gap between the toilet and the wall.

'Oh, madam,' says the cabin steward.

'Oh God,' I mutter.

Six

It would be cruel to laugh, wouldn't it?

In an attempt to not say something stupid, I say something stupid.

'Why are you dressed like that? It wasn't a formal night tonight.'

Fiona's only response is a wail.

'Madam, shall I help you out?' The cabin steward is a gentleman; I'm more interested in her dress. I haven't seen it before, although it's black like her other one, this one – what I can see of it – is more ornate and includes lace and a net petticoat.

'Yes, yes,' she hisses.

He steps into the bathroom, moves towards her then recoils before putting the toilet lid down and flushing it. Just as well he's still wearing the thin, blue rubber gloves all the stewards wear when they clean the rooms, a fresh pair for every room. He attempts to get his hands under Fiona's arms while I breathe down his neck – not my intention but that's what's happening.

'Stop, stop,' Fiona yelps. 'No, no. Pamela, you try. You might be more gentle than this brute.'

I feel the steward's hurt feelings as he backs away to let me nearer. I mouth, 'Sorry,' at him.

'How did you get down here?' I ask, as though she stuffed herself into this tight space just for fun; another stupid question.

'Does it matter?' Fiona spits, casting an eye at the steward, who then shrinks further back.

I grab her arms and pull, she doesn't move an inch, just yelps louder. Now I'm up close I can see why the steward recoiled; it wasn't just the toilet contents. Fiona's knickers and tights are down – well that seems logical, since I assume she *was* on the toilet – and I can see her nether regions clearly exposed. I lean in and move her dress around to cover her modesty.

'What are you doing? Just get me up.'

I grab her hands again but it's no good.

'I'll get help,' the steward says, glad of his opportunity to leave the scene.

'What did you bring him for?' Fiona snipes once he's out of our cabin.

'To open the bathroom door, you locked it, remember?'

'Of course I remember, of course I locked it; I was going to the toilet.'

Yes, I think we all know that.

The cabin steward returns with a colleague and, with a bit of shuffling I exit the bathroom and they enter. They have another go at pulling Fiona out from her hidey hole, but it's no good. They retreat and have a quiet conversation, so quiet I can't hear it.

'What are they saying? What are they saying? Tell them to speak English.'

I will not.

'Madam, we will get professional help.' They

47

disappear again.

'Professional help, what does that mean? Get me out of here, Pamela.'

I try, though not too hard because Fiona is squealing like a stuck pig.

A nurse comes into the cabin, she looks at me and smiles and I move out of her way so she can see Fiona.

'Hello. I'm Lizzie. What's your name?'

'Fiona.'

'How did this happen?'

'Does it matter? Just get me out.'

'Well, apparently it's too painful for you. Where exactly does it hurt?'

'I don't know. Everywhere,' snaps Fiona. 'Just get me out.'

'We're trying.' There's a nice professional smile as she opens her bag up on the vanity unit. She wipes, then stuffs a thermometer under Fiona's armpit, which isn't especially easy given her position. While she waits for that she checks Fiona's pulse and pulls out her stethoscope. I wonder if this is where they find out I've overdosed my cabin-mate on ibuprofen?

'Never mind all that,' Fiona says, 'Just get me out.'

'We will, I just need to ensure that you're fit enough. You are quite flushed.'

Whether the pun was intended or not, I feel a snigger beginning in the back of my throat. I have to leave the bathroom before it escapes.

The cabin stewards are still in the room, respectfully silent with their hands clasped in front of them, awaiting orders. There's a knock at the door. I'm nearest so I open it. Two burly men in boiler suits, one carrying a bag of tools, stand before me.

'Plumbers. Is Lizzie here?'

'Yes,' Lizzie calls from the bathroom.

One of the men steps inside where no conversation takes place because presumably one has already been had. He just inspects the toilet and Fiona and her situation.

'I see,' he says. 'We'll start from outside.'

I don't know what they're going to do, but my mind is working overtime. Can they take the wall down? Surely not.

They prop open the cabin door, and step outside. There's the sound of tools being used and I cannot resist a peek outside. They're removing a panel in the corridor; one I realise that is the other side of our bathroom. They started banging and clanking and then one plumber comes back inside – I have to jump out of his way.

'I need to break the seal,' he says to Lizzie who climbs into the bath to get out of his way.

'Oh, the indignity,' Fiona mumbles as the plumber bends down next to her and starts hacking at the mastic seal between the toilet and the wall with a blade.

'Done,' he bellows to his workmate out in the corridor.

'Done,' comes the response.

The man pulls at the toilet, Fiona yelps, and suddenly the toilet comes away from the wall and liquid and smells seep from the toilet pipe. Fiona's dress does a good job of mopping it up.

The plumber pulls the toilet out of the way and Fiona collapses in a heap into the space the toilet has vacated. That dress will be even wetter now.

'Do you think you can get up now?' Lizzie asks.

'No,' Fiona says, even though she's trying to push herself up at the same time smoothing down her dress.

Her skinny legs and her high heeled shoes flail about uselessly, but she cannot get up.

Lizzie looks pointedly at the plumber who has been gawping at Fiona; he nods and leaves.

'Guys,' Lizzie calls and the two stewards move towards the bathroom as I scuttle out of the way.

Because Fiona weighs next to nothing, they easily pick her up and sit her on the now marooned toilet. She yelps and moans the whole time.

'How do you feel?' Lizzie asks.

'In pain,' yells Fiona.

'Where does it hurt?'

'Everywhere.' There are beads of sweat on Fiona's brow and her previously red face is now white and waxen.

'Thanks, guys,' Lizzie says. 'If you could just wait outside.'

'Pamela,' yells Fiona. 'Pamela.'

'Yes?'

'Make sure my handbag is back in my bedside drawer.'

'Okay.' I cringe at her insinuation that the stewards might take it.

'Have you done it?' she calls.

I pop my head back into the bathroom. 'Yes. It's fine.'

I stay there as Lizzie lifts up Fiona's dress, her knickers and tights are halfway down her thighs, she was definitely on the toilet. Pee or crap, I wonder wickedly.

Lizzie pops her head out of the bathroom. 'Okay, guys, please bring the chair in.'

One of the stewards disappears and returns in seconds with a wheelchair which he bumps over the bathroom door sill.

'We're going to put you in the chair and take you down to the medical centre,' Lizzie tells Fiona.

'Oh no,' Fiona wails again.

In what seems like seconds they have Fiona in the chair and outside the cabin.

'Pamela, you come too,' Fiona's plaintive voice calls. I grab my bag and trot to keep up as Lizzie wheels Fiona towards the lifts.

'Don't worry, we'll close up for you after we've put the toilet back,' one of the plumbers says. I hadn't even noticed they were still here until he spoke.

I just manage to scuttle into the lift before the doors close and we whizz down to the lower deck where the medical centre is located.

It's just like a real hospital down here. I don't know why I'm surprised, but I am. The furniture is the same as our local, fairly new hospital and so are the beds. We could be in any NHS hospital in the UK. But we're not.

I follow Fiona into a side room where a doctor is waiting. It appears he's already been briefed. He starts to ask Fiona how this all happened and attempts to examine her. She squeals out in pain. Poor Fiona, she's just had enough.

'I think we need to X-ray you,' he says in a soft voice.

'No, don't move me again.'

Lizzie bends down and removes Fiona shoes before handing them to me. She's murmuring words of comfort to Fiona but I think Fiona is past caring. Next Lizzie removes Fiona's tights and knickers – they were halfway down anyway and hands everything to me.

'Perhaps you'd like to take a seat in the waiting room,' the doctor says to me. I can't scurry out fast enough. I hate hospitals at the best of times.

I ball Fiona's underwear up in my hand, balance the shoes on my fingers and sit down in the empty waiting room. It's quiet and the light is subdued.

Twenty minutes later Fiona is wheeled past me in a bed and taken to another room. I'm invited to join her.

Fiona is smiling when I enter the room, really smiling, I mean I haven't seen her smile like this since I met her. She's wearing a hospital gown and her dress and bra have been stuffed into a clear plastic bag and dumped on the end of her bed, because she's so small she looks like a little kid in an adult bed.

'How are you?' I ask, because she doesn't look as though she's in pain anymore. 'Have they sorted you out now?'

'Oh yes,' Fiona says, the smile on her face turning into a ludicrous grin.

'We've given her a little morphine for the pain.'

'Oh.' That's when I notice the tube thing coming out from her wrist. No wonder she looks so happy, she's away with the fairies. Still, better that than in pain.

'We were just telling Fiona that she's broken her leg.'

'No.' I can't believe it. 'Just from falling off the toilet?'

'Awkward fall.' The doctor shrugs. 'We'll have to keep her here until we get to Barbados. Then she'll have to go into hospital there.'

'Noooo,' Fiona says, but she's still smiling, almost laughing.

'But it's days until we reach Barbados,' I say.

'Yes, five. Fiona is fine, we're looking after her. She'll have an emergency hip replacement when we reach port.'

'A what?'

'Broken femur, that's how it's fixed.'

Fiona starts to laugh. 'What a hoot,' she says before leaning back in the bed and closing her eyes.

'Come back tomorrow to see her, you can pop in anytime, don't worry about the surgery hours, they don't apply to you,' Lizzie says. 'And you can bring down her own nightclothes, well a nightdress would be best, and toothbrush, washing implements, etc.'

'Okay.' I grab the plastic bag and stuff Fiona's tights, shoes and knickers inside with her dress. As I open the bag I get a whiff of pee. Not nice. 'I'll see you tomorrow, Fiona,' I say, but she doesn't reply. I don't think she can even hear me.

At least she's not in pain any longer.

♫♫♫

Back in the cabin it's as though nothing has happened. The toilet is back in its place and any spillage that Fiona's dress didn't already mop up is gone too.

I drop the plastic bag full of Fiona's clothes in the bath, get ready and go to bed.

I lie awake, wondering if it's all my fault, because she overdosed herself on *my* ibuprofen. If it made her confused enough to think tonight was a formal night, then maybe it affected her balance.

Yes, I'm definitely to blame. I'll have to be super nice to her to make it up.

Seven

I'm up early and already breakfasted by 8.30pm. I take the lift to the medical centre and attempt to push the door open. It's locked. So much for being able to pop in anytime I like. Maybe it's a sign and I should just skip off.

I hunt around until I find a bell, wondering if I should press it, daring myself. I do and I'm let in without any fuss.

I knock on Fiona's door; a meek little voice tells me to come in.

A nurse is with Fiona, not Lizzie, a different one.

'Eleanor,' Fiona says. 'How nice of you to come.'

'It's Pamela,' I say, in my nice voice because I have to be super nice now, don't I?

'It's Eleanor,' Fiona says, first to me while she narrows her eyes and then to the nurse. 'Eleanor Rigby,' she repeats.

I could punch her for looking at my passport.

'It's Pamela Rigby, actually.'

'Hello, Pamela, I'm Tracey.'

Fiona giggles.

'How are you?' I ask.

'I have a broken leg.' She giggles again and before long she's laughing like a hyena.

'The morphine,' Tracey says. 'We've taking her off it now. We're giving her something else.'

'Oh, don't do that. I love it.'

'Are those Fiona's things?' Tracey says.

'They are.' I offer over a carrier bag.

'Excellent. I'll get you a bowl, flannel and towel, and you can have a wash, Fiona.' Tracey turns to me. 'Perhaps you could help her.' With that she disappears only to return minutes later with the bowl. She whips Fiona's hospital gown off, while keeping her covered and smiles at me. Then she's gone.

I glance at Fiona who looks at me expectantly. I really don't want to do this and if Fiona wasn't morphined up she wouldn't want it either. Maybe she reacts badly to all painkillers, maybe this isn't *all* my fault.

I squirt a bit of shower gel into the bowl, swish it around and plop the flannel in, then wring it out and hand it to Fiona who doesn't take it.

'Could you do my private parts?' she says, whipping off the bedcovers to display her nakedness in all its glory. I don't know where to look. 'What's the matter,' she cackles. 'Have you never seen a fanny before?'

I smile and approach the bed. The fact is I haven't seen a fanny before, not someone else's anyway. Not even my mum's. Even when her dementia was at its worst she always insisted on 'doing me own ablutions', it used to make me laugh when she said that. My mum was a prude of the highest sort. Sadly, Fiona doesn't appear to be. Well, not in her drugged-up state, anyway.

I flannel one foot and lower leg, then the other.

Then rinse out the flannel and come back. The thigh muscle on her right leg, I assume it's the broken one, is taught and twisted, so I start with the left leg.

'Leave the other one,' she says, watching me. 'It's sore. But do me fanny and be careful not to dislodge the catheter.'

I do as I'm told, cringing with embarrassment for both of us. It's a cursory wash, but the best I can do, but probably better than she could do herself at the moment. Still makes me cringe though.

Get me out of here.

I rinse and repeat, moving up her body. I hope she doesn't make me do this every day. There's so little of her that it doesn't take long but even so. At least I now have her covered with the towel.

There's just her face to do.

'You'll have to get another flannel,' she says, seeing me hesitate.

'I will.' I take my opportunity to get out of the room.

When I come back, fresh flannel in hand, I glance at the wall clock. I've got fifteen more minutes before my watercolour class. I'll have to get a move on if I want to make it. I wet the flannel and give it to Fiona, surely to God she can wash her own face. She does.

'Toothbrush?' she asks, her voice sounding a little hoarse.

I smear toothpaste onto it and hand it to her. She waits expectantly for me to do something else. Oh yes. I look around for and find a paper cup – it looks unused – fill it with water from the en suite bathroom and hand it to her. After a lot of scrubbing, swilling and spitting she hands it all back to me.

'I need to get going soon.' I whip her nightdress out of the bag and roll it down so that she can put her head and arms through. I help her pull it down but when we get to her middle, I don't push it any further. I do not want to be responsible for harming that leg further. I pull the bedcovers up instead.

'What's in the other bag?' she asks, seeming not to answer my previous statement.

'My art stuff. It starts soon, so I need to get going.'

'You're still going?' The sound of hurt in her voice cuts into me.

A quick glance at her and I can see that she's blinking back tears. And I am supposed to be super nice to her, aren't I?

'Maybe not today. I don't *need* to go, do I?'

Fiona smiles a bit too quickly and I wonder if I've been played.

'Go tomorrow,' she says, as though she's giving me permission.

'Yeah.' I smile but I don't mean it. 'I do have to go by eleven though,' I say.

She frowns.

'I have an appointment.'

She frowns again, her face expressing puzzlement. I'll have to tell her because she'll see the results anyway.

'My nails. I booked it days ago, I have to go or I'll have to pay anyway. They need twenty-four hours' notice. Which, obviously, I couldn't give, because this happened to you just last night.' I'm not telling her the whole truth, given that I only booked the appointment last night. I probably could cancel, especially given the circumstances. 'But I won't be long,' I add.

'Lucky you. I was going to get my nails done, *that* won't be happening now.' She lets out a long theatrical sigh.

'There'll be other times,' I say, patting her arm which

just happens to be resting on her broken leg. She lets out a howl. I'm not sure quite how genuine it is.

Then she leans back, closes her eyes and dozes off.

It's just after 10am and I wonder if I could just nip into the back of the art class now? I tiptoe over to my bag, pick it up and head for the door. I have my hand on the handle when she speaks.

'Where are you going?'

'Just the toilet,' I lie.

'Use that one,' she says, pointing to the en suite.

'Oh yeah. I suppose I can.'

When I come out, even though I didn't actually need to use the loo, she's well asleep, her head back, her mouth open, and she's snoring. I can't quite believe the noise she's making, for someone so small she has one hell of a horrible, loud snore on her. It reminds me of an old motorbike Keith once had, he was tinkering with it in the back garden when he was home during his university holidays. He said he couldn't afford a new exhaust so we'd just have to put up with the noise and fumes – he said this to my mother and she slapped his face.

Served him right.

I wonder if I dare chance sneaking out again? I head for the door but Fiona does such a loud snore at that point that I'm sure she's going to wake herself up.

I won't bother. I slump down in the chair next to her bed and watch Fiona sleep.

She's still asleep when I sneak out for my nail appointment. Given the size of the ship I don't think I have time to go back to the cabin and drop off my art equipment so I take it with me.

I choose the nail varnish that needs ultraviolet light to set it and is supposed to last for weeks. It's such a novelty. With my job painted nails are never really an option. I keep my nails short too, because I don't like them full of dirt, but here, on holiday, they've already grown a lot in less than a week. I suppose that's the result of not humping clay pots about every day.

I leave the salon with a smile on my face. My hands have been paraffin waxed, soaked, massaged and my nails are a beautiful shade of maroon. Very dramatic. I resisted the temptation to have a pattern on them, thinking it too much, but now, I'm almost regretting that decision. Oh well, next time…

When I check the time I see it's after noon, I hadn't realised I'd been quite so long.

I suppose I really should go and see how Fiona is.

Or I could go for lunch.

I drop my art bag back in the cabin and take myself off to lunch. Not the buffet, but the restaurant, where I will be waited on.

I treat myself to a glass of wine. Just in case I need it.

♫♫♫

Fiona is reclining in her medical centre bed watching TV when I enter.

'Ah, the wanderer returns,' she says, without any attempt to hide her sarcasm. 'I see you took your art stuff so I assume you sneaked into the back of the class.' Is the woman psychic?

'No, I didn't. I was having my nails done. It was lunchtime by the time they were finished, so …' I shrug my shoulders and raise my hands and force a light laugh. I really don't know why I have to explain myself to her. We're not married, we're not even friends, not proper friends; we're travelling companions. 'Have you had any lunch?'

'Yes. I need all the insurance documents.'

'Okay. I can bring them down. Where are they?'

'That's the problem. They're in the safe.'

'That's not a problem, I'll get them out.' I have a horrible feeling I know where this is going.

'But you'll need the number.'

'I will,' I say and try my hardest not to smirk. She's going to have to give it to me.

'I can't give you the number.'

'Why not?' I sound indignant. I *am* indignant. 'I can't open the safe without it.'

'I can't give it to you. I told you before it's my secret number and I use it for everything.'

I sigh. 'I promise I won't tell anyone and I won't use it for my own personal gain.'

'No. I just can't. You'll have to take me up to our cabin.'

I laugh. How can I not? 'What, shall I give you a piggyback?' She's small enough and because of my job, I'm probably strong enough that I could.

'Don't be silly, I have a broken leg. There's a wheelchair in the corridor, I've seen it when the door is opened. Bring it in here.'

And I'm being silly!

'I can't do that.'

'Yes, you can. Go and get it now.'

'No.'

'Yes.' She gives me a look that I interpret as *this is all your fault anyway*, because I feel guilty. 'Yes,' she says again. 'Do it.'

I creep out of her room and glance about; the coast is clear. I snatch the wheelchair and bring it into the room and close the door behind me.

60

'Help me.'

'How? This isn't going to work. You've got that drip thing in your wrist for a start.'

'Oh that, pfff.' I can't quite believe my eyes as she rips it out and she doesn't even wince. 'Come on, help me.' She flings the bedcovers off and I'm relieved to see that her nightie is covering her *fanny*. She's wearing surgical stockings and they're compressing her tiny legs even further; they look like sticks now.

'They're because I'm not mobile,' she says, seeing me staring at them. Come on,' she urges, wriggling to the edge of the bed at speed.

If I don't catch her, she's going to fall. She must still be on a lot of painkillers, because she doesn't even flinch as she drags her broken leg towards the wheelchair which confirms my belief that she was playing me earlier.

I pick her up like a child and lift her into the wheelchair. She weighs even less than she looks.

'See, easy. Let's go.'

I open the door and peep out, still no one about. I turn to get behind the wheelchair but Fiona is already propelling it and herself towards me. I just manage to jump out of the way before she hurtles down the corridor towards the door.

I run to get there fast and open it almost at the same time as she hurls herself through it. We're at the lift in seconds.

'Press it, press it.'

'I have. I can't make it come any faster.'

She glances towards the stairs then at the wheelchair. She cannot seriously be considering…

The lift pings. The doors open. Out steps Nurse Lizzie.

Fiona urges me on with a series of frantic waves, and for one moment I think we're going to get away with it as I grip the wheelchair handles and start to enter the lift.

'Just a moment,' Lizzie says, finally realising and standing in front of us, barring our way. 'What are you doing?'

'We have to retrieve the insurance document,' Fiona says. 'Excuse us, we won't be long.'

'No. You cannot. You shouldn't be out of bed. You certainly shouldn't be in a wheelchair. How did you even get in it?'

'Quite easily,' Fiona says. 'We won't be long.'

'You need to be straight back in bed. Do you realise the damage you could do to your leg?'

'It's already broken.' Fiona does have a point.

'Yes, and it could be a lot worse, you could sever an artery doing this. Come on, back to your room.' Lizzie moves towards me to grip the wheelchair handles and for one mad, sad, insane moment I consider not letting go and just pushing past her and into the lift. Then I come to my senses.

Fiona's back in bed in minutes, a new bag is put up on the stand and the drip reattached to her wrist. A steward has been in and mopped up the mess caused when Fiona ripped the drip out and I am standing in the corner watching. I feel like a naughty kid about to get told off.

'Do not move,' Lizzie says in her best angry nurse voice.

Fiona scowls, I cringe, but we both stay put.

The chief medical officer comes in and tells us off, there's a mini-lecture about the possibility of Fiona losing her leg. The colour drains from her face.

'What were you thinking?' the doctor asks me.

Oh, so it's all my fault. Well, it's not.

'I wasn't thinking,' I retort. 'I was doing as I was told.'

He glances at Fiona who pretends butter wouldn't melt in her mouth, she's all little and hunched up and looking pathetic. And silent.

'This could have been very serious.'

'Tell her, not me. She insisted we go to our cabin.'

'*She's* on strong painkillers.'

So, it is all my fault. Yet again.

His eyes flick between us before he finally shakes his head. 'No more antics,' he says, as though we are naughty kids. He opens the door and steps through it.

'Then *you* can't have the insurance document,' Fiona spits, having finally found her voice.

The doctor stops in his tracks and spins round.

'*I* don't need your insurance documents, *you* do. This will all be charged to your on-board account. You'll also have to pay cash for your operation in Barbados.' He smiles and turns away again.

'Wait, what operation?' I ask, confused. I thought she had a broken leg; I suppose I hadn't thought much further than that. I'd imagined they'd just slap a load of plaster of Paris on it and she'd be back on board with a wheelchair and crutches.

'Fiona is going into hospital once we reach Barbados where she will have a hip replacement.'

'But she's broken her leg.' I don't understand.

'We explained it to Fiona this morning…'

'When you were off titivating,' Fiona cuts in, the sneer curling on her lip.

'Her femur is broken at the top and the only way to repair it is with a hip replacement. Quite expensive, so I suggest you,' he looks pointedly at me, 'Bring those insurance documents down ASAP.'

'I can't. They're in the safe and Fiona won't give me the number because it's her secret number she uses *for everything.*'

He looks at Fiona for confirmation but she's asleep now, or pretending to be. He indicates for me to leave the room with him.

'You can ask Reception to reset it. Just explain the situation.' He walks off and leaves me standing there, like the idiot I am.

Eight

The safe is open. So there.

I've pulled everything out and spread it on Fiona's bed, because the safe is tucked away in Fiona's wardrobe and unless I put my head on a stick, I can't see anything. Anyway, I don't want my head brushing against Fiona's clothes any more than she'd want that. Which reminds me, the plastic bag with last night's soiled evening dress and knickers is still in the bathroom, wedged between the spare toilet rolls and the sanitary bin, I had to take it out of the bath this morning to shower.

I jump up and run to the bathroom, hoping that the steward hasn't taken the bag away as rubbish.

He hasn't.

Actually, I'm wondering if it would be so bad if he had. Maybe I should just throw everything away.

Stop, that's not nice.

Back in the cabin I sort through the safe contents looking for the insurance policy. I find it easily enough – in a sealed envelope marked *Holiday Insurance Policy* in Fiona's tiny handwriting. So small I have to squint to read it, even with my reading glasses on.

I put the envelope aside and tidy what's left: my passport, my purse containing my currency, mostly US dollars, and my credit card. I pull the card out and look at it; it thrills me, I feel like a proper person. It's my first credit card ever and I can't quite believe that it has an eight-thousand-pound limit. Of course I'd never spend it because I'd never be able to pay it back, but still, it's nice to know someone thinks I'm good for that amount. Though God knows who or how, maybe it's a mistake, but what the hell.

Fiona's purse is there too, but I don't look inside – although it is tempting. I can't resist a peek at her passport though. She looked at mine without asking, so it's only fair. There's the inevitable horrible passport photo that is compulsory, no smiling, no hair on your face, and so on. Her passport is recent too, it must be a renewed one since she's such a seasoned traveller. No doubt her old passports are full of country stamps. I can't wait to get some of those, though not sure if that happens on a cruise; according to Cherry at work, it doesn't. Then I spot Fiona's date of birth. What? She said she was the same age as me, we'd joked about it, but she's not. Not if I'm working this out right. I grab my own passport and double check hers against mine. Yes, I'm right. She is ten years older than me, ten years older than she said she was.

Fiona is a big, fat liar. Well, a skinny, little liar.

Why did you lie, Fiona? I imagine myself asking her.

Ha. Maybe not.

I take the insurance document down to Fiona on my way to dinner.

'You look very nice,' she says, scrutinising my evening dress and sparkly shoes, both from eBay.

Tonight *is* a formal night and I'm looking forward to it, especially as I'm sitting on the fun table now.

'Thank you. How are you?' Stupid question really.

She gives me a withering look. 'Same. It's not going to get better on its own.'

'No. Anyway, I have the insurance thing you wanted.' I pull it out of my glittery evening bag – borrowed, at her insistence, from Cherry.

Fiona takes it and presses it to her chest as though it is precious, which I suppose it is now. She inspects the back of the envelope.

'Did you read it?'

'No.' It hadn't even occurred to me, even though I paid half. Fiona arranged everything and I've trusted her. Given her lies about her age I'm suddenly struck by the thought that maybe I shouldn't trust her so blindly.

She gives me a bland smile. 'The chief doctor is going to ring the insurance company and arrange my medical care for when we get to Barbados. He's telling them which hospital I should go to and which surgeon should operate on me.'

'That's good. Do you need me to do anything?' I don't know what since it seems to be all in hand.

'No, not at the moment.'

'Oh,' I say, pulling her phone out of my bag. 'I brought this down, I thought you might want to contact your family.' I hand it over and she gives me forced smile. 'Why?' she says.

'Let them know what's happened,' I offer.

'It'll only worry them. Anyway, who knows how much that will cost, ringing them, I mean.'

'Or you could WhatsApp. I could pay for the internet tomorrow.' I'm trying to help, I really am. 'Or you could email them.'

'Oh no, I couldn't ask you to do that. I really don't want to worry them.'

'Well, let me know if you change your mind. Do you want your phone? Shall I leave it here?'

'No, no, take it back. Maybe when things settle down…' she says. I'm not sure what she means by that, I don't see things settling down for quite some time.

'Okay.' I stand up. 'I need to be off.'

Fiona's mouth is pinched as she wishes me well.

♫♫♫

'Where's your tiny friend this evening?' Jockie asks as I take my seat at the table.

'Ah, well, bit of a disaster really,' I say, before telling them all about it, although I don't tell them that Fiona fell off the toilet, I just say she fell over.

'Oh no. Poor woman.' Everyone on the table is sorry for her.

'Trust she's well insured,' Shona says.

'I think so.' Maybe I should have looked at that insurance document, but I'm sure Fiona has everything sorted out.

'So they're going to replace her hip to fix her break, then?'

'I'm afraid so.'

'She'll be in Barbados quite a while then. Where does that leave you?'

'What do you mean?'

'You'll be getting off with her,' Jockie says.

'Oh, um…' I haven't even thought that far ahead.

'No, of course she won't,' Shona says. 'They're just travelling companions, aren't you?'

'Yes. That's right.'

'Oh, sorry,' Jockie says. 'I thought you were a couple. Mea culpa. Bit tough for her having to cope on her own there… but I'm sure she'll be fine.'

Later, in my cabin alone, having eaten and drunk myself merry and been to the theatre and allowed myself to be persuaded to go dancing, even though I can't, I start thinking about Fiona.

And worrying.

What the hell will happen when we reach Barbados? Will they just fix her and bring her back on the ship? I suppose, somewhere in the back of my mind that's what I certainly imagined before I knew about the operation. Now, I realise I haven't a clue.

♫♫♫

I've overslept today, so after breakfast I go straight to my art class. I tell myself that Fiona is being well looked after, they'll be feeding her and helping her wash the bits she can't reach so she won't mind waiting until I've finished. She's not my responsibility, I think, perhaps selfishly.

'Ah, the wanderer returns,' Fiona says when I bounce into her room.

'I've hardly wandered far, have I?' I almost snap.

'Well, you missed all the excitement, if you can call it that.'

'Oh?'

'Well, the doctor's made the call to the insurance company and they're sorting out the hospital details.'

'That's good.' At least, I assume it is.

'Yes, and the Customer Services manager has been down here giving me some advice about what is going to happen when we reach Barbados. Shame you weren't here to hear it first-hand.' She rolls her eyes just a little.

'Sorry, I was busy.' Anyway, what has it got to do with me, really?

'Well, we'll probably go by ambulance straight to the hospital and they'll probably operate later that day, depending on what time we dock.'

'Oh, that sounds good, will you be able to come back on the ship once it's done?'

Fiona stares at me as though I'm truly stupid.

'Are you joking?' she says, her eyes narrowing. 'I'll have had major surgery. Anyway, the ship's doctor has already said they won't let me back on. I'll just be a liability, to them and to myself. So, that's the end of our holiday.' She flops back on her pillows and sighs.

'Our holiday?'

'Well, yes, I'd assumed you were coming with me.'

When I don't answer she pales before my eyes, stares at me and blinks back tears, but her eyes are watery and I know she's close to crying. Oh God. She is genuinely upset.

'If you want me to,' I say, trying not to sound sullen.

'Oh, thank you,' she says, brightening instantly. 'For a moment there I thought you were going to let me down, abandon me in a strange land.'

I smile and fight back my own tears. For a moment there I thought I was going to have my holiday, the one I've saved up for for years, the only holiday I've ever had.

'Can I get you anything?' I ask, to distract myself.

'Yes, you can. Can you help me onto that bedpan please, I need to use it?' She points over at a cardboard bowl on the side.

'But you have a catheter, oh…' I finally realise why she needs the bedpan. 'I'll get a nurse,' I say, darting out

70

of the room and returning moments later to tell her someone will be along shortly.

'Why can't you just do it? You're strong, I'm small.'

'Because I might drop you or hurt you.' She's already moaned to me about how frequently they come in and move her about, even in the night and she says it's very painful. And they know what they're doing. Anyway, I don't want to.

'I suppose,' Fiona says, sulkily. 'I hope they're not too long because I don't know if I can wait.'

'They won't be.' I cross my fingers behind my back.

'That reminds me, what have you done with my dress and undergarments? You know, the ones I was wearing when this happened.'

'Um, nothing, yet.' I sound as sheepish as I feel. I don't tell her that I've seriously considered binning them.

'Could you wash them then please, otherwise that dress is going to be ruined and it's a designer piece.'

'Maybe I could send them to the laundry,' I offer.

'Oh, no.' Fiona's voice sounds pleading and surprisingly loud. 'No, they boil everything up down there, they think everything is a sheet or a towel.'

'I'm sure they don't.'

'Please, you wash them, by hand, in the bath and let the dress drip dry. Please say you will.' She's blinking up a few tears again. Am I being manipulated? Again.

'Okay,' I agree, thinking that I *will* send them down to the laundry even if I have to pay for it myself.

Two nurses come in wearing plastic aprons and rubber gloves and I take that as my cue to leave, excusing myself and telling Fiona I'm going to get her dress sorted out right now.

♫♫♫

Back in my cabin I enter the bathroom and find the offending bag full of pissy clothes. Or, at least, I hope it's only that and not something worse. I pull the bag open and gag, I really should have done something with these earlier because I think they're starting to ferment. I work with earth and plants and all sorts all day and I'm not usually squeamish, but this has moved on to another level.

I can't really send these down to the laundry now, can 1?

I start to fill the bath. I debate how hot the water needs to be; hot enough to kill germs and the smell, but cool enough to not damage the designer dress. That is, of course, assuming that's it's not beyond saving already.

The next debate is what to use to wash it in. I have brought some washing capsules with me but I had envisaged going down to the passenger laundry and using them there, not actually swilling my hands – and my lovely new manicure – in them. That's a point, I could take this lot down to the passenger laundry. I peek in the bag again and reel back. Maybe not.

I throw a couple of washing capsules into the running water and watch, mesmerised as they disintegrate and the liquid spreads through the water. At least *that* smells nice.

The bath is half full when I tip the contents of the bag into it. I screw up the bag and push it into the bathroom bin, mentally apologising to our cabin steward.

The dress, the knickers, the bra and the tights sink into the water. A good soak will do them the world of good, but unfortunately not every part of the dress is submerged. The net petticoat is sticking up. I look around the bathroom for something to use to push everything down. There's nothing.

Except… the toilet brush that is discreetly tucked away in its holder at the back of the toilet; Fiona's back must have been pressed against it during her ordeal.

Size wise it would be perfect, and it has a nice long handle which means I wouldn't need to touch any of Fiona's pissy clothes. I seriously consider it. Would it be so bad?

It's tempting, it really is. But I don't. I used Fiona's special shampoo and conditioner bottles instead because they're just the right size and my jumbo bottles are far too big for the job. I stamp them up and down over the washing to make sure everything is thoroughly wetted through before I leave the bathroom and close the door.

They'll need a good soak, I think.

Then I go off to a talk in the theatre about Barbados and all the lovely places I can visit. We're there for two nights and I've booked two trips.

Will I still be able to go on them?

Nine

Two hours later and the water in the bath is cold. I yank the plug out and let the water drain away. It's black.

I can't quite believe that her clothes were that dirty, so that means it's dye and they have faded. Oops.

I get the shower attachment and hose everything down. I don't want to touch anything until it's thoroughly rinsed. Using Fiona's shampoo and conditioner like tongs I turn everything over and continue hosing.

I use a hanger from Fiona's wardrobe and hang the dress up to drip dry. The underwear, I squeeze out and drape over the pull-out washing line over the bath. At least everything smells pleasant now and I can't see any actual fade marks on the dress. I didn't get a good look at it when it was bunched up around Fiona's body when she was wedged between the toilet and the wall, but the dress is rather nice. Although, given how small and skinny she is I do wonder if she might not have looked like a wicked fairy in it.

All that's missing is a black wand.

♫♫♫

I dutifully trot down to see Fiona on my way to dinner and give her an update on her dress, which, having spent the entire afternoon dripping away is now looking okay and drying nicely.

'Thank goodness,' she says, giving me a smile. 'That dress is designer.'

'Yes, you said.' Never mind thanking goodness, thank me.

I'm about to make my excuses and leave when Fiona tells me that they've speeded the ship up so we'll arrive in Barbados earlier than expected.

'That's good, then,' I say.

'Oh,' she says, waving her hand in a dismissive fashion. 'It's not for me, I don't warrant that. Some man has had a stroke and they need to get him to hospital as soon as possible.'

'Oh, that's awful. Poor man.'

'Yes. Of course they're focussing all their attention on *him* now and I'm just left here, unattended, for hours. So you could pop in more often instead of sunning yourself on deck.'

The word *selfish* is forming on my lips but I bite it back. 'I haven't been sunning myself at all.' Then I feel guilty, perhaps I am the selfish one, I can at least come and go as I please while poor Fiona is stuck here and in pain too. 'I'll come and see you straight after my art class.'

'Oh, what time is that?'

'It's ten 'til eleven, so I'll be here just after eleven.'

'No, that won't work. The customer services manager is coming down tomorrow between ten and eleven and you need to be here.'

'Do I? Why?'

'She's going to go through the arrangements for getting off. Obviously, that involves you.'

'Oh yes, I suppose it does.'

'Of course it does.' Fiona's tone is huffy. 'Just make sure you're here by ten. It's all a bit too much information for me to take in, especially with all these painkillers they keep giving me.'

I agree. Anything for a quiet life and anyway, it won't hurt to hear what the arrangements are. Fiona will need help, that's for sure, even if it does mean I'm going to miss my art class.

♫♫♫

I'm down just before ten but the customer services manager, Jill Pennyworth, doesn't manifest until quarter-past-eleven. She breezes in and I immediately take a dislike to her, not least because I've missed my art class while waiting for her glorious presence.

Stop being so selfish, I chide myself, Fiona is stuck in bed with a broken leg.

After introductions where she basically tells us her life story – not married, except to her job which she absolutely *loves*, and she'll be sixty on her next birthday – she starts to tell us what will happen.

'We'll be docking around midnight and Fiona will go by ambulance straight to the hospital.'

Fiona whimpers at the prospect.

'So you, Eleanor, is it, will need to pack a small bag for Fiona.' She points a finger and smiles at me and I dislike her even more. And Fiona.

'It's Pamela,' I say without even the hint of a smile.

'What do you mean by small bag?'

'Well, Fiona will probably be in hospital for a week, so probably just an overnight bag, toiletries and so on, everything else you can take in your suitcase. But remember, only take what you, *Pamela...*' she emphasises my name, 'Can carry because they'll be no one else to help you and obviously Fiona can't carry anything. And you'll have to manage it through the airports when you fly home.' She smiles and holds her hands in front of her like a snotty head girl who has just delivered a speech at assembly.

'I'm not necessarily flying home, I'll probably stay on,' I say.

'Oh but... I thought...' Her eyes flick between me and Fiona.

'We haven't sorted out the details yet,' Fiona says effectively closing down the conversation. 'Thank you, Jill.' If that isn't Jill dismissed, I don't know what is.

After she's gone Fiona slumps down the bed a bit further; I know what she's up to and I'm not going to bite.

'Shall we put the TV on?' I ask. 'There's a film on you might like, it's a newish one.'

'No. Thank you. I don't think I could concentrate on a whole film.'

Now it's my turn to slump down, but into the vinyl covered chair so beloved of all medical institutions. The air escapes from the seat as my weight hits it. So inelegant and so uncomfortable; I can already feel my legs starting to sweat. I could really do with getting lost in a film, I really could.

After a while of sitting in stilted silence, during which Fiona pretends to doze off and I consider sneaking out, she suddenly opens a gimlet eye and speaks. I almost don't take in what she's saying because I'm mesmerised by her winking stare.

'I think you might have to come with me…' Her voice is timid and at complete odds with the eye which is bold and challenging.

'Is there something wrong with your eye?'

She opens her other eye and pulls herself up the bed a little but she doesn't answer my question.

'Because of the insurance,' she says, finishing her previous sentence.

'What do you mean?'

'The insurance. We're on it together.' She doesn't look at me now, but stares towards the blank TV screen.

'Yes, but that's the same as us sharing a room, we do things, pay our onboard account and so on, separately. Don't we?'

Fiona blinks several times; the tears are coming and I feel guilty. I should too. She's afraid, she's broken her leg and is going to be tipped off the boat in Barbados. And, it's probably my fault for giving her the ibuprofen in the first place, although I didn't actually force feed them to her.

'The ship's docked there for a couple of days so I could come with you and get you settled.'

'Thank you,' Fiona squeaks.

'The insurance company will sort everything out. I'm sure.' I'm not, because my only experience of insurance companies was when Keith died. He had paid into a funeral plan insurance thing and they really didn't want to pay out the full amount because he'd only taken it out twelve months and four days before he died. Ironic really because if he'd died a week earlier, they wouldn't have had to pay out. They didn't have a leg to stand on but tried. It took weeks of wrangling with them to get it, and his funeral had been and gone before I got the money. It was lucky that he'd had just enough in his bank account to cover the funeral costs. Even so, the insurance pay out wasn't enough to cover the actual cost, it mostly went on paying off his credit card – God knows what he bought, and paying his utility bills. There certainly wasn't much left after that. It did however come with one of those M&S cards for £120 which he had put in a drawer and presumably forgotten about. I spent that on clothes for myself. Pretty much his only legacy to me.

'I hope they do,' Fiona says, before falling asleep, or at least, pretending to, only to wake up when a nurse brings in a menu for her to choose her lunch. I make my excuses and disappear for my own lunch.

I go back down on my way to dinner, having *actually* been sunning myself up on the top deck all afternoon because this is the first bit of proper sunshine I've seen on this trip. If I'm going to be accused of such a thing anyway, I might as well do it and enjoy it.

'Oh, hello,' Jill Pennyworth says as she answers my knock on the door when I go back to see Fiona. She's all bouncy and jolly and I could just slap her. 'We were just talking about you, um... El..'

'Pamela,' I say, helping her out.

'Of course. Yes. I was just telling Fiona that I've cancelled all the trips, so I've saved you having to worry about doing that. Just pop the tickets to the excursions desk and tell them I sent you.' She smiles and waits for me to congratulate her or at least, thank her profusely.

'Fiona hasn't booked any trips,' I say, knowing exactly where this is going.

'No, yours,' Jolly Jill says before turning to walk out.

'Just a minute, Jill. I didn't want them cancelled.' I can hear the annoyance in my voice so I know she can.

She shrugs, glances between me and Fiona again and leaves. She obviously knows more than I do.

I turn to Fiona. 'What was that about?'

'She just thinks it'd be better if you came with me.' Fiona looks sheepish.

'Yes, and I will to see that you're settled, I said I would.'

'No, she means that you need to stay with me. There'll be things that need doing that I won't be able to do.' Fiona doesn't look at me and I just know she's not telling me something.

'You'd better come clean, now.' I move right up close and stand in front of her. 'What are you not telling me?'

Fiona sighs and blinks several times. Here we go again.

'Don't bother with the waterworks.' Oh I sound mean.

'Well,' Fiona says, her voice timid again, 'To get the best deal on the insurance I might have implied that we were together.'

'We are together, travelling together.'

'No, not that…'

'Then what?' But I know what, don't I? Jockie had amazing prescience when he thought we were a couple.

'I might have put that we lived together. You know…'

'What, like married or something?'

'Maybe.'

'Give me that insurance policy, I want to read it for myself.'

Without a word Fiona hands it over and I snatch it

from her lying little hands and stomp off with it.

♫♫♫

'You're quiet tonight,' Shona says, giving me a little nudge. 'How's your friend getting on?'

'She's doing okay,' I say, not adding what a scheming little witch she is as I shovel my food into my mouth as fast as I can.

The leisurely pace we eat dinner at, which I usually find enjoyable, is driving me mad tonight. I just want to get out of here and read that damn insurance policy document.

'Actually,' I say, pushing my plate away. 'I need to go and see her, so if you'll excuse me.' I wipe my mouth and stand up.

'Oh, not coming to the theatre? It's a comedian, supposed to be funny,' Jockie says.

'Not tonight, maybe tomorrow. Night everyone.' I hardly wait to hear their goodbyes before I scurry away.

In my cabin I rip the policy out of the envelope and start reading it. There's way too much detail to take in, so after a few pages I stop and make myself a cup of tea. This might be an all-night job. Yes, she's put her address as our address but that's okay, surely, as she's the primary contact and all that.

After I've read more and finished my tea, I still haven't found anything that absolutely states that we are a couple or that we must get off the ship together. I keep going and going and finally I find it, just one little sentence, just a few words: *All parties must travel together at all times.*

I hunt through the documents looking for a phone number; I'm going to ring them, now, while I'm so incensed about it. I find the number and the office hours and realise that it will have to wait until tomorrow.

I'm frantically trying to work out the time difference, wondering when would be the best time to ring. First thing tomorrow morning? Before breakfast? Before visiting lying little Fiona. Then I notice that there's a 24-hour helpline, so I ring it immediately.

Ten

'I rang the insurance company last night,' I tell Fiona the next morning. She visibly winces as I say it. 'Yes, they've confirmed that I do have to come with you.' I wait for her to reply.

'Oh,' is all she can manage.

'So it seems I will be getting off in Barbados.'

Fiona sniffs but she doesn't look at me. Any minute now she will turn on the waterworks.

I really want to lay into her, really want to shout and rant about how she's spoiled my holiday, my once in a lifetime – quite literally – holiday which I'll never be able to afford again. But I can't, can I? She's just a little waif in a hospital bed in pain with a broken leg. The insurance company told me that Fiona had specifically gone for the cheaper option even though it was possible for us to be independent travellers which would mean I wouldn't need to accompany her. Apparently, it saved us fifty-two pounds, or twenty-six pounds each.

But what can I do? To be honest I don't particularly like Fiona, and I think the feeling is mutual, but I have no choice in this and there's no point in shouting or ranting about it no matter how I feel. And, if the situation was reversed, she would have had to accompany me.

She wasn't to know she'd break her leg.

I can't help feeling disappointed and resentful though, but I have to get over it. I have to stop feeling like this, and being selfish. That, it would appear, is Fiona's job.

There's a knock on the door and in bounces Jolly Jill.

'Morning,' she says, her best head girl voice filling the fragile atmosphere in the room.

'Hi,' I mutter and Fiona just nods.

'How's it going? Everything sorted? Have you taken those tickets to the excursion desk yet? Have you started your packing?'

'No,' I say. 'I haven't done either of those things.'

'Oh,' she says, smiling brightly, her head bobbing about as though it's on a stick. 'You'd better make a start.' She starts flicking through documents on her clipboard and pulls out a sheet of yellow paper. 'This is for your luggage, the luggage you can't take with you.'

'Luggage?' I echo and it suddenly hits me that if we can only take what I can carry then most of it will be left behind.

'Yes, what you can't take will need to stay on board. Don't worry, we'll off load it when we get back to Southampton and the baggage company will bring it to your door.'

'Ah,' I say feeling relieved.

'Yes, and it's only £35 a bag, plus VAT.' She delivers this as though she's just told us we've won the lottery.

'How much?' I swallow hard.

84

'Don't worry,' says Jolly Jill, 'The insurance will cover it, won't it, Fiona?'

'Oh yes, yes,' Fiona says, a bit too quickly.

It better had.

'So you need to make a start, you're getting off tomorrow night and I bet it took you longer than a day to pack it, didn't it?' quips Jolly Jill.

She's right, it took me weeks to assemble everything.

'What about the onboard spend?' Fiona asks. That's a point, it completely slipped *my* mind.

'Um, err,' Jill says, frowning away. 'I'll see if I can get it transferred to a future cruise. Then she skips off out through the door before we can ask any more questions.

I turn my attention to Fiona, languishing in her bed. 'Well, I'd better go and make a start,' I say, using this as my excuse to escape. I'm actually going to my art class as it's now evident there won't be many more for me.

'Okay,' Fiona's little voice says. 'When you come back could you bring me some paper and a pen, please?' There's a pleading tone to her voice.

'Yes, okay. Did you want me to bring your phone too so you can ring your family in Canada? Or email them. You can pay for the internet now that you won't be using your onboard spend. You can easily afford it.' I don't tell Fiona that I've already had the internet today so that I could google information about Barbados, hotels, the hospitals, everything I can think off. I've also discovered that the flight home will take eight or nine hours. I've never flown before and I wouldn't choose to start with a flight that long.

'No, thank you, just the pen and paper. I don't want to worry them.'

I skip off to my art class feeling like a naughty kid

escaping detention. I'm going to put all the forthcoming hassle out of my head and enjoy myself for an hour.

♫♫♫

After a relaxing session of watercolours – we've been painting sunsets over Barbados, ironic that, since I'll no doubt see enough of them – I'm back in our cabin pulling suitcases from under the bed and silently cursing Fiona for breaking her leg. I won't say anything to her because that would just be too hurtful, but I hate how she's ruined my holiday.

Stop being so selfish.

I pull my small case, the one I used just for my shoes, out of the big case I've stuffed it in and start to hunt through my wardrobe for my shoes. It's only after I've sat on it to zip it up that I realise I need to take some of those shoes to Barbados with me.

Bugger it, decisions, decisions – ones I shouldn't have to make. And I don't even know where to start with Fiona's belongings.

I leave the case as it is and flop down on my back on the bed, staring at the cabin ceiling that has become so very familiar – the air-con unit, the seam lines – in such a short time. My stomach rumbles, I'm ready for my lunch now, especially since I didn't bother with breakfast this morning because I was too wound up after my late-night phone call.

It's too soon for lunch but I can't face any more packing. Not yet, and I've hardly even started. Then I remember Fiona's request for paper and a pen. I'll pop them down to her now and then I can escape to lunch and not feel guilty when I don't go back to see her until late this afternoon.

'I thought you were never coming back,' she says as I enter her room.

'I've been attempting to pack. Anyway, I've brought you some paper and a pen.' I smile and present my offerings.

'Oh, you took too long,' she says, shaking her head. 'I've already got some, one of the nurses found some for me. I've made my lists.' She points to a sheaf of papers on the bedside cabinet.

'Oh, what lists?' I don't step forward to look.

'Well, here,' she says, twisting round so precariously to pick up her lists that she looks as though she's going to fall out of the bed. I can't have that, so I have to grab the papers.

There's what looks like a shopping list, line after line of Clarins products. Luxury indeed, the sort of stuff I've seen in Boots but would never stop to buy. It's all way out of my price range.

'What's this?'

'That's what I want you to go and spend my onboard credit on.'

'But it'll be transferred to your next cruise.'

'I don't care about that, I want my products, I've been looking forward to getting them.'

'Then why didn't you get them straight away when we got on board.' It would save me doing it now.

'Because they often have special offers and I wanted to wait, but I can't now, obviously. So you'll have to do it.' She says this as though I'm truly stupid. I think I am.

'But I can't use your card, they want a signature. Your signature.'

'Ah, well, that's all sorted too. Jill has arranged for a second card on my account. All you have to do is sign it.' Then from beneath the bedcovers she produces the second card and hands it to me. When I take it, it's still warm from being snuggled up in her lair. 'Sign it now,' she says. 'You have a pen.'

What choice do I have?

Once I've signed the card, I flick through the papers in my hand. 'What's this?'

'Oh, that's my packing list. Clothes and other items I simply must have in Barbados and how I want you to pack the rest of my belongings. There's a page for each suitcase so I've made it easy for you.'

'Thanks,' I say not attempting to hide my sarcasm, but Fiona doesn't notice, or, more likely, doesn't care. 'I'd better go and get started then.'

♫♫♫

In the shop I look around for all the items Fiona wants; it's a daunting task and this stuff is really expensive, nothing like the £1.99 SPF15 supermarket brand moisturiser I use every day.

'Can I help you?' The assistant is young and heavily made up.

'Um, yes, I have a list.'

'Oh, shall I…?' She holds out her hand and after a bit of fumbling I give her the two pages which are Fiona's shopping list. I see her eyes light up. She turns to me and smiles. Oh that's a big smile. 'Why don't you leave this with me and I'll get it all ready for you. You can pick it up later.'

Now it's my turn to smile a big smile. 'Oh, thank you. That would be such a help.'

I leave happy that I don't have to spend all my time finding these items. We've agreed I'll come back this evening, which means I have the whole afternoon free.

No, I don't, I have to pack. Oh well.

I head up to the sundeck for lunch, it's my intention to at least see some daylight today. I choose pizza and salad from the al fresco food bar and start to look around for a vacant table.

'Pam, Pam, over here, join us.' Shona and Jockie are sitting in the sunshine, eating their lunch and each with an empty cocktail beside them. I sit down at their table and soon I'm telling them what's happening and how tomorrow will be my last day on the cruise. Jockie calls the waiter over and orders another round of cocktails and this time includes me. I'm not sure it's a good idea with what I've got planned for this afternoon, but I *am* supposed to be on holiday.

'So Fiona has you doing all her luxury shopping for her,' Shona says, laughing.

'Well, fortunately the assistant is doing it, her eyes lit up.'

'I bet they did, she'll be on commission,' Jockie says.

'Good. She deserves it. It's one less thing I have to do and I'm grateful.'

'What are you going to do with *your* onboard spend?' Shona asks.

'Well, I'm desperately hoping that the insurance will cover the cancellation so I can book again, probably next year,' I sigh at the prospect of waiting a whole year before I can go on holiday again and negotiating the extended time off work, again, and that's assuming the insurance will pay up. 'The customer services manager is going to get it transferred.'

Jockie and Shone both roll their eyes before Jockie shakes his head. 'Get and spend it, lassie,' he says. 'We've all heard stories about transferring onboard spend and most of them don't end well.'

When I ask him what he means he says that invariably the cruise companies wriggle out of giving you the full amount.

'Anyway,' Shona adds, 'You'll get new onboard credit with your next cruise, so you should just go and spend what you have for this one.'

'Buy some jewellery, always a good investment,' Jockie adds, before calling the waitress over to order another round of cocktails, which I insist on paying for, since it will come off *my* onboard spend.

I'm almost tempted to use Fiona's card.

♫♫♫

Back in the cabin I yank Fiona's cases out from under the bed and examine her lists. They're very comprehensive. Very.

Two hours later I've finished, each case is zipped up, labelled as per Jolly Jill's instructions and wedged between Fiona's bed and her wardrobe. I have, as instructed left enough space in one case to add her *luxury products* as she calls them. She's definitely better at this packing malarkey than I am, but I suppose she's had plenty of practice since she's been on so many cruises. She's even told me exactly what to pack in her carpet bag which she's taking to the hospital with her. I admit, I might have been a bit cavalier when following all her instructions, but I'm just going to blame the cocktails if she complains – which I'm sure she will.

Unfortunately for me, I've had to pack some of her stuff into my case, the case I'm bringing with us, since I can only manage the one case and Fiona's carpet bag. There really isn't much space left for my clothes, but I'm going to worry about that tomorrow. The sun is still shining and it's warm outside, too warm to be trapped in my cabin any longer and I've just realised I haven't even been in a swimming pool on this ship yet. I find my costume, pull it on, wrap a towel around me, grab my bag and head for the pool deck.

I'm supposed to be on bloody holiday after all.

Eleven

No one says anything about my lobster-red face at dinner. People have definitely noticed it, even the waiter has done a double take. Serves me right, I suppose.

Thinking about it now I know it was stupid, I should have used sunblock. But all these years of working outside in all weathers made me think I was immune to sunburn. My skin is weathered – I know this because Cherry commented on it one day. I think she meant weather-beaten. Anyway, turns out I'm not at all immune to the sun, not the nearly-Caribbean sun in the South Atlantic Ocean anyway.

I've covered my face in moisturiser and make-up but the fact remains the glow is still shining through. I've even taken a pink bomb in an attempt to soothe the burn – and I haven't fallen off the toilet, yet.

I decline the invitation to join my table companions at the theatre, not because of the sunburn but because I've decided I'm going to follow Jockie and Shona's advice, and Fiona's example, and spend my onboard credit.

I've never felt so decadent.

When I arrive at the shop to pick up Fiona's luxury products, the shop assistant greets me with a smile, then a frown.

'Oh dear,' she says. 'Is that sunburn?'

'Mmm,' I say, not really wanting to discuss it.

'I've got just the thing for that; it'll calm it down and take away the redness. By the morning you'll hardly be able to tell. It's pricey though. Still I don't suppose that'll bother you after spending so much already.' I don't correct her assumption that all these products are for me.

She dabs a sample on my hand that she claims is a miracle worker and before I know what I'm doing, I've agreed to buy it. She goes off to find a tube while I sign for Fiona's shopping.

She pops my cream in the bag with Fiona's products, smiles and walks away.

'I need to pay,' I call after her.

'Yes, you did. I added it to your bill.' Then she's gone, busily serving another customer and leaving me standing with two bursting and very heavy bags and a feeling of guilt.

At the jewellers I buy myself a watch, nothing ridiculous, but it's very nice and then a ring, while gold with a beautiful pale stone. I don't even know what the stone is — I don't care either — I just like it. The ring looks especially elegant on my manicured hands, so I keep it and the watch on. Let's face it, once I'm back home I won't get many opportunities to wear jewellery like this, not when I'm humping pots around in the garden centre.

I call into Reception and get a statement for each of our accounts, something which Fiona had written on her *to do* list for me. I've spent all of my onboard credit.

Oh well.

Fiona is watching some old film when I knock on her door. I'm glad she's still awake as it's now heading towards 10pm.

'Hello, stranger,' she says, her tone a little snidey, before her eyes alight on the shopping bags.

'I thought you might like to see what you've bought before I pack it.'

Fiona pulls herself up the bed and flaps her hands towards the bags.

'Did you get everything?'

'Yes, apparently. The store assistant did it.'

'Really. Not you? I'll have to check. Have you got my original list?'

'Not with me, no. I think the store assistant still has it, it's probably in the bin now.'

Fiona frowns. 'Mmm, all right.' She starts rummaging through the bags, her eyes lighting up like a kid's on Christmas morning. 'What's this?' She holds up my magic sunburn cream; the tube is tiny.

'Oh, that's mine.' I grab it from her.

'I hope I didn't pay for that.'

'Ah, yes, I think you did. I owe you.'

'It's thirty-two pounds,' she says, scrutinising the bill. 'You definitely owe me.'

I'm about to argue, about to say I don't have any onboard credit left and she does, because I've just seen that she's still got a fair bit unspent but decide it's not worth the trouble. I'll pay her back then I'm not in her debt. That's fair.

'I'll give it to you later.'

She gives me a look that means that she'll be making sure that I do.

'Have you spent yours?' she asks.

'Yes. I bought myself jewellery.' I flash my hands in her direction showing off the ring and watch. 'Very nice,' she says, sounding a bit peevish. 'Just as well you spent it as Jill's been back and said it's proving difficult for her to transfer our credit to another cruise. She *might* be able to do it but she's not sure.'

'Oh.' Why am I not surprised? 'Ah, here's your statement, I nearly forgot.' I pull Fiona's statement from my bag and hand it over. She reads it slowly, running her finger across every line.

'They haven't added my medical expenses yet,' Fiona says, her voice little. 'I haven't seen a bill yet but I asked them how much it's likely to be and they said around four-thousand.'

'Pounds?' I can hardly believe it.

'Of course,' Fiona snaps.

'Maybe you should have kept your onboard spend and used it towards…'

Fiona holds up her hand to silence me. 'No, they don't allow that. Jill already told me. It's going to max out my credit card so I'm definitely going to need that thirty-two pounds you owe me.

'Don't worry, I'll pay you back. Better be off now, then. I've got to get this lot in your luggage.' I grab her shopping bags.

'Make sure you pack the shower gel, face wash, and my special shampoo and conditioner from the bathroom in my hospital bag, won't you?'

I smile my agreement.

'And the moisturiser. Oh, and I need my card back.'

'Of course,' I say, fumbling in my purse for it. I feel unfeasibly guilty and Fiona evidently doesn't trust me not to go and spend what's left of her credit, not that I know when she's going to spend it on herself, unless she does manage to get it transferred to another cruise. I don't need to do that, I think, glancing down to admire my ring.

Back in our cabin I follow Fiona's instructions, packing everything into one of her suitcases which is continuing on the cruise and putting the required items in her hospital bag. I've rinsed off the shampoo and conditioner bottles after using them as washing tongs, but it still makes me smirk when I think how Fiona would react if she knew. I zip up the bag and weigh it in my hands – with all those bottles in it, it weighs an absolute tonne.

Good job I'm strong.

I climb into bed happy that I've packed all of Fiona's things, even if they are taking up over half my suitcase, but slightly panicked that I've hardly started on my own.

I wake up at five am and start throwing things into my suitcases. I won't need many warm clothes, not my coat or my boots, the ones I wore when I got on the ship. Just as well because they are heavy. I do stuff a fleece for each of us in my Barbados case, Jolly Jill suggested this in her best head girl voice. Trouble is they take up a lot of space but at least they're not heavy.

By the time I've finished packing my cases which are staying on the ship, I still have a large pile of clothes that I want to take to Barbados with me. I start to pack them into my case and soon realise that Fiona's essentials and the fleeces are taking up more room than I have left for myself. I start to sort through her things but what can I really take out? I've no idea what clothing she will need once she's had her operation but I do know that she will be up and out of bed quickly as that's what they do with hip replacements apparently.

She's also told me, via her lists, to bring her incontinence pads as once the catheter is out, she may have a little problem. The packs take up a lot of space. My space.

I have to pare down my own clothes, there's nothing else I can do. I stuff my surplus into one of the ongoing cases, zip up the one I'm taking – after sitting on it for a long time – and lift it off the bed.

'Ah,' I yell to no one but myself.

The case is so bloody heavy.

I haul it back onto the bed. I'm going to have to cull my stuff some more. I have my jumbo shampoo and conditioner in there, as well as shower gel. I pull them out, I'll have to use the hotel's toiletries, they're usually nice, aren't they? They certainly are on this ship and I've used them every day instead of the ones I brought with me. By the time I'm finished I have enough clothes for four days, but at least I have a week's worth of underwear. The case is still heavy, but manageable. I'm just glad it has wheels. I imagine myself hauling the suitcase, Fiona's weighty carpet bag and my own handbag which will be stuffed with our travel documents, passports, my tablet computer, my phone, and my purse full of foreign currency around Barbados without – as Jill has described it – any help whatsoever.

After breakfast I go to my last art class. Silly really when I won't be able to carry on, but I've so enjoyed these few lessons, maybe I'll take it up when I get home. I had thought that I might take my art materials to Barbados with me, but I now know that I dare not add one little thing to that damn case. Not one. It seems my watercolours will be continuing their holiday even if I'm not.

♫♫♫

Fiona is dabbing her eyes with a tissue when I enter her room the next morning. She's alone and the TV is off.

'Are you okay?' I ask.

'No, no, I'm not.' She sniffs then blows her nose.

'What's wrong.' I hope it isn't her leg. I hope it's not worse than they thought. 'Is it your leg? Is it hurting?'

'No, it's not that.' She dabs her eyes again.

'What is it then?' I wish she would just spit it out.

'Jill's been in. You missed her,' she says, accusingly.

I refuse to feel guilty. 'And…?'

'I have to pay the ambulance that's taking me from the ship to the hospital in cash, in US dollars. I haven't got any US dollars. I was going to get my currency on the ship but I can't now.'

'Can't Jill arrange for you to get currency? I'm sure she can.'

'No. Well, maybe. But they've just given me the bill for all this.' She waves her arms around in the air. 'It's almost five thousand pounds and that's my credit card limit. My card is officially maxed out. I haven't got any money to pay for the ambulance.' She starts to wail now, proper loud, snotty sobs.

I think about the three-hundred-and-fifty US dollars in my purse still in the safe. It would be mean not to, wouldn't it? 'It's okay, I have some cash I can lend you. How much is it?'

Fiona looks up, her sobbing stops immediately. 'Two-hundred-and-twenty-five US dollars.'

I swallow hard. 'Okay,' I say. 'I can cover that.'

'You'll get it back off the insurance,' Fiona says, brightening up immediately. 'Have you packed everything? Have you packed my bags in accordance with my list?'

'Yes, I have.'

'Jill says you have to be down here by nine this evening at the latest with all the luggage we want to take. And can you bring my phone down before then I want to use the Wi-Fi before we get off, who knows what it'll be like in Barbados.'

'Yes, I'll bring it after lunch. I expect you want to let your family know what's going on.'

Fiona's smile is tight-lipped as she nods her head in agreement.

At least she has family to tell, I don't. And it's not as if I'm going to let work know what's happened, that can wait until I get back.

Twelve

I have the audacity to go for dinner before I go back to Fiona's room.

'You're late,' she says as I struggle my suitcase, her carpet bag and my handbag in through her door.

'Ten minutes,' I say, glancing at the clock on her wall.

'But Jill said nine, be here by nine. She's been in asking where you are?'

'Really?' Even Fiona must hear the sarcastic tone in my voice.

'Yes. *Really.*' There's no disguising *her* sarcasm.

'Well I'm here now. It's not as if we're getting off in a minute, is it? We're still miles from land.'

'Yes, but…' She glances at my face and stops talking, even Fiona knows what she is saying is silly.

I flop into the plastic seat, the air whooshing out with the force of my weight, it's not an attractive sound. We sit in silence for a minute or two, it's neither pleasant nor companionable. Fiona gives in, finds the remote control amongst the dishevelled covers on her sickbed and switches on the TV.

We both stare at the screen though neither of us is really watching it. I lean back and rest my head against the head rest. I'm tired, I feel as though I've spent the last few days running around mindlessly doing stuff I don't want to do. I just want to put my feet up and relax. The sticky plastic seat is so uncomfortable and it's making me sweat. I lay my suitcase down and use it as a foot rest, then close my eyes. We're not getting off for hours; I could have a little doze.

'Ah, you're finally here.' Jill's irritating voice jerks me awake. 'Making yourself comfortable, I see.'

I glance at the clock; I could only have been asleep for a minute or two.

'Are we getting off now?' I ask.

'Well, obviously not, we're still at sea.' Jill looks at me as though *I* am the stupid one.

'So what's the urgency?'

'I like people to be early so we're not hunting them down when the time arrives. It does happen you know.' She shakes her shoulders at me as if that explains it.

'I'm not people and I can tell the time.' I'm getting sick of all this. I've spent all afternoon sorting our Fiona's bits and pieces, ensuring the room is clear, ditching yet more of my clothes to accommodate her stuff, getting another printout for her because the one I got earlier didn't have her hospital bill on it. And she wasn't even particularly grateful when I brought her phone down, just dropping it on her lap and giving me a look that told me I was dismissed from her presence. I'd even charged her phone up for her, not that she thanked me or even acknowledged it.

'I expect she went for dinner with her friends,' Fiona spits.

'Oh, well…' Jill starts and I glare at her, daring her

to say something nasty about me. 'Probably just as well, who knows when you'll get another meal.'

'What?' I start but Jill talks over me.

'The arrangements are that when we land, you'll be second off. The ambulance will take you straight to the hospital. You, Pamela, can ride in the front of the ambulance. You're going to spend the night in Fiona's room, they've got a bed for you.' Jill gives me a thin smile then turns to leave.

'Hang on. I thought, I assumed, I'd go to a hotel.'

'You will, eventually. Obviously, it's not ideal to have you turn up at a hotel in the middle of the night, is it? Anyway, I'm sure you'll want to make sure Fiona is settled and comfortable. She's our top priority at the moment, aren't you Fiona?'

Fiona does a little smile, like a kid who just managed to steal a sly sweetie.

'Great,' I say.

'It'll be fine,' Jill says, this time skipping out of the room before I can say anything else.

'I hope you don't snore,' Fiona says.

'I hope you don't,' I snap back.

'Of course I don't.' She turns her eyes back to the TV while I lean back and close mine.

I'm not sure whether either of us snored before all this happened. It seems such a long time ago that I can hardly remember.

♫♫♫

'You're next,' Jill says, popping her head around the door. We already know this as we've seen the ambulance crew for the man next door hovering in the corridor while the ship's medical staff got him ready to move.

'Thank you, Jill,' Fiona says. 'You've been such a help. Thank you so much.'

Jill smiles her acknowledgement at Fiona then looks at me, waiting, I suspect for more gratitude. I just smile back; Jill frowns then closes the door.

I stand up and shake the sleep away. I've had at least an hour but it's been on and off. Fiona and I have hardly spoken but since I'm a little more refreshed than I was earlier, I hold out the olive branch because I know this cannot be easy for her and it's potentially going to be a lot more difficult.

'Have we got everything?' I ask, my voice sweet.

'I think so,' she snaps back. So that's how it is. 'You could have said thank you to Jill, she's been amazing.'

'Has she?' And I haven't, I think. I'm feeling resentful. I have to stop it.

The door bursts open and the ambulance crew for Fiona, a man and a woman, breeze in. They're young and fresh faced.

'All ready?' the woman asks, her voice a long drawl.

I bumble around with the case and bags and get out of the way so they can bring in the stretcher.

'I'll wait outside.'

Fiona looks on with apprehension, I suppose the prospect of being moved is an alarming one when you have a broken leg. Fortunately, her tiny frame and miniscule weight means it doesn't take them long to flick her onto the stretcher and we're soon trundling out of the ship's medical centre. When we get to the gangway, I'm shocked by how steep it is. I imagine the case running away from me as I struggle with the bags.

'Let me help,' a voice says from behind and one of the ship's doctors takes the case. 'Whoa, what have you got in here?'

'Don't ask,' I mumble, wanting to add that most of it isn't mine.

He leaves my case outside the ambulance as I watch Fiona being loaded into the back. The ambulance isn't what I was expecting and from the wide-eyed look of horror I glimpsed on Fiona's face before she disappeared into the back, it's not what she was expecting either. It's not much bigger than a people carrier; I had imagined something akin to our NHS ambulances, so well equipped, they are mobile trauma units.

A door is slid open for me and I wonder where I'm supposed to sit. There is a seat, just the one, the other two are filled with oxygen cylinders.

'All right?' the male paramedic asks me. 'You sit there?'

'Err, yeah, my case…'

He grabs it and hurls it up on top of the oxygen cylinders. There's a resounding clonk as they all knock together. I climb in with our bags on my lap and he slams the door across so it's shut. I fumble around for a seat belt but cannot find one.

'All right?' he calls once he's in the driver's seat.

'All right,' the reply comes from behind me. I'm quite impressed, the female paramedic is large, very large, but agile, and she has squeezed herself into the back with Fiona, probably wedging the stretcher in since there doesn't appear to be anything to secure it to.

He starts the engine and we roar off, the wipers on full speed, because it's raining here, something else I wasn't expecting. We hurtle out of the port at break neck speed, although I don't think it's necessary and he hasn't put the lights or siren on. The road is bumpy and

I'm starting to feel travel sick, something than didn't happen on the ship despite us spending five days sailing across the Atlantic and crossing the Bay of Biscay which was as still as a millpond when we crossed it.

The driver flicks on some music, then turns the air-con up, the fan so strong, the temperature so low that my lips turn blue as they flap about. I feel as though we are taking off and I'm being subjected to a hell of a G force.

If I had a sense of humour about this, I'd take a selfie. I imagine posting it on Facebook, my lips flapping about like a galloping bloodhound's.

After less than ten minutes we lurch to a halt outside a low building. The driver jumps out and runs around to my door and flings it open before he runs to the back of the ambulance and yanks open the rear doors. I'm still struggling to get my case off the top of the cylinders as Fiona is being wheeled through the doors of the Oceanside Hospital.

When I catch up with her she is parked in front of the reception desk behind which another large woman is wielding a clip board at a whimpering Fiona.

'Pamela, Pamela. Can you deal with this?' she bleats as I fall through the doors with the luggage.

The receptionist immediately thrusts the clipboard in my direction and I have to almost jump to catch it. I can see she's busy, has other patients to deal with, but really, is that necessary? Fiona is one of four patients sent here from the ship, the others got here even quicker than us because, apparently, they came by taxi.

The clipboard has copious forms in different colours clipped to it.

'Not more forms,' Fiona moans. 'We've already done so many on the ship.'

She's right, we have. Or, to be more accurate, the ship's medical staff have filled in lots of forms which Fiona has signed, they've also given us copies.

I fill in what I can as fast as I can and hand the clipboard back.

'We've already done this one,' I say, pointing out a pale pink form which needs details of the medical assistance company the insurance company are using.

'Do it again, we need it.'

'But I have a copy…' I really don't want to copy it all out, there are three pages.

The receptionist holds out her hand and flaps her fingers at me as I fumble in my bag for the copy. Once I find it she snatches it from me and disappears into a back office returning minutes later with a copy, she thrusts my copy back at me and waves at the paramedics to take Fiona up in the lift.

I shuffle my suitcase along to go with Fiona.

'No, not you,' shouts the receptionist as everyone in Reception falls silent and stares at me.

I turn and blink at her in question. It's gone one in the morning and I'm tired and disorientated. I shuffle back to the desk.

'You need to pay,' she says, holding out her hand.

'Pay?'

'Yes.' Her eyes widen. 'Sixteen-thousand dollars.'

'What? I don't have…'

'Eight thousand US,' she says.

My mind is spinning. Are eight thousand US dollars less than eight thousand pounds, my credit limit on my brand-new card?

'But the insurance company will pay for everything…'

She shakes her head. 'This is a deposit against the

insurance company. They are too slow to pay.' She holds out her hand. 'Credit or debit card?'

'Credit,' I say, feeling as though I want to cry. But what can I do? Fiona has already maxed out her card on the ship. I haven't spent anything on mine because I used my onboard credit. I really don't have much choice. Reluctantly, I hand over my card, watching in horror as the receptionist feeds it into her machine and waits for me to tap in my pin number.

A few minutes later I'm getting out of the lift and looking for Fiona. A smiling nurse ushers me along a dimly lit corridor to Fiona's room. Hovering outside are the ambulance crew. Big smiles spread across their faces when they see me. The woman is flapping a small book.

'Would you like to pay by cash or card?' she asks.

'Cash,' I say, wondering for a second or two what she means then remembering the fee for the ambulance ride. Minutes later I am two-hundred-and-twenty-five US dollars lighter and holding a signed receipt, complete with a postage stamp stuck on it! I need to make sure this doesn't get lost.

I find Fiona in her hospital bed and under the startling glare of ceiling strip lights.

'Hello,' Fiona says, her voice tiny.

'Hello,' I say, my voice coming out in a long sigh.

'Everything done? All the paperwork?'

'Yes. It's fine.' I don't tell her about the eight thousand US dollars. 'Where am I sleeping?' I ask.

Fiona looks away and shrugs. The room isn't especially large and Fiona's bed takes up most of the space. I spy a black plastic chair and my heart sinks.

'I'll get your bed,' a nurse behind me says as she enters the room.

'Thank God for that.' I'm so bloody tired.

Thirteen

The bed is a folding contraption, in the closed position it's tied together with bandage. I watch with a mixture of horror and awe as the nurse opens it out, it's an action which could easily chop off fingers. Clean sheets are produced and the bed made. The bed is wedged between Fiona's bed and the wall, but it's still better than a plastic chair.

I climb in with all my clothes on because Fiona is hot and has the air-con on full blast. Admittedly it's not quite as cold and hurricane like as in the ambulance, but it's wearing nonetheless. I've turned the strip light out and the only light now is coming from the window above the door which leads onto the dimly lit corridor, so it's not too bad. But even in the dim light I can see rust running along the underside of the Fiona's bed.

'Hello,' says a woman as she bursts into the room, flicks on the lights and bustles over to Fiona. She introduces herself as a doctor and proceeds to do Fiona's pre-op checks, including blood tests. She manages to do these by sliding up and down the small gap between Fiona's bed and the window. Fiona, the doctor tells us, is to be operated on first thing tomorrow.

Fiona whimpers at this news. I do feel sorry for her, it must be pretty daunting even though this is exactly why we came here, why we got off the ship.

Finally, the doctor leaves, I turn off the lights again and we attempt to settle down. I'm just dozing off when I realise that Fiona is crying. Proper crying, not the sympathy seeking, manipulative crying that she's really rather good at.

'It'll be okay,' I say, reaching up in the half light and squeezing her hand. She yanks it away and whimpers some more. 'It will be okay,' I reiterate. 'You won't feel a thing.'

'I know that,' Fiona snaps. 'It's hurting now though. They've taken me off my painkillers because they're operating in the morning. I'm nil by mouth.'

'Oh, sorry. I didn't realise that.'

'No, well, no, you wouldn't.'

There's nothing I can say to that. I wonder if now might be a good time to tell her she owes me sixteen thousand Barbadian dollars?

♫♫♫

I manage some sleep, I think Fiona does too, but it ends at six in the morning when the curtains are yanked back and two cheery nurses bring in a trolley.

'We're here to get you ready for your procedure,' they tell Fiona who's as blinking and confused as I am.

'Oh, I'd better move.' I shuffle to the end of the bed, since that's the only way off it, and attempt to stand up. The bed is low and my limbs are weak from lack of sleep. I manage it eventually.

I'm no sooner off the camp bed than one of the nurses folds it up, reties the bandage that keeps it closed and wheels it out of the room. The other nurse rips off Fiona's sheet and, almost simultaneously whips off her nightie. Fiona is laid bare in all her glory and I don't know where to look, and neither does Fiona.

'I'll sit outside,' I mumble, hunting around for my handbag and stumbling out of the room. I sit on another plastic chair outside and pull my phone out. There's Wi-Fi, so I go down to the reception desk and ask about a password. I'm hoping that it's not too expensive to get on their internet because the signal is very strong. Happily, it's free for patients and visitors. Fiona will be pleased; it means she'll be able to contact her family in Canada easily.

Ten minutes later I'm back on the plastic chair and the nurses are leaving and I'm told I can go back into Fiona's room.

She's lying on the bed wearing a hospital gown and looking shell-shocked.

'Are you okay?' I ask, fearing the reply.

'No. I'm in pain. Especially after that. They scrubbed me from top to toe and it felt as though they were using sandpaper. Could you put all my things back in my bag please?' Fiona points over at the sink in the corner where her toothbrush and toothpaste are on the side. I tidy everything away. 'I feel as though they scrubbed my tonsils when they cleaned my teeth. I wanted to do it myself but they wouldn't let me.'

I don't know what to say but fortunately I don't need to say anything because a knock on the door precedes another person coming into the room. The anaesthetist, or as he calls himself the anaesthesiologist. He proceeds to ask Fiona a lot of questions about her medical history and I feel I should leave the room again but the opportunity to do so tactfully just doesn't arise.

'Are you allergic to anything?' he asks, dropping his pen and then fumbling around on the floor looking for it. In the end I have to find it for him.

Fiona waits until the pen is retrieved before giving her answer. 'No, I don't think so.'

'What anaesthesiology have you had in the past?' He takes his glasses from his pocket and puts them on his face, they're too big and slide down his nose. He tilts his head back to see through them properly and stares, goggle-eyed, into Fiona's face.

'No anaesthetic,' she says.

'Are you the next of kin?' he asks me suddenly, dropping his clipboard now.

'No,' Fiona and I say at the same time as I quickly pick up his clipboard and hand it back to him.

'Your next of kin is on their way?'

Fiona hesitates. 'No,' she says. 'It's not convenient.'

'Ah. All right, I'm sure it'll be fine.' With that he breezes out of the room.

'Did you hear what he was saying? They're not going to put me under, just give me a spinal block. What is that?'

I don't really know so I have to bluff it. 'I think it's like what they give to woman having babies. I think.'

'Oh,' Fiona says, giving me an odd look. 'I never had anything like that.'

Nor me, I think.

'They're going to sedate you too, so it'll be fine.' I hope it will, surely it will.

'He's going to sedate me,' Fiona says, her tone scathing. 'That idiot who drops everything and wears someone else's glasses. Did you catch his name?'

'No.'

'Well it sounded like bumbling fool. Mr Bumbling Fool.'

'I think that's probably racist,' I say.

'No it's not. Would you like to be at his mercy?'

'He must be qualified and everything. He must be,' I mumble, but no, I wouldn't like to be at his mercy.

At that point the door bursts open and in walks the surgeon, Dr Patel. He's large, exudes confidence and charms us both with his smile. Fiona simpers under his attention.

'We're going to give you the Rolls Royce of hips, little lady,' he tells Fiona.

I swear Fiona blushes and flutters her eyelashes at him. It's both comical and sickening. But at least she's reassured.

'We're ready to go at ten, all your bloods are done, we're just waiting for the insurance company to give us the go ahead.'

'But they've said everything is fine. I spoke to them just yesterday,' I say. 'They said they'll be covering everything, they emailed me to confirm too.' Though they're not, it would seem, paying the deposit for this place.

Dr Patel smiles at me then picks up the phone on Fiona's bedside cabinet. He talks quickly into the mouthpiece while facing the window, I can only catch the odd word. Finally, he's off the phone.

He shakes his head at Fiona. 'We don't have the right paperwork yet. We don't have their explicit go ahead. We can't perform your procedure until we do.'

Fiona gasps and I feel her pain, both physical and mental.

'Don't worry,' he says, patting her arm. 'It'll work

out. It's not unusual.' Then he leaves while Fiona and I sit open mouthed and shocked.

'We'll have to ring them,' she says. 'Have you got the policy?'

I rummage around in my handbag until I find it, and the relevant phone number. I pull out a pen and draw a circle around the number to make it easier for Fiona to see it. I hand everything over to her, including my pen in case she needs to make notes. She stares at me blankly.

'Can't you do it?' she says, her voice tiny.

I put my hand out for the paperwork.

I always thought the dialling code for the UK was 0044, that's what you see on national company phone numbers, don't you? 0044 then miss off the leading 0 on the area code. And, I googled it before I left home, just in case I needed to ring the UK, although I don't really know who I'd need to ring. I try this several times but to no avail.

'It just doesn't connect,' I tell Fiona and ask her to check that I'm putting the right number in.

'Keep trying,' she says, using her little voice again and lying back on the bed and sighing.

I remind myself that she's in pain and try again, same result, that is, no result. In the end I google how to ring the UK from Barbados and find that it's not 0044 but 011 44. Well, that makes sense. Not.

I spend a whole hour on the phone being passed from one part of the insurance company to the next, making notes on the policy document and not quite losing my temper. Eventually I'm through to Andy, our claims handler who sounds about twelve. I'm told that Fiona shouldn't have gone to The Oceanside Hospital because it's private, she should have gone to the public hospital. I tell him we had no say in where she went. I also tell him that really, it's not like a private hospital in the UK, not that I've ever been in one but I don't think rusty beds are the norm in UK private hospitals. I also remind him that the insurance company has already agreed to pay all the medical costs and I have an email to prove it. I'm so angry by then that I spit out the part about the sixteen-thousand Barbadian dollars deposit just so we could get through the door, and the reason why. There's silence from Andy but Fiona coughs and splutters her shock. Damn, I hadn't intended telling her just yet and certainly not like that.

'We've filled in everything we've been asked to,' I tell Andy. 'It's all your end now, we need you to tell the hospital to go ahead. Fiona is in pain, her leg is broken, it's been broken for days. We can't go on like this.' I'm tired and Andy is getting the sharp end of my impatience.

'We don't have the paperwork back here yet,' his monotonous teenage voice says.

'It was sent by the ship's medical team days ago. Check again.'

'Ah, it's just come through on email,' he says. Of course it has. Just now, right this minute. Lazy, little lying toad. 'I'll get the medical team to check it and we'll get back to you.'

'How long will that take?'

'Well, I don't know.'

'Chase them then, hurry it along. Fiona is in pain here, they've taken her off all the painkillers because they were planning to operate now, this morning.

'I'll ring you back,' he says, sounding desperate to get me off the phone.

'No email me, I want it in writing. Bye.' I end the call

and see Fiona staring at me.

'Sixteen thousand dollars?' she says. 'Is that true?'

I nod slowly. 'Sorry, I wasn't going to tell you just yet.'

'But how did you pay it?'

'Credit card.' I force a smile. Yes, my brand-new credit card that I've barely used myself, except in Tesco's the night before I came on holiday when I treated myself to some suntan lotion, own brand, of course, just to make sure the card worked.

Fiona studies my face for a second or two before speaking.

'You must have a high limit.' It sounds like an accusation.

'Mmm.' I'm not explaining to her that it's my first credit card ever and I don't know why the limit is so generous. She should just be grateful it is.

'The insurance company will reimburse you,' she says without looking at me.

'I hope so. And I hope they don't take too long about it because obviously I can't afford to just pay it off when the time comes.'

'You need to get onto the port agent to sort you out a hotel,' she says, ignoring my comment. 'You can't sleep in here again tonight.'

Fourteen

I walk into the lobby of the Charlotte Bay Beach Hotel, it's lovely. If I were here on holiday I'd be delighted. The port agent has done me proud, but my arrival here doesn't feel like a holiday. Jill had given me the port agent's card and exacting instructions to contact her about a hotel. It's taken all day to get it sorted. All day in the hospital with Fiona who still hasn't had her operation. Poor Fiona.

My credit card takes another hit as I have to pay for four nights up front; breakfast is included but dinner is not. A wrist band is slapped on my wrist quicker than a policeman's handcuffs and I'm shown to a room a long way from Reception, but it's just a stone's throw from the beach. There are two double beds, which will be great if Fiona has to come here. They're high though, so high I almost take a run and jump to get onto mine. I'll have to lift Fiona onto hers if she does make it here, though I'm hoping we'll just get on a plane and go home instead.

When I left Fiona at the hospital, she was looking happier than she had all day. That was mainly down to being put back on painkilling medication and given something to eat. I've had nothing all day, not that Fiona noticed. Dinner here isn't for another hour, plenty of time for me to have a shower and change out of the clothes I've been wearing since yesterday morning.

The approval for Fiona's operation from the insurance company finally came through at four pm, too late for surgery today, so it's now scheduled to start at seven tomorrow morning. I've been told not to ring to find out how she is until after eleven. If I'm honest, I'm relieved. Selfishly, I could do with some time to myself, some time away from Fiona.

I don't think she'll miss *me* either.

The shower is hot and certainly refreshes me, but I see I've made a major mistake in not bringing my own toiletries. There is only shower gel here, no shampoo, no conditioner, they had to be ditched to fit everything else in. I couldn't even fit them in the suitcases that were staying on the ship, so I've asked the cabin steward to pass them on to anyone who'd like them.

I wonder if Fiona will let me borrow hers? She has them in her hospital bag and it was me who carried them there for her. I'll have to pick my time to ask. In the meantime, I have to wash my hair with shower gel and hope for the best.

Once I'm dressed, I fluff up my hair with the hairdryer – not difficult given it's fairly fluffy anyway without conditioner and I know I can always tie it up in a bun like I do for work if all else fails. I apply a little tinted moisturiser over the top of the expensive cream to hide my sunburn. A quick slick of lip gloss, because that's all I've brought with me, and I'm ready.

Dinner is served, or self-served to be precise since

it's a buffet, in an outdoor restaurant overlooking the sea. Fortunately, it's not far to go, I'm both dog-tired and starving. As soon as I've eaten it's bed time for me.

'Hello, my darling,' the restaurant manager greets me from behind his podium. He's wearing a brightly coloured shirt with Barbados written all over it, it's both comical and clichéd. 'Room number?' And, after glancing at my wristband asks, 'Will you be paying cash or adding it to your bill?'

I hadn't even thought about that. 'My bill?' I venture, thinking about my credit card limit. Will it be enough?

He smiles. 'We're very busy, you'll have to wait for a table. Perhaps you'd like a drink.'

I sigh, it's loud and long and he looks at me, reading my face, perhaps.

'It's on the house,' he says, with another smile. So smooth, so practiced. 'White wine or red? Here, sit at the bar.' He pulls out a stool for me and I climb on. I could cry, with exhaustion, hunger, stress, worry about Fiona, the whole damn lot.

He calls over the bartender and whispers to him. Promptly a glass of red wine is put before me.

'You look like a red wine kind of girl.'

I laugh. Who wouldn't? Being called a girl when you're fifty is just hilarious. He gives me a wide smile, the kind of smile I would guess he uses on all the *girls*. He's not young, but he's younger than me. He sidles back to his podium.

I knock the wine back far too quickly; it goes straight to my head. It's fortunate that the glass isn't too large nor the wine too strong or I'd be dancing on the bar by now. I chuckle to myself, what a sight that would be. Maybe I'll have another. I look to catch the barman's eye.

'We're very full this evening,' the manager says, having returned to my side before I can get my second drink. 'Would you mind sharing a table?'

'Sharing?' I echo. Sharing, do I mind? 'No, that's fine.' I just want food and sleep.

'Come with me.' He steps back and crooks his finger.

I slide off the bar stool and follow him, my legs wobbling just a little.

'There's a table of ladies who are happy to make room for you.'

I smile my thanks. As long as they don't want any conversation, I don't care where I sit, I think, as we make our way to a table overlooking the beach.

'Pam?' a male voice calls, but I ignore it, because he can't mean me, no one knows I'm here and certainly not anyone I might know. 'Pamela Rigby?' the voice says again. 'Is that you?'

I stop, turn and frown in the direction of the voice but I can't see who spoke. That wine has definitely gone to my head, that's what you get for drinking on an empty stomach. I shrug and continue following the manager.

'Pam?' the voice calls again. 'It is you.' A hand is placed on my shoulder and I nearly jump out of my skin.

I turn and stare into the eyes of a man, a complete stranger.

'It is you, isn't it?'

'I'm sorry,' I say, with just the hint of a slur. 'I don't think I know you.'

'Carl, Carl Fisher. We went to school together.'

'Do what? Did we?'

'Yes. Don't you remember me? I remember you. You've hardly changed. I'd recognise you anywhere.'

'Bullshit.' The word slips out of my mouth and is swiftly followed by a hiccup.

Carl Fisher laughs. And in that instant I realise that I do recognise him. His laugh is distinctive, infectious, but it's his perfect teeth that confirm recognition. Among crowds of kids with goofy, wonky, gappy teeth his were beautiful, shining white in a perfect arc.

'Your teeth are still good,' I say, sounding like a drunken idiot.

'You do know me,' he says, laughing as he spots the recognition in my eyes. 'Why don't you join me for dinner? We can have a good old catch up.'

'Okay,' I hear myself say.

'Are you sure, madam?' the manager asks, a concerned frown playing across his brow. No more *my darling* now.

'Yeah, it'll be fine.'

'As you wish, madam.' The manager signals to a waiter to set a place for me at Carl Fisher's table. It's just the two of us, so that's nice and cosy.

'I've had my starter, so if you want to get yours, I'll wait.' Carl flashes me his famous smile.

I think for a moment. I am starving, but despite that I don't think I can manage three courses and I'd much rather have a pudding.

'Nah, you're all right,' I say. 'Where do we go?'

He shows me the way inside to the buffet and I fill my plate with a strange assortment of pasta, roast beef, Yorkshire pudding, and assorted Caribbean vegetables.

'Watch those,' Carl says, pointing to the vegetables as we sit down to eat. 'I had them last night and they're spicy.'

'Okay. Thanks.' I really just want to eat and go to bed. I take a big gulp of cold water; grateful it has appeared on the table while we've been away.

Carl waves at a waiter and asks for another wine glass; he has a bottle of red already on the table, and his own glass.

When the other wine glass arrives and is placed in front of me, I'm tempted to refuse it, but the truth is, I feel as though I've earned a drink.

'Thank you,' I say, taking a big gulp after I've chomped on a mouthful of beef.

'You look like you could do with it.'

I shake my head. I can't decide how to react to this, is it a compliment? No. So what is it? An insult.

'When did you arrive? Did you come in on the Virgin flight this morning?'

I shake my head again, partly because I don't really want to talk about our trip here and partly because I have a mouth full of Yorkshire pudding.

'Ahh, you're not on the all-inclusive either?'

'No.' Another shake of my head. Then I ask, 'Are you on holiday?'

'Not really. Well sort of having a bit of a holiday now.' He smiles. Those teeth. 'If you remember my family come from here.' He waits for me to agree.

'I thought your family came from Jamaica,' I say.

'No. Here. Barbados. Of course my immediate family live in the UK. That's home. That's where I grew up. But my extended family, what's left of them, is here. I've been to a funeral. My dad's sister. He's too old and frail to attend himself, so I had to come.' He rolls his eyes in a theatrical way. 'And then to get over the trauma I had to have a little break.'

'I'm sorry,' I say. 'Condolences.' It sounds so trite.

'Oh I hardly knew her, met her once when I was about eleven. Actually, it was around the same time I met you.'

I laugh. He's got a good memory, better than mine. I do remember him from school, though mainly because of the teeth. Everyone envied him his teeth, while half the school had braces, or worse, gaps, wonks and goofs and no chance of a brace, he had perfect pearly whites. And he still does. If he says he was eleven when we first met, then I believe it. I have no idea. He was just there, like all the other kids in school, especially the boys. They all roll into one from this distance, well, mostly, with a few notable exceptions.

Carl Fisher comes from a big family of boys and if I'm remembering correctly, they all had teeth like his.

'Are you on holiday on your own?' he asks, breaking into my thoughts.

'Not really,' I say, aware of how cryptic that sounds.

'Oh. Okay. Is there a Mr Rigby with you? Of course he wouldn't be Rigby, would he?' He takes a sly look at my wedding ring finger, and I think he smiles when he sees it's bare. I do the same to him, also noting an absence of wedding ring, not that that really means anything or matters much to me.

'There's no Mr Rigby, or whatever,' I say, taking another gulp of wine. 'I've never married. You?'

'Yes, I was married. Fifteen years and three kids, but that's in the past now.'

'Oh, yes, I remember. Didn't you marry Jackie Corcoran?' I remember seeing their wedding photo in the newspaper. It was in the days when photographers used to send them in. No one bothers now, they just post a picture on Facebook. Sometimes I stalk old schoolfriends on Facebook, but the wedding photos now are not theirs, but their children's, a generation away, completely removed from me. It's amazing how some of those sons and daughters are the image of their parents when I knew them.

'I did. She invited you to the wedding. You never came.' He frowns.

'It was a long time ago.' I smile and try to forget why I didn't go, why I couldn't go.

'It was.' His eyes glaze over and I think he's remembering old times, maybe better times.

'How is she?'

'Yeah, fine. I don't really see her much. We're on good terms, because of our sons, but we only really see each other at family occasions.'

'Three sons. Didn't you come from a family of all boys?'

'Yes. You do remember.' He laughs. 'I'm the youngest of five.'

'I didn't know that.' Well, at least I don't think I did.

'Yes, my oldest brother, Brent, he's the same age as your brother, Keith, isn't it? How's he?'

'Dead.' It comes out of my mouth so bluntly, so harshly, I can't quite believe it myself.

'I'm sorry.'

'Yeah. Me too. Although we weren't close, we were all we had, each other, after our parents died.'

'Was it recent?'

I find myself telling him about Keith and his sudden, untimely death, how I had to clear up his life. I feel sad when I think about it. Very sad. It must be the wine because I actually feel sadder now than I did at the time. I sniff back tears; no one wants that at dinner.

'So you're all alone?' It's a question and a statement.

'Yes.' Another glug of wine. I need to watch myself

and I'm sure this glass was empty when I last looked.

'No children?'

I hesitate before I answer. 'No. It's just me.' Then to divert attention away from me, I ask, 'So what do you do now? Where do you work?'

He tells me about his job in the council planning department, how he loves it but it's stressful, then I tell him about my job in the garden centre, how I love it and it's rarely stressful.

'I often shop in Jolliffe's,' he says. 'I've never seen you in there.'

'I'm out the back in amongst the plants and pots.'

'I heard they were closing down.' After he's said it, he grimaces. 'Sorry.'

'There're always rumours, gossip about a buyout. Hasn't happened yet, but it will.'

'What will you do?'

'I don't know.' I stop for a moment. I've never really given it any serious thought. I've certainly never considered what I would do if I lost my job. 'I've no idea. Work in a supermarket, maybe. I have experience of that.' I shrug and push my vegetables aside. 'You're right, those are spicy. Too much for me.'

'So,' he smiles over at me. 'You didn't say how long you're on holiday here for.'

'I'm not on holiday, not anymore.'

'Oh?' He waits, waits for the explanation I hoped I wouldn't have to give.

'Well, it's a long story…' I begin, and tell him about Fiona, our travelling companionship and her fall from grace. Perhaps it's the wine, or the fatigue or the stress, I don't know, but when I've finished, I'm crying. And I never do get my pudding.

Fifteen

I have misgivings about this morning; I've agreed to meet Carl for breakfast.

When we parted last night, it was much later than I had planned. I'd had too much to drink and I was a mess. Telling him about Fiona just tipped me over the edge, then I thought about Keith and that made me worse. Carl had asked if one of Fiona's sons was coming over to be with her. I'd told him that I didn't think so. Carl voiced something which I suppose I felt but didn't want to admit. He said it wasn't fair that I should assume so much responsibility for Fiona's welfare. He's right, we hardly know each other, but I can hardly abandon her, can I, if her family can't come over?

It was only after I got back to my room, went into the bathroom and saw myself, that I realised I had a big red wine stain on my white top. Typical. How long had that been there? After soaking the top overnight, it's now hanging out to dry on my balcony.

'Morning,' Carl says, when I answer my door. The teeth are on full display again. His mouth is so wide that

I think a smiley face is his default, unlike my *resting bitch face*. I feel like a bitch now too after slating Fiona the way I did to Carl last night, he's basically a perfect stranger.

'Hi, just get my bag.' I wonder if it was wise to give him my room number? I don't know him. Not really.

Just because we met at school nearly forty years ago doesn't mean I can trust him. What could he want from me? Once I'm out of the door I take a good look at him, his hair is in the sharpest haircut I have ever seen on a man of his age. Clipped around the back and sides and slightly longer on top it's very smart. He had an out of control afro at school, but that is now firmly oiled into place. It's still dark too, mostly. What could he want from me? Certainly not *that*. He's like a film star to my short, mousey woman.

He sees me looking at him.

'Do you think it's too much?' he asks. 'The hair?'

'Um, what do you mean?'

'One of my lads is a barber, he gave me a *cool cut* before I left, said he didn't want me showing the family up. Said he would hide my grey, by shaving it off.' He laughs.

'Well, I can't see any grey. Unlike my own,' I add before he does.

'Your hair isn't grey, more ash blonde.' He grins at me. 'It's not so very different in colour to how it was at school.'

'More bullshit,' I say and manage a grin back, but secretly I'm flattered.

'And I like that fluffy little style you have; it really suits you.'

I'm not going to tell him it's fluffy because I've washed it in shower gel and don't have any conditioner.

It feels horribly dry too, but he won't be touching it so he'll never know.

We head off to breakfast, but we're not going to the beach restaurant where we ate last night.

'Where are we going? The restaurant is the other way.' I feel a tickle of alarm.

'Breakfast is served at the other end of the complex. It's a bit of a trek from here.'

He's not joking; we walk to the far end, as far away from the beach as possible, then take a lift up five floors, then across a little bridge, around two corners and finally, we're here. I would never have found this place on my own. We wait to be seated, then help ourselves to another buffet, breakfast this time.

'How's your friend doing?'

'I don't know, I have to wait until after eleven to find out. I just hope it went ahead and everything is okay.' I have no idea what happens once she's operated on. When she will be able to leave hospital. Will she come here or will we fly straight home?

'Well, it's barely nine, so after breakfast we could take a stroll along the beach.' That certainly sounds appealing.

I'm just finishing my breakfast inside the restaurant when a little bird lands on the table, its breast as yellow as the sun. I jump involuntarily. Carl laughs.

'There are no windows, just shutters and they'll all open, so the birds come in.' He points to another table where a small black bird sits, its head darting from one side to the other, watching, curious, cautious.

'Hygiene?' I ask, thinking about the restaurant in Jolliffe's, and how if a bird got inside there the whole place would be closed down for disinfecting immediately.

Carl shrugs and laughs. 'I suppose that's why the buffet is in another room behind closed doors.'

I suppose it is.

After breakfast I take him up on his offer to walk along the beach. We pick our way along the water's edge, my feet sinking into the soft, wet sand. I imagine myself floating in the sea, it looks so inviting with the sun glinting off it.

'You need shoes on to go in there,' Carl says. 'There's coral underneath.'

'I doubt I'll have time.' I sound as world-weary as I feel. I have to stop feeling like this, there's nothing wrong with *me*, it's poor Fiona I have to worry about.

We wend our way further along, through trees like a little forest growing in the sand, then retrace our steps back to the beach bar and help ourselves to iced water from the cooler. Carl chatters on about his sons, their wives, his grandchildren.

I have nothing to say back.

'I need to go and make that phone call, then go to the hospital to see Fiona.' I stand up, so does Carl.

'I'll walk you back to your room.'

'There's really no need.' No one has ever walked me back to my room, or back to anywhere for that matter. 'What are your plans for the day?'

'Bridgetown. I need to get a few things, souvenirs mostly.' He laughs. 'Is there anything you need?'

'I can't think of anything.' Shampoo and conditioner? Maybe not.

Outside my room I worry that Carl is waiting to be invited in, instead he asks for my phone number and gives me his, then says goodbye.

I ring the hospital from the room phone, perching on my unmade bed. Fiona is fine, still in recovery but I can come in an hour when they bring her back to her room.

What now, I wonder?

A knock on the door makes me jump. Is it Carl? But when the door opens all I see is the cleaner, here to make up my room. I have nowhere to go yet so tell her I'll sit on the balcony out of her way. I want to use the hotel Wi-Fi to check my emails, see if there is anything further from the insurance company. There isn't.

I lean back in the shade and close my eyes. It's warm, there's a little breeze, it's quiet apart from the soft rush of waves on the sand; I could almost doze off.

'Wah!' I screech, jumping up.

'Sorry, madam,' the cleaner says before grinning at me. I don't know if she deliberately meant to slap her wet mop over my feet.

She carries on mopping and the smell of disinfectant is so strong it's making my eyes water. Open mouthed I watch her finish the balcony then back away into my room, where she continues her mopping. Finally, she finishes, leaves and closes the door and I am marooned where I stand until the floor dries and it will be a while, judging from the wet high sheen.

I'm bloody sure she did that on purpose.

♫♫♫

Fiona's propped up in bed smiling like an idiot when I enter.

'Pamela, my friend,' she says, but I know it's the drugs talking. 'I've missed you. Where have you been?' Was that a dig?

I choose not to answer. I'm really not in the mood for Fiona's jibes, especially after the taxi ride from hell.

It's little more than a five-minute journey, though it cost ten US dollars, and rattling around in the back where the seat belts had been snipped off as though they were a nuisance has left me feeling shaken and sick. What is it with today? I had to ask the receptionist at the hotel three times to get me a taxi, but she was too busy admiring her inch-long nails to fit it in to her busy *tapping the counter top* schedule. When finally she did ring, and the taxi appeared within seconds, she beckoned me with one of her talons then pointed out of the window, all without a word. In a very short time I've become fascinated by so many of the receptionists' nails, they all seem long and elaborately decorated. When I was signing in yesterday one of the receptionists told me that her nails were 'real, all my own.' I had a job not to laugh, they were hanging off her fingers like Wolverine's claws and no one can grow their natural nails that long without them curling. I thought my own were showy, but I'm not in the same league as the reception girls.

Fiona coughs, I think it is to get my attention. She's hooked up to drips and monitors and the smile never falls from her face. It's so unlike her, or what I know of her. Maybe she's normally jolly, to be fair I've mostly seen her in pain.

No, she was a miserable cow before she fell off the toilet.

'Did it go well? Is everything okay?' I ask, not sure if Fiona is best placed to judge.

Fortunately, before Fiona gets a chance to answer a nurse bursts into the room to *check Fiona's vitals*. A phrase which makes me smirk. There's very little that's vital about Fiona.

'You've made us all laugh,' she says to Fiona, while

smiling at me. 'We hear you were singing during your surgery.'

Fiona giggles like a little girl.

'Singing, really?' Now I know it's the drugs. 'What were you singing?'

Fiona doesn't answer, but the nurse does. 'Eleanor Rigby. That old Beatles one.'

'Oh God,' I say, flopping down into the black plastic chair.

'It was quite tuneful,' the nurse says, laughing. 'And she knew all the words.'

'I bet she did.' And I bet if she didn't before she met me, she made it her business to learn them once she discovered my name.

Fiona grins at me and I'm sure her eyes twinkle.

'What happens now?' I take the opportunity to ask the nurse.

'Oh, not for me to say.' She smiles, finishes up and leaves.

Great.

'How do you feel, Fiona?'

'Mmm,' Fiona says in a sing-song voice.

Do NOT start singing that bloody song.

'Yes, very good,' she says, increasing the brilliance of her smile.

'Good.' Now what do I say?

A knock on the door saves me from making small talk and in walks the surgeon, Mr Patel.

'And how are we feeling now, little lady?' he asks.

Fiona simpers in her bed; I swear she's fluttering her eyelashes at him.

'You brightened our day with your singing,' he says.

'What happens now?' I ask, diverting him from the singing nonsense. To be fair *I* would find it amusing if she hadn't chosen *that* song.

He turns and looks at me as though he's only just noticed I'm here, which, given that I'm slumped low in the sticky, black plastic chair, maybe he has.

'The physiotherapist will mobilise Fiona tomorrow, all being well she should be able to go home in a week. You'll have to put some work in, little lady,' he says as Fiona blinks at him several times, her smile never fading, her cheeks pinking up.

Pass the sick bucket.

'Thank you,' I say because he seems to be waiting for a response and Fiona doesn't seem capable of giving him one.

He nods, turns and leaves and then it's just us, Fiona and me.

Then Fiona dozes off and it's just me, my legs sticking to a hot plastic chair and I'm wondering if it's too soon to scoot off back to my hotel? I could lie on a sun lounger rather than sitting here watching Fiona sleep.

I pick up my handbag and get ready to creep out when a nurse bursts in through the door carrying a tray.

'This is lunch for Fiona,' she says, smiling at me.

'She's asleep,' I offer as the smell of the food makes my stomach rumble.

The nurse sets the tray down on the overbed table then starts to shake Fiona until eventually, she wakes up.

'You must eat, you need to build up your strength and you've had nothing since last night. Yes please.'

Fiona groans and attempts to go back to sleep.

'No, Fiona, you must wake up.' With that the nurse whips off the metal cover on Fiona's lunch, gathers up a forkful of meat and pushes it into Fiona's mouth.

Fiona splutters at first, but then chews and swallows, all with her eyes closed. The nurse repeats the process twice more. 'Well done. You must eat.' She turns her attention to me. 'You can carry on feeding Fiona, yes please?'

What can I say?

'Yes, please,' I mumble, unpeeling myself from my chair.

Sixteen

I'm not completely convinced that Fiona was asleep, I think she just liked the attention.

I've finished feeding her now although she woke up enough to eat the pudding herself, a fruit thing with sauce on it. It looked delicious and made my mouth water. All I've had is a large glass of iced water, there's plenty of that and visitors are allowed to drink it.

I'm back in my chair watching as Fiona, now fully alert, flicks through the channels on the TV looking for something to watch, not that I can see it because my chair is positioned beneath the TV which is high on the wall.

'Is there underwear in my bag?' she suddenly asks.

'Yes.'

'Does it include *everything*?'

I'm tempted to ask her what she means by everything, because I know she means incontinence pads, but I'm not that mean.

'Everything,' I say with a smile. And about another hundred of them in *my* suitcase.

'Good, because once I'm mobile I won't be able to

walk about with that.' She points to the bag hanging off the side of the bed, the urine bag.

'No. Anyway, you'll be glad to be up and about after all this time lying in bed,' I say cheerfully so that she doesn't start talking about her catheter or her fanny, I'm still reeling from the shock of having to wash it that first day.

'I will, yes, I will.' Her eyes move away from me and back to the TV screen above my head. 'Oh,' she says, 'This is one of my favourite films and it's just starting.'

Lucky you, I think, but don't voice it.

'I expect you'd like to escape back to your hotel,' she says, giving me an out. 'When you come up tomorrow do bring your computer tablet because we'll need to start pushing the insurance company to get us out of here. I'll see you tomorrow.' With that she turns the TV up. That's me dismissed then and I couldn't be happier.

I sit in the hospital reception for twenty minutes before the taxi the receptionist has called finally turns up. It's another hell ride at break neck speed while I roll around in the back without a seat belt. What is it with the seat belts? I notice the driver is wearing his.

Back in my hotel room I add the cost of today's taxis to the list I've started with all the items I've had to pay for, not forgetting the eight thousand US dollars at the hospital. I hope the insurance company pays quickly because I just don't have the money to settle the credit card bill when it comes and I can't afford to pay the interest. I'm also concerned about the taxi fares; I've just counted up my US dollars and I only have just over fifty left. That's five journeys, that's two and half days. I can't see Fiona being ready to leave in a couple of days.

I wonder if they'll accept pounds? I have twenty-seven pounds; I don't think that'll last long either.

It's too late for lunch and too soon for dinner. I could sunbathe to pass the time, or swim in the sea, but I don't have any suitable shoes to combat the coral and I daren't attempt to buy any, even though I noticed the gift shop next to Reception sells them. I can't afford it. I don't have enough cash and can't risk putting anything else on my credit card, I have this hotel bill to pay and I don't know how much longer I'm going to be here.

I make myself a cup of tea in my room, grateful that I'm able to, and eat a couple of biscuits from a cellophane wrapped packet. They're very similar to the ones on the ship. The ship, that floating palace of entertainment and endless food, is still docked in Barbados but will soon sail away to other islands without us.

I shake myself, shake off the self-pity. There's a pool just below my room, I could go for a swim. I rummage through my suitcase, pushing through the packs of incontinence pads, looking for my swimming costume but I can't find it. I think I accidently discarded it when I realised my case was too heavy to carry. It couldn't have weighed much.

I run my hands through my hair, I'm so fed up. This was supposed to be my holiday of a lifetime, but it's turned into the nightmare from hell. It's not Fiona's fault, I remind myself. It's not mine either.

'Shampoo,' I say aloud, feeling how coarse my hair is. I noticed a little parade of shops about a quarter of a mile up the road. The taxi hurtled past so fast that I don't know if there was anywhere there that sold shampoo but, if nothing else, the walk will fill the time between now and dinner.

I trek all the way to Reception then leave the air-conditioned iciness and step outside. Half a dozen steps and I'm already sweating. It's hot, so much hotter than I realised. I've spent so much time inside with air-con, even the tatty taxis have super freeze air-con, that I haven't really appreciated how hot it gets here as the day goes on. Walking along the beach after breakfast with Carl, the sea breeze cooling us off, seems like another country compared to this searing heat.

I'm sure I can make it to the parade of shops. I'm sure I can. It's so bright that even with sunglasses on I'm squinting. I don't think I can afford a hat and I didn't bring one with me, that too is still on the ship.

I walk for five minutes, though it feels more like twenty. Trickles of sweat are running down between my shoulder blades, between my breasts, from my hairline and into my eyebrows. I'll be needing another shower before dinner tonight. I can feel my shoes, flip flops that I actually did have the foresight and space to bring with me, slipping around on my feet, they are definitely going to rub something raw by the time I get back.

A black car slows as it approaches me. I carry on walking. Young lads, young Barbadians, hang out of the windows and wave while the driver beeps his horn several times as they pass me by. I look behind me, to the side, ahead. I am the only person walking along, alone. What is the matter with them?

I carry on. It happens again, this time from behind. I check my dress isn't tucked into my knickers. It's not. I cannot believe this. These are young men, handsome men, what could they possibly want with me? I'm old enough to be their mother.

I reach the shops, a sticky, sweaty mess. I'm used to varying temperatures, sometimes in the garden centre it can get very hot especially when I'm humping pots and bags of compost about, but this beats anything I've ever experienced. I stumble into the first shop I see, a gift shop of sorts, selling swimming costumes and hats – oh that I could afford such luxuries – and tourist knick-knacks. I can't afford any of it.

'Madam?' a smiling assistant greets me. Another young beauty with extravagant nails.

'I'm looking for shampoo,' I venture, sure there is none here.

'No, madam.' She shakes her head and turns her attention back to the phone she was obviously scrolling through before I came in.

'Okay. Thank you.' I slip slop out of the shop and head towards the next one.

A hair salon, the pictures in the window show elaborate braids and beads, keratin straightening, and nails. I finger my own pale, fluffy strands and doubt they could do much for me. They must sell shampoo though, even if it might be expensive. I grab the door handle but the shop is shut. Then there's a bakery, the sweet spicy smell reminding me how hungry I am. I move along to a shop selling strange parts for cars; oversized headlamps and coloured stickers. I wonder if they sell replacement rear seatbelts? Finally, there's an undertaker. So, no shampoo.

'Hey lady, you want a ride?'

I'm tired, it's hot, it's tempting.

No, it's not.

'No, thanks,' I say to the young man. His smile shows his teeth just like a crocodile's, his hair is long and braided, maybe he's just been in the hair salon, before it closed.

'No problem.' He shrugs.

I march past him as quickly as I can, heading

towards the road, back towards the hotel. Rushing makes me hotter and sweatier. I glance back but he hasn't moved, he isn't following me, he's leaning on the bonnet of his car, watching, and at the same time, not watching.

I march on and get another beep. What is wrong with these men? Another car behind me, it slows down, I walk faster. Go away, go away. It passes. I sigh with relief to myself and slow my pace. The car stops. The driver door opens. I glance behind me. I glance across the road. I'll cross, that's what I'll do. I'll cross and scurry away as fast as I can.

'Pam,' the voice calls as I step into the road, my face turned away from him. 'Pam, it's me, Carl.'

I stop.

'Carl?'

It is Carl. He's smiling, his perfect teeth grinning at me.

'What are you doing walking along in this heat?' He comes towards me, the grin never diminishing.

'I need some shampoo. I saw these shops. I thought…' I let my voice trail away and shrug.

'No good?'

'No.'

'Come on, I'll take you back to the hotel and then I'm going to buy you a big, cold drink in the bar.'

I laugh and groan simultaneously and clamber into his car, oh, the air-con coolness.

'Shampoo?' he asks. 'Don't you have any?'

'No.' Then I tell him how I didn't bring it with me because I had to travel light, how my suitcase is full of Fiona's things, but I don't tell him what those things are. I tell him how I'm using shower gel. He laughs. Trust a man not to understand.

I almost don't want to go to the bar with him, I'm sweaty and dusty from my trek. But I'm also thirsty. I settle for a diet coke with ice and lemon when he offers. When it comes I almost down it in one. It certainly hits the spot.

'I need to go and have a shower before dinner,' I say, standing up. 'Thanks so much for the drink, I really needed that.'

'My pleasure.' The look on his face is genuine. 'I have some shampoo you can use.' He stands up too. 'Come with me.'

We head towards his room, in a block just like mine but on the other side of the complex. More walking, my feet slopping about in my sweaty flip flops. I think about asking him to bring it to me, then decide not to.

When we arrive at his room I hover outside, I don't want to go in.

'Come in.'

'No, I won't. I need that shower.' I wipe my brow in an exaggerated movement to prove my point.

He hands over the bottle, a two in one shampoo and conditioner. Better than shower gel.

'Thank you. So much.'

'Will you join me for dinner again?'

'Yes. Please.'

'I'll call for you.'

We agree a time and I scuttle away with his shampoo, promising myself a long soak in the bath before I see him.

Back in my room I peel off my clothes, the odour from my armpits makes *me* gag. What must Carl have thought? I cringe.

I fill the bath and climb in, using Carl's shampoo is definitely an improvement on shower gel but it does smell very manly. Oh well. I use the hotel's shower gel to scrub my sweaty self and when I've finished, I climb out, but I don't let the water out. Because I've brought so few of my own clothes with me, I need to wash everything I've worn today in case I need to wear them again. Who knows how long we will be here? And washing them in the super scented, even if masculine, bath water seems like a good idea. I hope it is, I hope I don't wash more bad smells into them.

I dunk my clothes and give them a good scrub, followed by a rinse and then hang them over the line above the bath to drip dry.

♫♫♫

'You look lovely,' Carl says when I answer his knock on my door.

'Thank you.' No doubt I do, considering that I was a mass of sweat and heat when he last saw me, not to mention the smell, which, thankfully, he doesn't.

We're quickly shown to a table overlooking the ocean, not that we can see it, the sun has long gone down even though it's barely past 7pm.

Carl orders a bottle of wine and I don't protest when my glass is filled.

'Do you still live in our home town?' I ask, realising that we never discussed this before, I just assumed he did because he said he'd been in Jolliffe's.

'No,' he says, mid sip of his wine.

'Oh.'

'Well, no and yes. I live in Lyffingdon, so not far.'

'Ah. Nice.' I've heard it's nice, a quaint old pub on a village green, thatched cottages, that sort of thing; I've never actually been there.

'I moved there after my divorce. I like it, it's quiet, well apart from the birds and the occasional tractor roaring through the village. I bought a newbuild, it's not very big, just two bedrooms and a bathroom upstairs, kitchen-diner and lounge downstairs, but it suits me. I was lucky there; they don't build many new places in villages like that and I could never afford one of the older properties.' He rolls his eyes and laughs. 'What about you?'

'Nothing as grand as you.'

He laughs. 'My place really isn't grand.'

'I live in a one bed council flat. Been there for years. Well, it's housing association now, but you get my meaning.'

'Funny, in my head I imagined you living in your parents' place. Of course you wouldn't still be there now. That was a nice house, wasn't it? Nice street, I remember.'

'Have you ever even been there?' Has he?

'Yes. I walked you home once, don't you remember? Maybe you don't, you were rather the worse for wear as I recall.'

'You walked me home? When?' I have no recollection of this.

'It was after a party, in that house near the park. I think you might have had too many fruit punches.' He laughs again, a light little laugh of embarrassment as though he wishes he hadn't brought it up.

'I must have done. I didn't go to many parties.' Only that one and it changed my life. I pick up my wine glass and study the contents as though it were a book.

'How was the shampoo?' he asks, reading my signals.

'Ah.' I grab it out of my handbag. 'Lovely. Really good…except for the smell.'

'It smells nice.'

'On you. Now I smell like a man, a well-groomed man.'

He takes the shampoo and sets it on the corner of the table.

'Yes, it's one of my son's choices. I didn't think about the smell.'

'I need to find a shop that sells ladies' shampoo. There was a hairdressers in that shopping parade, they weren't open but I'll try them in the morning.'

'Or I could take you to a supermarket, I'm sure there'll be more choice and probably cheaper too.'

'I couldn't ask you…' I don't finish the sentence. He's offering.

'We'll go after breakfast. Save you walking in the heat.'

'Save me having young men hanging out of their cars and beeping me.' I say this as a joke, and follow it with a laugh.

'Were they? I suppose they would.'

'Why? I don't get it. I'm old enough to be their mother.'

'I don't know. Mostly they're just being friendly. Some might have a motive.'

'A motive to murder….' I laugh again.

'No, to marry you. They think white women of a certain age, on holiday here, are rich widows.'

Now I really laugh. 'They'd be sadly disappointed.'

He forces a smile but his teeth don't show, which looks strange. Then he orders another bottle of wine because we've already drunk a whole one between us and we haven't even had anything to eat yet.

♫♫♫

We're having a lovely evening, it's heading towards midnight, it's still warm and we've eaten and drunk far too much. We're on brandy now, a nightcap, Carl says.

'It's late,' I say, twisting around to see the clock behind the bar.

'It's early in the morning at home.'

'Well, if you put it like that.' I laugh, we've done a lot of that this evening. I don't even know what we've been laughing about. Nothing, something, I don't know. I suppose that's what drink does to you, makes you laugh at nothing and everything.

Two cups of coffee appear at the table, Carl has ordered these in an attempt, he says, to sober us up. I don't feel drunk, not that out of control, swaying head kind of drunk, but maybe that's because we've drunk as much water as wine.

'What happened to you at the end of school,' he says out of nowhere. I'm stunned and don't know how to answer. 'Only, if I remember rightly, you disappeared before the exams.'

Where do I start? Do I even want to start? There are things in my past that are best left in the past.

'Officially because my dad was dying.'

Carl looks horrified. 'Oh, God, I'm sorry.'

'He wasn't. Not then, anyway.' No, that would come a few years later, after he'd held his pending death over us, over me, blaming me for his weak heart, never himself, never his sixty-a-day cigarette habit.

'Ah,' Carl says as though he knows something, but I know he doesn't. Having finished his coffee he picks up his brandy glass, there's such a tiny amount in the bottom that I wonder why he bothers.

'I had a baby.'

Carl splutters, spreading the tiny amount of brandy all over his face, it dribbles down his chin. He grabs a napkin and dabs himself.

'I'm sorry, I thought you said…'

'I did,' I cut across. Evidently, I *am* drunk, far drunker than I thought I was. I never intended to tell him that. I haven't spoken about it to anyone, ever. Never, ever. I don't even allow myself to think about it too much, just occasionally when the maudlin feelings get the better of me.

'What? How?' He can't even ask the right questions.

I shake myself back into my sensible mode. I've already said far too much.

'Ignore me, I shouldn't have said that. I don't want to talk about it. I think it's time I went to bed.'

I stand up and call the waitress over, sign my bill and leave. I say a polite goodbye to Carl but I decline his offer to walk me back to my room.

Me and my big mouth.

Seventeen

Carl knocks for me for breakfast. He has that look of someone acutely embarrassed. I can tell he wishes he'd never asked me. He wishes I'd never told him I'd had a baby.

Not as much as I do.

We trek up to the breakfast buffet without speaking. I suppose it would have been odd if he hadn't knocked for me, if we hadn't breakfasted together. Or would it? We hardly know each other. It's not as though we're on holiday together.

'How's your friend? I'm sorry, I forgot to ask yesterday.'

'Fiona. She's okay. They're getting her up today. I'll have to get up to the hospital later this morning to see her.'

'I could drop you off, after we've been shopping for your shampoo.'

I'm about to refuse his offer, to say no thanks, I don't want to be in a car with you in case you ask me questions about my past. Then I remember how little cash I have, how expensive and downright frightening it is rolling about in the back of a taxi with no seatbelts.

'Thank you.'

He doesn't ask. We hardly talk in his car, in the supermarket; on the way to the hospital we only exchange pleasantries. It's awkward. On the plus side I now have a bottle each of shampoo and conditioner and at a reasonable price too.

He offers to pick me up later. I hesitate but then accept his offer. Every dollar counts. I hope he doesn't think I'm using him. We agree that I'll message him when I need him to come for me.

♬♬♬

Fiona is dressed in her own clothes and sitting in my black plastic chair when I go into her room. She's sitting on a pillow so she won't stick to it, and it should make it more comfortable. It's also been moved to the far side of the room, giving her a good view of the TV. Where will I sit now?

'Ah, the wanderer returns,' she says.

I don't bite. 'How are you today? I see you're out of bed.'

'Yes, been for a walk, well ten steps but it's good to be upright after all these days lying in bed. I can sit on this chair for a few hours. I'm lucky, because I'm so small this one is just the right height, otherwise it would have been a bigger, higher, harder one.' She pulls her shoulders up in what she thinks, I assume, is a cute pose. Oh, look at me, I'm so little and sweet. 'It's so good to be up,' she says again.

'I bet it is.' I glance around for somewhere to put my bags, settling for the floor in the corner where the chair previously was.

'Been shopping?' Fiona asks, her voice seeming to accuse me of something.

'Just for shampoo. I didn't bring any with me.'

'That was a bit stupid, wasn't it? You certainly had plenty of it on the ship. Your jumbo bottles almost took over the entire bathroom. You should have brought them with you.'

I force a tight smile. I won't agree with her but I can't argue with her either, I can't put the blame back on her.

'I'm glad to see that you remembered to bring the correct toiletries for me because I'm having a shower and hair wash tomorrow. And it's long overdue, I can tell you. Did you bring your tablet computer?'

'Yes.'

'Good. Let's send an email to the insurance company, I don't want them slacking on getting us home.'

I fish my tablet out of my bag then look around for somewhere to put it, somewhere to sit. I consider the bed, but think it wouldn't be right to sit on it, anyway, it doesn't look particularly comfortable, the mattress is wafer thin. It probably doesn't bother Fiona with her sparrow like proportions but I imagine my bones would soon be aching if I had to sleep on it.

'Why don't you go and find a spare chair,' Fiona pipes up, as if reading my thoughts.

I take the opportunity to get away from her if only for a few minutes. There are, of course, no spare chairs anywhere. I approach the nurses' station where half a dozen nurses and doctors are either on computers or making notes in folders and wait until someone looks up at me. It feels wrong to interrupt them for something so trivial as a chair.

The nurse who looks up and raises her eyebrows at me is older than me, with grey wavy hair and the palest of complexions. I expect her to have an Irish accent because she reminds me of the nurse, long ago, in Holby City, the BBC hospital drama, or was it Casualty? I don't know, it's such a long time ago.

I'm so engrossed in my walk down TV memory lane that when she speaks in a strong Barbadian accent, I'm shocked.

'I'll bring you a chair,' she says with a brief smile. 'Fiona's room. Yes please?'

'Yes. Please.' I hover. 'I'll go and wait then. There.'

'Yes please,' she says again already back focusing on her computer screen.

'No chair?' Fiona's irritated voice asks.

'It's coming.'

'When?'

'When they have time, I would think. It's not exactly a medical emergency, is it.'

'They don't have medical emergencies in here, it's all planned ops. Despite the tatty décor this is a private hospital. Have you seen how many of them there are? Never get that in the NHS. I had another good scrub down by a nurse this morning, 6am though. Could have done without it that soon. Lovely breakfast though, too early for me, but there you go. I'm going to buzz for them to bring the chair, should have done that in the first place.'

'Nooo,' I call, but it's too late, she's already pressed the button on a long cable which is wound around the arm of her chair.

We wait a few minutes until someone comes in, it's the *Irish* nurse and she's carrying my chair. She sets it down without a word, then walks over to the wall where the light is flashing after Fiona pressed the button and flicks a switch to cancel it.

'You need something?' she asks Fiona.

'We needed the chair, but you've brought it now.'

I hate Fiona's tone, it's so rude.

The nurse nods at Fiona, scowls at me as though it's my fault and leaves without a word.

'Thank you,' I call after her. I turn to Fiona, 'That really wasn't necessary, was it?'

'They've got nothing else to do, there's hardly anyone here.'

'How do you know that?'

'Well, it's obvious, isn't it?'

'Is it?' I say more to myself than her as I position my chair, flip the cover over on my tablet and sit down ready to do her bidding.

'Log onto the hospital Wi-Fi,' she instructs. 'The signal is strong.'

'Ah, have you managed to contact your family, let them know how you are, told them about your op.'

'Yes,' she says, her tone curt. 'Thank you.'

Fiona dictates a sharply worded email to the insurance company telling them that she wants them to start sourcing flights to get us out of here. She tells them she expects to be fit to travel in six days. I assume that this is what the surgeon has told her. Six days. I'll have to extend my stay at the hotel, I hope I can afford it. After she's finished and I have read it back to her several times and she has tweaked it, I move my chair away and prepare to send it.

'What are you typing?' she snaps.

'I'm putting their email address in.' I'm not telling her that I've written that although the email comes from my address it's actually from Fiona, I don't want them thinking I'm as rude as she is. 'It's sent,' I say.

'Good. I wonder how long it'll be before they reply?'

'Tomorrow, probably. Don't forget the time difference.'

Fiona rolls her eyes at me and sighs. 'Supposed to be a twenty-four-hour service,' she says slowly, as though I am dim.

'Yes, well in the garden centre we're open very long hours but the office isn't staffed for all of them,' I say, equally slowly back.

Fiona gives me a look that screams, 'You know nothing,' but she doesn't actually say anything.

This is awful, I think our relationship is deteriorating even further. I had hoped that once Fiona was on her feet, on the road to recovery, she might not be so nasty, but, if anything, I think she's worse.

The door bursts open and the *Irish* nurse comes in with a tray. Fiona's lunch. Lucky Fiona. It smells delicious. The nurse sets it up on the overbed tray, then moves it towards Fiona in her chair.

Fiona eats her lunch and I browse Facebook on my tablet. I had imagined posting the odd exotic picture of my holiday by now, we'd be moving onto a different Caribbean island every day. I imagined my colleagues at Jolliffe's being impressed, even Richard would find it hard to criticise lush vegetation and bright blue skies. I suppose I could post one of Barbados. I could do that every day, no one would know the difference, they wouldn't know it wasn't one of the other islands.

'Have you had a reply yet?' Fiona suddenly snaps. She's eaten some of her lunch, but pushed the rest away.

'No, not yet.' I haven't even looked and I'm not going to because we can save that treat for tomorrow, it's not as if we'll be leaving that soon.

'Oh, then what are you studying so hard?'

'Oh, nothing, just Facebook.'

'Humph.'

'What did your family think of all this?' I nod at her hip.

She shrugs. 'They were busy. They'll ring me later.'

'I suppose there won't be such a big time difference between here and Canada, not like between here and the UK.'

She shrugs again. 'No.'

End of that conversation then.

She looks away before picking up the remote control and switching on the TV, she starts to flick through the million channels on offer. I watch her face light up when she finds something she wants to watch. Not that I can see it because I'm back in my position underneath the TV.

A different nurse comes in and tells Fiona it's time to get back into bed for a rest. I watch the agonised movement Fiona makes as she's helped back into her bed. My, that looks painful. Poor Fiona. The nurse leaves and takes Fiona's lunch tray with her.

Fiona looks over at me, or maybe it's the TV.

'You don't have to stay you know,' she says.

'No?'

'I'm sure you've got things to do.'

'Not really.' What the hell does she think I do when I'm not here. I don't want to be stuck here on this one island. I take a deep breath to stop myself from feeling self-pity and being selfish. *I'm* not the one with a broken leg and in pain.

'Well, you can go,' she says, dismissing me.

'Okay.' Then I bloody well will. I stuff my tablet

back into my bag, grab my shopping and stand up, unpeeling myself from the sticky plastic chair.

'I'll see you tomorrow.' I feel as though I should kiss her goodbye, but that also feels totally alien.

'Don't forget your tablet computer tomorrow, we'll need a response from the insurance idiots or we'll need to chase, but either way, bring it.'

'Okay.' I glance over to the side and notice her phone on charge. 'Shall I bring your phone over to you, it's out of your reach.'

'No. Thank you.'

'Okay. I'll be off then.'

'Oh, before you go can you grab that bag there,' she points to a clear plastic bag.

I pick it up. It's her knickers. I hold it up waiting for instructions, dreading them.

'Can you take those with you and give them a rub through please. I had a little accident earlier. And be careful with them, they're my good ones. Oh, and can you leave the bag here please, it's the only one I have.'

I try not to shudder, try not to grimace my disgust, try to remember that it's not her fault. She's a little bit incontinent, I already know that. I nod slowly then wonder where I'm going to put them. Not in my handbag. I drop them slowly from her plastic bag into my supermarket bag containing the shampoo.

'Bye then.'

♫♫♫

'I didn't expect you to leave your friend so soon,' Carl says when he picks me up from the hospital.

'Me neither. I was dismissed.' I laugh, with relief. 'I'm not sorry. We're not the best of friends.'

'Oh?'

'We're not enemies or anything like that, it's just that we're not best friends. We only teamed up to come on holiday together to make it cheaper, for the room and the insurance. That worked out well, didn't it?'

He starts the car and pulls away from the hospital and doesn't say anything until we're driving along the road.

'Well, her loss is my gain. And if you hadn't ended up here, in the same hotel as me, we might never have met up.'

'No.' And I might never have blurted out that I'd had a baby when I was a teenager and churned up feelings I've tried to keep at bay all these years.

'Fancy lunch? I know a lovely little place overlooking the sea, not too far to drive and we could paddle in the sea afterwards, and you can go in barefoot there too, no coral.'

'Why not?' I look over at Carl as he drives and then I remember. 'Oh, no, maybe not. I really can't afford it.'

'My treat. I invited you.'

'Yes, no, you don't understand.'

'Then make me understand.'

I tell him how I have little cash, how my card is almost maxed out, how I'm already worried about the hotel bill and how I really can't afford lovely lunches.

'My treat,' he says, smiling. 'I invited you. And if you get stuck for cash I can help.'

'Thank you,' I mumble into my lap. 'I couldn't...' but I don't finish the sentence in case I do have to borrow money from him. Heaven forbid. I kick the supermarket bag in the footwell, nudging my shampoo away from Fiona's stinky knickers.

We eat lunch overlooking a beautiful bay, we sit

under an awning with a sea breeze cooling us. Neither of eats a lot, both mindful of the hotel buffet later, no doubt. It's just nice to sit here with a long, soft drink and pretend I'm on holiday.

Afterwards we stroll alongside the beach, wandering past little kiosks.

'You need a hat,' Carl says, laughing as he plonks one on my head. He's right, I do, I can feel the sun burning my scalp through my hair. I have the perfect thing on board the ship, deep inside one of my cases. 'It suits you,' he says before whipping it off my head and turning to the stall holder. Before I can argue he's bought it and is placing it properly on my head, adjusting the angle. He stands back and admires me in the hat.

'Thank you,' I say, but bite back my words of protest about how he shouldn't have. He wanted to, and I do need a hat.

We edge our way across the sand and along the water's edge. It's cool and refreshing and Carl ventures in up to his knees. He beckons me. I step towards him, hoisting up my dress and laughing. The water is soon up to my thighs and I scream with delight and shock. I can't remember the last time I was this deep in the sea. Probably never, or maybe on one of those day trips to Bournemouth, so many years ago. It's exciting and exhilarating and I feel like a child.

'Ohhh…' I yell as I see a wave approaching.

Carl turns and sees it too and grabs my hand and urges me inland. We laugh as the wave hits the back of our legs, splashing up onto our clothes. He's still holding my hand long after the wave ebbs away and he doesn't let go and I don't make him.

I find I quite like it.

'Should have brought our swimming gear,' Carl says.

'Not me.'

'Oh?'

So I have to tell him how I left that behind on the ship too.

'Then we'll go and get you one now, here, and then we'll go back and we can swim in the pool. You'll enjoy it, come on.'

So that's how we spend the afternoon, bobbing around on giant floats, laughing and giggling like a couple of giant kids, and lying on the hotel sun loungers to dry ourselves off.

Eventually, as the sun goes down, we weave our way back to our rooms. I need to wash my hair again, this time with the lovely shampoo and conditioner.

And, I have Fiona's knickers to wash, or rub through, as she put it. Cringe.

Eighteen

Oh no, she's shat in the knickers. I wasn't expecting that.

I can't handle them now. I'm showered and hair washed and lovely and fresh and the last thing I want to do is rub through Fiona's drawers. I squirt a bit of shower gel on the offending area and drop them in the bath, wash my hands and get the hell out of there. It's not like she needs them tomorrow. She has a bag full of knickers and I have more of hers in my case. Many more.

♫♫♫

'There's a live band tonight,' the restaurant manager tells us when we arrive for dinner.

'Okay, sounds good,' Carl says, with a hint of diplomacy to his voice as he glances over at the stage. 'Could you sit us over in the far corner?'

The manager raises his eyebrows and smiles. 'Certainly, sir.'

'You don't like live music then?' I tease as we sit

down.

'It's a steel band. No disrespect to my heritage but the sound reverberates in my eardrums.' He glances around us to ensure no one is listening, 'And I don't like it.'

I laugh. 'What, the music or the sound?'

'Both,' he whispers before laughing. 'It must be my age.'

We're halfway through our meal before the musicians make an appearance, quickly setting up their drums and plugging in their microphones.

They start to play and I stop eating instantly, my fork in mid-air.

'What's wrong?'

'They're playing Beatles stuff,' I say, hurriedly pushing food into my mouth. I cannot believe it.

'Well, everyone knows it, I suppose.'

'Yeah, of course.' I can't say any more. I can't bring up my irrational fear of them playing Eleanor Rigby just in case it makes the inevitable happen, like a jinx. Who knows, maybe they won't play it, it's hardly jolly holiday music, is it? No, it's fine, they won't play it.

The music stops, everybody claps and the band moves onto another song. Another Beatles song.

We go and grab our pudding; I'd like to finish my meal and escape. I now dislike steel bands as much as Carl does, but for an entirely different reason.

When we get back to the table another bottle of wine has appeared.

'I thought it might help us ignore the music,' Carl says, when I query the wine's arrival.

'Okay, well pour me a big one.' Perhaps they won't play *my* song.

'We could go somewhere else,' he says. 'Once we've

finished eating.'

I think about where else we could go. This is the only eating place open in the evening, the only bar. There are a few tables and chairs around the pool but I don't much fancy that and I certainly don't want to go to Carl's room or have him back to mine, especially with Fiona's knickers soaking in the tub.

'No. I'm fine.' I raise my glass and take a swig before delving into my pudding, a peach crumble with custard, it seems an odd pudding in the middle of the Caribbean, I was expecting something exotic, maybe a giant pineapple stuffed with spices.

'The music carries anyway, I could hear it in my room the first night I was here,' he says.

After another glass of wine, the steel band has faded into the background. Carl was wise to ask for this table as we are just about as far from the music as it's possible to be.

I can hear myself chattering on inanely and I see Carl's smile flash over his face. It looks genuine, or he could just be humouring me. I've wittered on endlessly about Fiona and how she is now onto the insurance company, via my email. I've told him how she's out of bed and desperate to get mobile enough to go home. I've told him how I'm dreading the flight home because I've never flown before and this is going to be one hell of a long flight. He nods and smiles in all the right places.

I don't normally drink much, or very often. The truth is I don't have much of a social life. By the time I've finished at the garden centre I'm tired and hungry and usually just have a quiet night in with the TV. I occasionally go out to an event organised through work, Christmas, a birthday – even my own occasionally. I go to the odd pub quiz, Richard allows me to be on his team but only as a reserve, so I'm not expected to turn up unless he tells me first. That suits me, it's not every week, it probably averages once every six weeks. It suits me very well. Yet, here I am drinking every night, dining out every night and now spending all my time with a man, albeit one I knew at school.

Carl pours the last of the wine into my glass.

'Are you trying to get me drunk?' I giggle.

'Trying? Succeeded,' he says, laughing. 'Shall I get another bottle?'

'No. No. Not for me. I'll be unconscious.'

'Seems to me that you need it to unwind,' he says, summing me up in one little sentence. I don't know if I like it.

'Really.'

'I didn't mean anything by that. What I meant was you have a lot to cope with, your friend, her operation, all the hassle of dealing with the insurance, getting home and so on.' He's certainly been listening.

I look into his eyes; I hold his gaze too long. He doesn't look away.

'He wasn't yours,' I say, out of nowhere.

'No,' he says, instantly knowing I'm talking about the baby, my baby boy. 'I know that without a shadow of a doubt,' I continue. 'Even if I slept with you that night, and I can't remember if I did, I know he wasn't yours.' I pause, take another drink, aware that I'm saying things I don't want to say but cannot stop myself. 'I know by the colour, you see. He was such a pale baby, with bright blue eyes.'

'I know he wasn't mine,' Carl says, his voice soft. 'You and I never did that. I just walked you home that once. Is that when it happened, at that party?'

I hear a big hiccup come out of my mouth. I think I might be crying but it's silent, just the tears, apart from the hiccup.

'Yep. Don't really want to talk about it.' I attempt to stand up. Sit back down, then stand again, this time successfully. 'Oh, listen, they're playing my song.' Right on cue they've got to it, as I always knew they would. "Eleanor Rigby".

'Would you like to dance?'

'To this?' I shriek, but despite myself I start to sway in time to the music and Carl jumps up and wraps his arms around me and we're dancing, me with my head against his chest.

When the song finally finishes we stay exactly where we are, still swaying slightly.

'Why do you call it your song?'

I pull away from him. Is he fucking joking?

'"Eleanor Rigby",' I say. '"Eleanor Rigby".'

'But your name's Pam.'

I could kiss him, right here, right now, just for that. Instead I have to correct him. What the hell is wrong with me?

'It's Eleanor, my dad named me after that song. I'm Eleanor Pamela Rigby.'

'Oh. I never knew. You've always been Pam to me. Why are you so bothered by it anyway?'

'Well, you know. Lived on her own, lonely, all that shit.' My voice is far too loud and people are looking at us. 'It's a self-fulfilling prophecy, isn't it?'

'That's not you,' he says, his face filled with kindness.

'It is. I am. My dad cursed me with my name. Made me alone.'

'It doesn't have to be like that. You can change it.

Change anything. Be who you want to be.' He's being kind. And trite.

The band starts to play another song, a catchy one, *Ob-La-Di, Ob-La-Da*. Carl grabs my hands and dances me in time to the music. I go with it. Why not?

The music stops and we sit back down. He pulls his chair up to mine, calls the waiter over so he can order coffee and more water, both of which I definitely need.

'Eleanor's quite a nice name.'

'Shut up.'

'It is.'

'Not with my surname.'

'I doubt anyone would even notice.'

'You must be joking. Fiona spotted it in my passport, she brings it up at every opportunity, sneering and teasing.' I tell him about how she sung it while sedated for her operation, how the whole hospital enjoyed her performance.

He laughs, far, far too much. And I find myself annoyed because he's belittling my lifelong torture. How dare he?

'Oh, you don't understand.' I start looking under the table for my handbag; I need to go back to my room and sleep this off. 'It made me odd.'

He laughs, a little bitter laugh. 'Everybody's odd.'

I look at him with his perfect teeth, his sunny smile, his trendy haircut. He has a family, sons, an ex-wife. Somewhere along the line there will be grandchildren, if there aren't already.

''You don't understand,' I mutter again.

'Now you're the joker. I was one of only three black kids in our school year. Can you remember the others? Being a black kid, in the seventies in the middle of Wiltshire, that was quite odd.' He stares at me, daring me to argue.

'I never noticed,' is all I can manage.

'You certainly didn't. You didn't even notice when I walked you home after that party when you were incapable and upset. Though now I'm beginning to understand why you were so upset. And why you never noticed me.'

'I didn't notice you were black.'

He looks at me, searching my face, checking if I'm genuine.

'Yeah, well I never noticed your surname or connected it to that song. Anyway, you only had eyes for one boy at school. That football player. Is he the father?'

'David Woodward.' My tongue betrays me.

'That's the one.'

There's a silence between us now. A hush everywhere. The band is packing up, the steel drums are being taken away. People are starting to head back to their rooms. The air feels cool and still, heavy with moisture. Maybe it's going to rain. I take a long sip of my coffee.

'Do you keep in touch with anyone from school?' What a stupid question, why am I asking?

'Him, you mean?'

'Him. Anyone.'

'No, not really. I've bumped into the odd person in Asda, but not recently. I saw Alan Wilson once.'

I gasp at the mention of his name. Alan Wilson. I put my hand up to my mouth, I feel hot and cold all at once.

'Was it him?' Carl asks, his voice incredulous.

I nod. I shake my head. I nod again. 'I don't know. Him. Or the other one.'

'The footballer?'

'Maybe.'

If it's possible for a black man's face to turn ashen, Carl manages it.

'Tell me,' he says. 'Tell me everything.'

I don't want to. Not really. I don't want to think about it or talk about or tell anyone anything. That's how I've got on with my life, by not going there. But once I start there's no stopping me, it all comes tumbling out in one long, continuous speech and I'm back there, living that night, the night that would change my life for ever.

Ruin my life for ever.

I was barely sixteen, but I was popular. Certainly, some boys had told me they fancied me and Alan Wilson definitely liked me. I wasn't so bothered about him; he was small and scrappy with lank hair. I was there for one boy only, the footballer, David Woodward. I adored his golden curls, his muscular legs that were often on display because he swanned around the school in his gym kit. He, of course, had never expressed any interest in me, probably hadn't even noticed me. Until that night. He was the only reason I had agreed to come to the party at all. Maria, my best friend at the time, wanted to go because her almost boyfriend was going but she didn't want to go on her own. So I went, when she told me David Woodward would be there.

There was alcohol, to be expected. Cider, beer, some cheap nasty wines. Then there was the fruit punch. In my naivety I didn't really appreciate that fruit was a joke for spirit. God knows what was in it but after once glass I was dancing, after two I was singing, after three I lost all my inhibitions.

I ended up in a bedroom with the two of them. On a double bed that must have belonged to the parents of whoever's party it was. The three of us rolled around in an ungainly manner. And it was over before it had barely begun. Then they went back to the party and I went to the bathroom to be sick.

'That's where I found you,' Carl says after hearing me out. 'In the bathroom, being sick. I cleaned you up and took you home.'

'Thank you.' I cannot look at him.

'Was it both of them?'

'Yes.'

'Which one first?'

'Does it matter? David Woodward.'

He leans back and sighs. 'Yes, that sounds about right. Alan Wilson nipping in afterwards, fits what he was like.'

'Well, now you know.' I reach under the table and grab my bag, pulling it up onto my lap.

'They were in the wrong, you know. They shouldn't have taken advantage of you like that.'

'They were stupid boys. I was a stupid girl. No one took advantage. My father called me Lolita when he found out.' I let out a bitter little laugh. 'I had to look that up in the library, we didn't have the internet then, remember? He meant I was sexually precocious. It was all my own fault.' I stand up. 'I'm off to bed now. I'll see you for breakfast in the morning?'

'Yes. Yes.' Carl stands up.

'Don't mention it again though, will you?' I turn and walk away, waiting until I'm at the entrance to the restaurant before I chance a glance back. Carl is still standing at our table, staring, not at me, just staring.

Nineteen

Despite my revelations of last night, I've slept amazingly well. Maybe it was all the wine. I check the time then go into the bathroom. I've time for a quick shower.

A glance in the mirror makes me yell. My face is covered in blotches and on closer inspection I can see that they are bites. A shower should cool these angry lumps down. Unfortunately, Fiona's nasty knickers are still in the tub. I really cannot face attempting to wash them, however I can't leave them here either, the cleaner will think they're mine.

I fetch the supermarket carrier bag from my bedroom and use it to scoop up Fiona's knickers. I tie it in a knot and leave it on the side of the bath so I can have a shower. Only when I take off my pyjamas do I see that my legs have been bitten to bits too. And, judging by the state of some of the bites I've been scratching them in my sleep.

Once I've finished in the bathroom, I go back into my room and hunt through my case for some bite cream. Needless to say, I don't have any, even though I know I brought some on holiday with me. It, like so much of my stuff, is still enjoying a Caribbean cruise.

So annoying.

I check the time again on my phone and notice a message has arrived.

Fiona: *Bring some more of my things with you.*

Me: *Which things in particular, specific clothes?*

Fiona: *I have plenty of clothes. Bring 'things.'*

Finally, I understand what she means. Me: *Okay.*

Back in my case again I find a pack of Fiona's incontinence pads. If I take a whole pack they should last her a few days. Then I come across some of her underwear, three packs of knickers to be exact, six in each pack. Unopened and brand new. And they're exactly the same as the pair she wants me to wash. That decides it. I was going to wait until I came back this evening, so that I could wash them and hang them to dry and the cleaner wouldn't have to see them either wet or dirty. Now, I think the best place for them is the bin.

Not that I want to put them in the bin in my room.

I've just finished dressing when there's a knock on the door.

'Oh no,' Carl says, his face etched with concern when he sees my blotches.

'I know. I woke up like it.'

'Was that last night outside or in here.'

'I don't know, but they're all over my legs as well as my face. And some of them are very itchy.'

'Do you have repellent or bite cream?'

'Of course not,' I snap. 'I have a suitcase full of incontinence pads.' Me and my big mouth.

He frowns and looks embarrassed.

'They're not mine, they're Fiona's.' I hadn't intended

telling him that either but I can't have him thinking I need them.

'Of course,' he says, looking so embarrassed it's almost laughable. 'Breakfast?' He holds out his arm for me to link, and after I've grabbed my bag and the carrier bag, and closed the door, I do.

'What's that?' He frowns at the carrier bag.

'Don't ask. I just need an anonymous bin.'

'Right, umm?'

'I told you, don't ask.' I am *not* going into detail about Fiona's poo-pants. 'This will do,' I say, spotting one by the lifts and stuffing the bag deep inside.

♫♫♫

'Do you have the pox?' Fiona shrieks as I walk into her room.

'Mosquito bites.'

'Oh. You need one of those machines like that.' She points to the corner of the room where a little red plastic machine containing a blue mosquito repellent tablet is plugged in next to her charging phone.

'Yes, I know. That's why I bought one this morning.' I don't tell her how Carl, my new-old friend took me to buy one after breakfast, or how I purchased repellent for my skin as well as antihistamine cream. I'm also not telling her that the only reason I could afford to buy any of this is because Carl is fast becoming my personal taxi and saving me the taxi fares. We've already arranged a pick up time. I've left my shopping in his car and used yet another carrier bag in which to discreetly carry Fiona's pads.

'Is that why you're so late?'

'I'm not late. It's mid-morning.'

'Have you got my *things*? Are they in there?' She nods at the carrier bag.

'Yes.' I hand the bag over. 'But I need the bag back.'

She glances inside the carrier, nods, then hands it complete with its contents back to me. 'You can put those in my carpet bag.'

'Okay. How are you today? Have you been up and walking?'

She tells me she has, she's done half a circuit of the corridor, which is pretty impressive. Now she needs her rest before lunch, with that she flicks the TV on. She also tells me she's had a shower, and that even though she had to sit down it was still better than being scrubbed raw by one of the nurses.

'I washed my hair with my special shampoo,' she tells me.

'Cool,' I say, because I struggle to think of anything else. Her hair looks exactly the same as it did yesterday – old lady curls.

The chair I had yesterday has gone, but since she's not using it because she's in bed, I sit myself on her plastic chair. At least here I can see the TV. Fiona is busy flicking through the channels, she's going so fast that I don't know how she can choose, but when she stops, I realise she was looking for something specific. Most of the programmes are American, the one she's stopped on is a US version of Long Lost Family – adopted adults trying to find their birth mothers. Wow, what timing. I feel sick.

'What's the matter with you?' Fiona asks.

'Bit of indigestion,' I say, getting up and heading into her bathroom where I wash my face in cold water. I'll have to pull myself together because I can't stay in here for the duration of that programme. Maybe she'll tire of it and put something else on. I open the window and take gasps of air, but it doesn't really help because it's hotter outside than it is in here.

Eventually I sidle back into Fiona's room. She's asleep, snoring away and clutching the remote control. The dreaded programme is still on and I daren't prize the controller away from her because she is sure to wake up. After some pondering, I do the only logical thing; I yank the TV plug out of the wall, then push it back in again. Thankfully, the TV does not come back on.

While Fiona slumbers on I help myself to a glass of water and scroll through FB and emails on my phone.

Fiona only wakes up when her lunch arrives. She shakes herself awake and hauls her tiny frame up the bed ready to eat.

'What happened to the TV?'

'It just went off.' Such an easy lie.

I help myself to another glass of water while Fiona tucks into her lunch.

'That looks really good,' I say, because it really does, not what I'd expect of hospital food.

'It is.' The catering manager comes up every day and asks me what I'd like and what I thought of yesterday's food. It's a very good service, much better than at home.

'It's a private hospital. I've never been in a private hospital at home. Have you? Maybe that's what they're all like.' I've only been in hospital once in my life and that was to give birth. That's not an experience I like to think about. Neither the actual birth nor what happened afterwards.

'No, I haven't,' Fiona admits. 'Have you rubbed through my underwear yet?'

I'm tempted to lie, to say I have and that her poo-pants are now spotless but I decide to be honest, well, mostly.

'It won't come out. Not without going through the boil wash in a washing machine. I could send them to the hotel laundry, but I can't afford it.'

'Oh. Have you tried bleach? That's why I buy 100% white cotton, so they can be bleached.' Is she serious?

'I don't have any bleach,' I say in my most flat voice, hoping she'll get the message.

'Well maybe if you hadn't bought the mosquito machine…' her voice trails away. I think this is more because she's seen the look of anger and shock on my face rather than she realises how selfish she's being.

'Do you have any cash?' I ask, fairly convinced she's already told me she hasn't but I have to ask, just to emphasise the point.

'No.' She looks sheepish, and so she should. She returns to her lunch without saying anything else and I settle back down thumbing through my phone, I'm not really paying any attention to what's scrolling past my eyes, just trying to distract myself from Fiona.

She finishes her lunch and pushes her overbed table away.

'Did you bring your tablet computer?'

'No. Sorry, I didn't even think of it.' I genuinely didn't, what with her knickers and my bites.

'Oh, well how are we going to reply to the insurance company?'

'There's nothing to reply to yet, they haven't responded to yesterday's email.'

'They might have done since you've been here.'

'No, I've just looked. They haven't.'

A little frown of puzzlement passes over her face

before she speaks. 'Oh, on your phone?'

'Well, yes.'

'Ah.'

'Actually, why don't you take over the conversation with them? That way you can respond whenever you like and say whatever you want, save you dictating it to me. What's your email address and I'll forward their response as soon as it comes through, because it might be this evening. Who knows?'

She looks at me as though I've said something stupid. Maybe I have. Maybe in her secret civil service world she has a secretary who does such things for her, that's why she treats me the way she does, as a cross between a servant and a secretary. But now I've hit on this good idea, I'm pursuing it.

'So, what's your email address?' I hover my fingers over my phone, waiting for her reply.

'Um. I can't remember.' She shakes her head. 'So we can't do that.'

I stand up and walk around her bed, unplug her phone from its charger and hand it over. 'Look it up and tell me.'

She leans back on her pillows and sighs. 'I'm feeling very tired and I have to keep my strength up for another walk this afternoon.'

'It won't take five minutes. Let's just do it.'

'No. Not now.' She hands the phone back to me.

'I could look it up for you,' I say as I swipe the screen. 'Oh, it needs your number to unlock it.'

'I can't give you that, I've already told you it's the secret number I use for *everything*.' She gives me her gimlet stare and purses her lips as though I'm the stupid one.

'You type it in, I'll look away, then give me your

173

phone and I'll find your email address.'

'No, no, I really don't want to do that. You handle the correspondence with the insurance company.'

'This is silly,' I say, plugging her phone back in to charge. 'But if the reply comes after 2pm today, you'll have to wait until tomorrow to read it.'

'2pm? Why?'

'Because that's when I'm leaving. I have a lift arranged.' I'm not telling her it's Carl.

'You can cancel a taxi and rebook it. Do it now. I need you to stay and reply to the insurance company when they come back today.'

'I can't.' I could, but I'm not going to. 'Anyway, the insurance company might not answer today.'

'Then we need to chase them again. I know what these insurance companies are like. We'll chase them now. Sit down and I'll dictate an email to you. And if there's no reply by 2pm, you'll have to cancel your taxi.'

'It's not a taxi,' I say too quickly. I could bite my tongue out, but the words are out there now, waiting for Fiona to grab onto them. She doesn't disappoint.

'Not a taxi, not a taxi? Are you catching a bus?'

I could lie. It would be so easy; I could say that I *am* catching a bus and there's only one a day. But much as I don't love Fiona, I don't want our fragile friendship to be based completely on lies, I already feel guilty about her knickers.

'No, it's a friend, doing me a favour.'

'A friend. You have a friend here? No wonder you can hardly bear to visit me. No wonder you arrive so late and are in such a rush to leave. That explains everything.'

'There's nothing to explain,' I snap back. 'I bumped into an old schoolfriend who's here on holiday.'

'How nice for you while I've been stuck in hospital.'

I hold my tongue, biting back the words. I really want to tell her that's it's not my fault she fell off the toilet, broke her leg and needed a major operation, but I don't, because it would just be mean. There's a tiny part of me that does feel guilty about her overdosing herself on ibuprofen, even though I know that's not my fault either because I did warn her.

'Well,' she says, taking my silence as her triumph. 'Cancel your friend and get a taxi.'

'I can't afford to get taxis; I'm running out of cash.'

'Then don't keep going shopping.' She folds her arms across her chest in victory.

This is so wearing. Is now the time to have the big argument about how much all this has cost me, both financially and emotionally? I look at Fiona's skinny little body in bed and think, perhaps not.

'Let's get this email done then,' I say. It will benefit me too, the sooner we get back home, the sooner they will settle the claim, and the sooner they will pay me back. 'Although it would be so much easier if you just handled the email yourself, then you wouldn't be reliant on me.'

'I don't do email on my phone,' she snaps. Then, realising her mistake she corrects herself. 'I don't like doing it.'

'But you email your family from your phone, don't you?'

There's a long enough silence from her that I know she's fighting with herself.

'No, no. We text.'

'What? From here? That must be costing you a fortune. You should use WhatsApp; you can do it on the Wi-Fi for free. In fact, you should WhatsApp me

175

instead of texting, it costs me money to reply to you too.'

'Yes, yes, that's what I meant. That's what we do.'

But it's blatantly obvious that she doesn't know what I'm talking about.

She's a worse liar than me.

Twenty

When Carl picks me up from the hospital, I tell him about my conversation with Fiona. He asks if I think she's lying about texting her family. I tell him yes, because I know a liar when I see one. I'm an expert; I've spent most of my life living a lie even if mostly by omission. Carl can't really argue with that and instead suggests we go to a beautiful beach he's found and have a swim. We stop off at our hotel to pick up our swimming things then head back out.

'It's like paradise here,' I say as I lie on my back, spread like a starfish and floating in the sea. The sky is an unbroken deep blue, the water is warm, and once I'd got over the initial sting as the salt hits my bites, it seems to be calming them.

'But you'd rather be on your cruise,' Carl says, and I don't think he's fishing for compliments.

I have to consider this for a moment or two and don't reply immediately.

'That's a hard one to answer.' I laugh and swim away from him. This is all getting a bit too intense. What do I say? That if I hadn't bumped into him it would have been the case, but not now, because now I'm actually enjoying myself. *This* feels like a holiday, one that is only minimally impacted by Fiona's oddities.

He swims to catch up with me. 'We could go somewhere else for dinner tonight. Not the hotel, I mean.'

'Yes, but if we do that you won't be able to drink because you'll be driving.'

He nods slowly. 'True.'

'Or is that your plan, stay cold stone sober while getting me drunk so I can spill out more revelations about my miserable life for your amusement?' I really don't know what made me say that.

The forced smile that plays across his face suggests that nothing was further from his mind.

'Is it miserable, your life? Are there more revelations?'

This is definitely too deep for me. 'Not miserable, no. I was quite comfortable in the humdrum of my daily life before I left home, quite content.' It's the truth, even Richard's odd little quirks and sulks didn't bother me too much because I could always escape to my plants and pots. My life was tidy, orderly, I had my routine. I turn to face Carl as the water laps softly around us. 'And no, there are no more revelations. Let's face it, not much could top that.'

'No. I suppose not. Have you ever tried to find him?'

'Who?'

'Your baby?'

'God, no.'

'Oh.' He nods slowly then swims towards the shore, back to our sun loungers under the shade of a straw umbrella. I follow much slower behind him, his swimming skills far exceeding mine.

I lie back on my lounger, my face in the shade, allowing the hot sun to dry off my body. Salt settles in little circles on my swimming costume, it's navy blue with enormous flowers of bright orange and pink. I would never have bought something so loud at home, but here, in the startling sunshine, it doesn't seem loud at all. I love it.

'Is that possible?' I ask, as Carl beckons a waiter over.

'What's that? Would you like a drink?'

We order and then I hope that Carl forgets what I asked. Of course he doesn't.

'What were you asking me before the waiter came?'

'Oh nothing.' I close my eyes and fish around blind in my bag for my sunglasses and put them on, something to hide behind.

'We should have worn these in the sea.'

I open my eyes and frown at Carl. What he's talking about?

'Our sunglasses,' he says. 'Here's our drinks.'

We sip long, cold drinks full of fruit, straws and umbrellas. They're mocktails, so no alcohol. I watch Carl as he drinks, his throat pulsing as he swallows. He's a nice man. I think he was a nice boy at school. He walked me home that night. What a shame I hadn't spent the evening with him instead of the other two. I would have no sad and shady past then, I think.

'You weren't allowed to keep the baby?'

I can't answer. Can't speak. He didn't ask if I wanted to, or not, just assumed that I couldn't. Assumed that I wanted to keep him. I reach into my bag for a tissue, can't find one so use the corner of my towel, well, the hotel's towel.

'I'm sorry,' he says, reaching over and squeezing my knee. 'I'll keep my mouth shut.'

'No, I wasn't allowed. I should have put up a fight, but…'

'You were sixteen. It was a long time ago.'

'It was the 80s, not the 50s. I could probably have got a council flat, gone on benefits, kept him.' I've thought about this for the past thirty-plus years. I saw others do it after me. 'I should have been stronger.'

'We all have regrets.'

'I suppose. But I should have stood my ground, not been pressured into giving him up. I look back and I seem pathetic, just allowing my parents to decide for me. I've kicked myself a million times since then, but it's too late now.'

'Would it help if you traced him, found out how well he is, that sort of thing? Would it make you feel any better?'

I can't answer. I have no answer. I've had a little fantasy for years, ever since he turned eighteen, that one day there would be a knock on my door and my son would be there, smiling and happy. But what if that's not the case? What if giving him away, letting him go without so much as a fight to keep him, has ruined his life as well as my own? And, who's to say that staying with me would have been any better for him. Look at me now, I just work in a garden centre and I only have myself to look after, how could I have managed a child too? What would have happened when my dad had his stroke and my mum got dementia? Maybe it was always meant to be, me not keeping him so I could look after them. I shrug in answer to Carl's question and take a final slurp from my almost empty mocktail.

♫♫♫

Back at the hotel, after a shower and a liberal amount of insect repellent I sit on my balcony and check my phone. There's a text from Fiona asking if the insurance company have replied. They have. It's a long email saying that they can't arrange flights home for us until Fiona has a fitness to fly certificate and that needs to come from the surgeon. There are also a lot of questions about her needs, her capabilities with regard to flying, that the flights only go to London, so what transport will she need to carry on her journey home. There is no mention of me. My needs, my onward journey are quite different to hers.

Fiona texts me again to remind me I haven't replied.

So, I do, telling her that I've received a long email, too long to tell her about in a text and if she will just give me her email address, I'll forward it so she can read it and reply to it herself.

She doesn't reply, nor does she text me again.

I ready myself for another evening with Carl. Tonight, neither of us mentions my past, very wise. I ask for, and he shows me, photos on his phone of his sons, their wives and his grandchildren – he does have grandchildren, of course he does. Something else I'll never have. His eyes glow with pride when he shows me the photos.

Our evening is muted and we only manage one bottle of wine between us, which given how much we've drunk on previous evenings is not much at all.

He sees me to my room, the perfect gentleman. I sleep well and when I wake the next morning, I don't have any new mosquito bites because I plugged the little machine in – even if Fiona does think it's an extravagance.

♫♫♫

'Oh, finally,' Fiona snaps, when I enter her room. 'I thought you were never coming. Been having a nice time with your friend? There's some more washing for you over there.' She points to the side where the clear plastic bag holds the clothes she wore yesterday. She has texted me several times this morning asking where I am and I replied to the first one saying I would be along as soon as possible. I ignored the rest as I had nothing else to add. I am not accountable to Fiona, despite what she thinks.

'Thanks,' I say, before leaving the room to find myself a chair since Fiona is sitting on the only one in her room now. I do wish the nurses would just leave *my* chair in here.

'Well?' she says as I clomp a chair back in.

'Yes, I'm fine, thank you.'

'I didn't mean you. I meant the email from the insurance company. Show me. Show me.'

I get my phone out of my bag and scroll through until I find it. I can see Fiona watching me, willing me to hurry up and hand it over. I find it, glance through then turn to Fiona.

'How are you? Have you been up and about this morning?'

'Yes. Yes. Twice around the corridor. What about the email? What does it say? Let me see.'

This is so ridiculous. Am I the one being unreasonable here? I feel annoyed with her, and, if I'm honest with myself. Seeing Carl's family photos last night, and a video at breakfast which he received this morning showing his two-year-old granddaughter dancing, has really brought home to me what I've missed out on in life. Last night Carl asked me if I'd ever married or had a long-term relationship. I had to confess that I hadn't.

Why haven't I? He never asked, but I could see the question on his face. Instead he asked me what time I wanted a lift to the hospital?

'Well,' Fiona barks, bringing me back to the present.

I start to read it out. She listens but I can tell that she is bristling with irritation and impatience, desperate to read it herself. When I've finished she demands my phone.

'I can't give it to you, it's private.'

'But that email is about me.'

'I've read it out.'

'Yes, but I need to study it before I dictate my reply. Why didn't you bring your tablet computer?'

'It's out of battery and I forgot to charge it.' This is true, but I could easily have brought the charger and socket converter with me and plugged it in here. It just never occurred to me. It's ancient and slow and my phone is more convenient and faster. 'Just give me your address and I'll forward the email to you.'

'I told you I don't like doing email on my phone.'

'Why not?'

'Because…' she purses her lips and looks out of the window; she has a nice view of the blue and sparkling sea from here.

I sit and stare at her, my expression expectant. She keeps her eyes on the sea. We could sit like this for hours.

'Just let me read it.' Her voice is whiney.

'No. I'll send it to you and then you can read it as

often as you like.'

'I CAN'T DO EMAIL ON MY PHONE,' she shouts.

'It's a smartphone, of course you can.'

'*I* CAN'T.'

So now we get to the truth.

'Do you have an email address?'

'Of course I do, but I use my desk computer for that.'

'Do you know your email address?'

'Yes. I'm not stupid.'

'And your password.'

'Yesss.'

I get up and grab her phone from the side, it's still plugged in although it's fully charged. I unplug it and hand it to her.

'Put your secret number in then, so it's unlocked, then I'm going to load your email onto it. Then you can be in charge of the insurance emails.'

She cups her hand over her phone and stabs in her number, even though I look away at the appropriate point. She hands her phone to me, her face like a child in full sulk.

I sit back down in my chair and hunt around for the email app, ask her for her email address and password which she won't give me, so I force her to type it in herself, before she hands the phone back to me. I watch as her emails load up, they don't take long; there aren't that many. My inbox is full of adverts and newsletters and emails from online shopping, hers has only a few. She obviously doesn't spend all her time shopping online or accepting friend requests from strangers on Facebook.

I pick my own phone up and forward the insurance

emails, all of them. I check they have come through on her phone and I'm about to hand it back to her when I do something I really shouldn't. I check her texts.

The only ones sent, the only ones received, are mine.

She isn't texting anyone, least of all her sons in Canada. Then I check her call log – no calls.

'Shall I load WhatsApp on too?' I ask. 'Because it'll be better for communicating with me, and your family in Canada.'

'Okay,' she says without looking at me. 'Thank you.'

Twenty-one

'This is early, I was really surprised to receive your message,' Carl says as I climb into his car.

'I was dismissed early,' I say, with a snigger. 'Now that Fiona can talk directly to the insurance company, I am of no further use. Well, until tomorrow when I have to collect more of her dirty washing.' I wave today's about before dropping it in the footwell.

Carl turns and frowns at me before starting the car.

'I loaded her email onto her phone.'

'Right. She didn't have that already?'

'Nope.'

'O-k-a-y,' he says slowly. 'Well, her loss is my gain, we can go out for lunch early enough not to spoil our dinner.'

'We can,' I say, without even the slightest feeling of guilt. Fiona basically told me to leave as she had things to do and programmes to watch and more exercise to undertake – those were her exact words. I couldn't get out of there fast enough. Am I a bad person? Maybe, but no worse than Fiona.

'What's she going to do when she gets home?'

'What do you mean?'

'Well, I'm guessing, and I don't know because I've never experienced anything like the op she's had, but I'm assuming she'll need some help to start off with.'

'Will she?' The thought had never occurred to me. I just assumed that the hospital wouldn't send her home until she was back to normal. 'Well, she's already up and walking about. She has physio every day.'

'That's good. Have you seen her walking?'

'No. You're worrying me now.'

'Have they said when she can fly?'

'No, not yet but soon. And surely being fit enough to fly means she'll be fine when she gets home.'

'Yes, probably,' he says, not sounding very convinced. 'If not, she'll have to get a friend round to help, failing that one of her sons will have to fly over from Canada.'

'I don't think she's told her family in Canada what's happened. I took a sneaky look at her phone and I can't see anyway she's been contacting them. Thing is, she told me she'd texted them and they were ringing her back, but her phone says otherwise.'

'Maybe she doesn't want to worry them.'

He's right, she probably doesn't. She actually said that on the ship and only agreed to contact them because I urged her to. It's probable that she didn't contact them at all, just told me she had to shut me up. Well, I suppose that's understandable if she doesn't want to worry them, maybe she's waiting until she's back home and almost recovered. Perhaps I'll suggest that she contacts some friends back in London, that way, if they do need to help her out it won't come as such a shock. I wonder if she's told her employer? I wonder how long she's going to need off work? I know that officially we're still on holiday for another three weeks, but should she return then? I just don't know.

♫♫♫

We head back to our hotel after a long, lazy lunch in an air-conditioned restaurant overlooking the sea. I offer to pay, Carl refuses and I feel guilty and relieved, promising that I will make it up to him when we get back to the UK. He raised his eyebrows and smirked when I said that. I felt myself blush, actually blush, at my age. Now, back in my room, alone, just the memory of those reactions makes me smile and makes my stomach flip just a little. I really don't know what's going on with me. With Carl.

I've come back to my room primarily to sort out Fiona's washing. I pull her clothes out of the bag and ready myself for today's horror. I hold the clothes at arm's length but after having a good look I can see that there are no noticeable stains, no horrors today. On closer inspection I can find nothing at all. They don't need washing, not immediately and certainly not in my hotel bath. I fold up the clothes, and put them aside. I've put most of Fiona's clothes away in the drawers and I know how many outfits I have for her, they're mostly cotton tops and loose trousers, as per her instructions. Depending on how long we are here, and assuming she doesn't stain anything, I think there are enough clothes to last her without me washing any, then they can go in her washing machine when she gets home.

Wish I could say the same about my clothes. I have one more clean outfit then I will need to start re-wearing them after a dunk in the tub. On the ship there was a launderette with washing machines, tumble dryers and irons. Here there is the laundry service but I daren't chance using it in case I end up staying here longer than I anticipate because every night is another one I have to pay for. Tonight is my last official night, so I need to extend my stay again. They've already popped the bill under my door, even though I've already paid for my room but I still need to pay for my meals. I'm wondering how close to my credit limit I am? I should have downloaded the credit card app so I could check my balance. Too late now, doing it from here would probably look dodgy and they would put a block on my card – I can't risk that.

I'll go to Reception before meeting Carl for dinner – not that I can imagine being hungry by then after the lunch we ate – I don't want to end up homeless. I pack Fiona's washing in amongst her *things*. She hasn't asked for any more so presumably she has enough to last her for now.

I'm on my way to Reception when I bump into Carl; he's been out for a stroll, probably trying to work up an appetite. I tell him where I'm going when he asks and he says he'll accompany me because once I'm finished, we can have a drink in the bar near Reception.

Carl goes and sits in the lounge area where a giant widescreen TV is showing American football, while I sort out my bill. They insist I pay for the meals I've already had before booking me in for three more nights. I just hope that's enough.

I watch as the girl on Reception stabs away at her computer with inch long talons – it's fascinating. I make fists with my own hands to hide my chipped and scruffy nails. Between the sea, the pool and the beach, my nails are looking pretty sorry; they haven't lasted quite as long as I expected.

'We have a salon and spa that could sort out your nails,' the receptionist tells me, evidently having seen my attempt at concealment.

'Thank you.' I smile and hope that will be the end of her help.

'I could give you a discount voucher. Let me see.' She hunts through a drawer beneath the reception desk and pulls out a voucher. 'Twenty percent discount. There you go. Yes please?'

'Oh, thank you.' I take the voucher and drop it into my bag. The only way I could afford a manicure is with a total discount. I just need a bit of nail varnish remover, not something I brought on holiday with me because I never have any need for it. On the ship I could easily have got some.

'Okay, that's all done for you.' She gives me back my credit card and I wonder again how much of my limit is left. At least I have three more nights paid for. Maybe that will be enough. I hope I can afford my meals. On the ship they were included, endless buffets or served food, how lovely that was and no extra cost. Now I'm constantly worrying about money.

Stop complaining, I tell myself, it could be so much worse. The sun is shining, the hotel is pleasant enough, you're fit and healthy, unlike poor Fiona, you've met Carl. That thought lingers on my mind as I turn away, suddenly finding him standing right behind me.

'Oh, didn't see you there.' I laugh, nervous that he has read my thoughts, which of course he hasn't.

'Got a bit sick of the football,' he whispers as we walk away. 'Did I hear the receptionist mention a spa?'

'Oh yes. Not much use to me. I can hardly afford that. She did give me a discount voucher.' I pull it out and wave it at him. 'Just need to find a bin for that.' I laugh and glance around.

'Give it here, I'll find one later.' He takes the voucher from me and tucks it into his pocket as we head off for dinner.

♫♫♫

'The surgeon says I can go home in five days' time. I'll be fit to fly. He's going to write a letter for the airline,' Fiona says all this before I'm barely through the door.

'Oh wow. That's great news.' I think.

'I've told the insurance company to get a move on. I've told them to book us on a flight. I'll have to travel business class. I need the space and the comfort. It's a long flight.'

'Yes. Good.' I wonder where I'll be put, in the cargo hold? 'I'll just get a chair.' I leave her room and commence my daily chair hunt. When I come back Fiona is sitting with a pinched look on her face, annoyed, I suspect, because I interrupted her victory speech. I hover with my chair, mid-room, while she resumes her monologue.

'It's so much better now I have control of the correspondence with them, don't you think? I'm so much quicker with email than you.' She smiles at me, it's so brief that I wonder if she's passing wind.

'Yes. Great.' I struggle to believe the cheek of her, only yesterday she couldn't even do email on her phone, now she's an expert. 'How have you been?'

'Yes, walking and stuff. I'm really quite mobile, of course it helps that I'm not a big, overweight thing. Who'd have thought being so small would come in useful one day. I'll need you to bring some more of my *things* tomorrow.'

'Okay.' Why do I feel as though the big, overweight thing is me? I'm neither of those things yet I feel as though she's getting a dig in. So the things aren't lasting as long as I thought. I hope there are enough to last, I wouldn't know where to buy them here or if I could afford them.

'As soon as we know the flight, we'll sort out the transport this end. I told them we'd do it because they were getting twitchy about who to use. I don't want anything holding us up, certainly not because they couldn't organise transport to the airport.'

'Can the hospital help with that?'

'Yes. They can send me in an ambulance. No room for you though. You'll have to get a taxi. I can't think about it now, I'm too tired from all this organising.' She leans back in her chair and sighs.

'When did all this happen?' I wonder because I know the time difference means it's not normal working hours in the UK yet.

'Yesterday, afternoon and evening.' She looks smug.

'You should have messaged me with the good news.'

'Oh, I didn't want to disturb you and your *friend*.' The smug look increases.

'You wouldn't have.' I ponder for a moment before I mention her family, should I, shouldn't I? 'Have you emailed your sons and told them about your progress now that you're almost ready to go home?'

She glances at me, a sly look that I know precedes a lie. 'Yes, they're delighted.' She flicks on the TV and turns the volume up while I position my plastic chair and flop down into it.

An hour must pass while I look out of the window, staring at the horizon where a blue sky meets a blue sea and Fiona intermittently dozes in her chair as the TV drones on above my head. All this organising and exercising must be tiring for her. There's a hospital walking frame in front of her, better than crutches she has told me. I wonder how we'll manage at the airport, on the plane? I try not to think about it, try not worry about it, imagining myself lugging my case, our bags, and propping up Fiona.

My phone vibrates in my bag.

Carl: *Can I pick you up early?*

We've agreed that he'll pick me up at three because, despite being dismissed by Fiona yesterday I feel guilty about leaving her on her own for so long. It can't be much fun, stuck in here.

Me: *Not sure. Why?*

Carl: *Just thought we could do something nice. Pick you up at 1pm?*

Fiona's still asleep, it's just approaching noon and I'm desperate to agree.

Me: *I'll have to let you know. Sorry.*

Maybe she will dismiss me early again.

Carl: *No worries.*

The door bangs open and Fiona's lunch arrives. The noise wakes her up and she gives me a look that screams annoyance. I'm not sure if it's me she's annoyed with or her lunch bringer. Then she frowns at my phone in my hand.

I watch her eat; I'm not hungry, having eaten a lot at breakfast, but I am bored. It must be boring for Fiona too. And tough. She's still hooked up to IV painkillers and fluids. I wonder if she has to drag them along with her when she takes her exercise.

'Do they disconnect those when you go for your walks?' I nod at the bags on the stand.

'Of course,' Fiona says, as though I'm stupid, which I suppose I am. She pushes her tray table away. 'Can you get my walker back please. I need the toilet.'

I swop everything over and hope and pray that she doesn't need any help in the loo.

I watch as she shuffles towards the bathroom, to be fair her movement is quite impressive considering what's she been through. I pull the door open to make her journey easier.

'You might as well go,' she says. 'Physio will be here at one then I'm going to need my rest before I start on my next round of correspondence with the insurance company.'

'Okay. If you're sure.' I try not to smile too much in case she changes her mind.

'Yes. You can go now. I need some privacy.' She slams the bathroom door shut behind her.

I message Carl immediately. '*1pm okay*.' Then I grab my things and scuttle off; I can wait down in the reception area.

Twenty-two

'I have a treat for us,' he says as I climb into the car.

'Oh, what's that?' Just being away from that hospital room and Fiona's sour face is a treat as far as I'm concerned. Not that I'm going to confess that to Carl.

'It's a surprise. You'll enjoy it.'

When we arrive back at the hotel I imagine we're going for lunch and I wonder if I can manage eating another meal. I'm sure I'm eating far more than usual and I'm not getting the exercise I do when I'm at work. I'm going to get home and look like a house end.

'You'll need your swimming costume,' Carl says as we head into the hotel. I'll knock for you in about ten minutes. 'Oh, put the costume on.'

Back in my room I slide into my costume, pulling it into place and feeling a little grateful that whatever his surprise is, it doesn't include food. I think. I hope. I pull my sundress back on top of my costume and grab my towel. As I do so I suddenly realise that in her haste to get rid of me, Fiona forgot to give me her dirty clothes. Oh well, there's always tomorrow. Carl knocks on the door.

'Ready?'

'Yes.' What sparkly eyes he has, they're very dark but they twinkle.

'You won't need a towel.'

'Okay. Intrigued now.'

He grins.

As we walk back to Reception, he takes my hand in his and I don't resist. I like it. It's not something I'm particularly used to. We veer off before we reach Reception and I finally see where we're going. The spa.

'Oooh. No.' I want to say I can't afford it, because I know I can't.

'My treat,' Carl says, pulling me in through the door. 'And no arguing or you'll spoil our afternoon.'

'Okay. Thank you.' I need to add up how much he has spent on me, what with his insistence on paying for lunches and bottles of wine, I must owe him a fortune. I'll have to pay him back when we get home – once the insurance company has reimbursed me.

The spa receptionist greets us and tells me we're both booked in for a massage later. I feel hesitant, nervous even; I've never had a massage. In the meantime we should take advantage of the steam rooms, the sauna and the jacuzzi. She gives us slippers and robes and points the way through. Carl grins at me and I follow him in.

'I've never been anywhere like this,' I whisper as I stuff my handbag and dress into a locker.

'You'll love it.'

He's right, I do. There are several steam rooms, each one scented with different oils, it's hot and definitely steamy but it's so relaxing. The sauna is unbelievably hot and I can hardly bear the hot air in my lungs. I'm glad of the cool shower after we get out. The jacuzzi is a whirl of bubbles playing on my muscles and relaxing them, even though I didn't think they were tense.

'Time for our massages,' Carl says.

I follow him along to the treatment rooms' waiting area and fill in the form I'm given about my health. Then my massage therapist, Alicia takes me into a room and suggests I take off my wet costume and wear the paper knickers she hands over. She discreetly leaves while I change. When she returns I'm lying on the bed face up with a towel covering me. I don't know if I'm going to like this, I don't know what's expected of me.

Nothing, as it turns out. I just have to lie here and enjoy it, and turn over occasionally. It's actually blissful and not at all intrusive. So blissful that I doze off. I'm guessing that's a good thing.

When I catch up with Carl afterwards, I can't stop grinning.

'Well?'

'Lovely. Never experienced anything like it. And I smell *so* nice.' I sniff my arm, then sniff Carl's shoulders. 'So do you too.'

'You have another appointment,' he says, 'While I go and rest in the chill out room.'

'Oh?'

'Nails,' he whispers and pushes me towards the nail area, where they are, indeed, waiting for me.

I'm given a full manicure which, obviously includes the removal of my old nail polish. I'm offered nail polish, gels or acrylics – too much choice. I smile as I imagine myself with nails like the hotel receptionists' inch long talons. In the end I opt for clear polish because who knows what will happen to it by the time I've manhandled Fiona and our luggage through the airport and home.

'You didn't go for a bright colour then?' Carl comments when he sees my nails afterwards.

'No. Not practical.'

'Who says you always have to be practical?' He laughs and nudges me.

'I do.'

'Come and lie in the chill out room before we get ready for dinner. I don't know about you but I've quite worked up an appetite.'

In the chill out room I lie on a warm, soft bed and listen to birdsong, waves crashing and soft rain falling. It's piped music but they could just as easily have opened the windows because these sounds, except the rain, are all around us. It's tempting to doze off again, but I don't want to do that.

'Have you enjoyed our little treat?'

'I have. I have. And I can't thank you enough. I owe you. For everything.'

'The pleasure of your company is payment enough.'

'Yuk,' I say.

'Sorry, couldn't resist, but it is sort of sincere.' He laughs, his eyes crinkling as he does so.

'Sort of sincere?'

'Don't fish.' He laughs again. I like his laughter. So I join in.

♫♫♫

Another buffet dinner, including the obligatory crumble and watery custard for pudding, although I'm strangely addicted to it. Another bottle of wine, white this time and I insist it goes on my bill, I'm crossing my fingers I can afford it.

'Have you given any more thought to finding your boy?' Carl asks as we have a late brandy before bed.

I almost choke on my drink before I answer. 'No. Yes. I don't know.' Why did he have to bring that up? I was enjoying myself.

'I did some checking on the internet this morning while you were at the hospital, the first step is simply to register to say you're open to meeting your son.'

I frown at him. I don't know what he means. I don't know if I want to open this can of worms. I feel guilty and sad about losing my baby. It ripped apart what little of a relationship I had with my parents. I've never really forgiven them for making me give him away. I've never forgiven myself for being so weak.

'You just register. That's all. If he also registers, then they match you up.'

'Like online dating,' I say, dismissing the idea.

'Well, not really.' He smiles and leans over the table and takes my hand. 'You don't need to do anything. I'm just saying if you wanted to, you could. I got the impression – correct me if I'm wrong – that you didn't realise you might be able to trace him, if he wants to trace you, that is.'

'No. Yes. I don't know.'

'Well, something to think about.'

We go our separate ways back to our rooms but not before Carl kisses me softly on the cheek. I can still feel the brush of his lips against my skin even after he's gone. How silly of me.

I wish Carl hadn't dropped the bombshell about finding my baby so late at night. I won't be able to sleep now, I'll toss and turn and wonder if I should pursue it, wonder if my son would even want to see me. Why would he? I abandoned him. Gave him up as though he were worthless.

I'd put to the back of my mind how much this all

hurts, how angry I was with myself, with my parents. I resented them until the day they both died. In fact, I still resent them. They'd said giving up my baby was for the best, that I could put it all behind me, live as though it never happened. I'd never find anyone to love me if I was, as my dad put it, *saddled* with another man's baby and tainted goods.

I refused to tell them who the father was, not that I was even sure myself, not that they really wanted to know. My refusal was accepted without any further questions. I realised later that they didn't want the complication of another family involved in the decision. They, my parents, especially my dad, had already made the decision for me. My mum said it was for the best, I could find myself a nice man to marry when the time came.

I shudder at the memory. I should have fought them. I really should. Being a single mother then wouldn't have been so bad, it didn't carry the stigma they thought it did, not then. That was the problem with having such old parents. They were so old-fashioned, so out of touch with what was really going on in the world. Dad was still working; he'd stayed on after retirement to see me through school. I didn't really understand that, it was not as though they were paying for me to go to school, although I suppose I still cost them for clothes and food. Without the burden of a baby I could get a job straightaway without returning to education. I already had my two O'levels, English and Art, taken early. I could get a job of some sort.

I never got a job, not a proper paying one, anyway. Dad had his stroke less than a week after retiring; we found him bent over his spade in the garden as though he was bending down to grab a weed. His face was contorted, his eyes glazed. I thought he was dead.

He spent a month in hospital, hovering between life and death then came home to a bed at the dining room end of the lounge and two full time carers. Me and my mum.

We became a benefits family, with Dad's state pension, Mum's somewhat reduced state pension and some kind of allowance Mum managed to get for me, not that I ever saw it, she said it barely covered my keep. My days were spent helping my mum look after my dad. Even then the irony wasn't lost on me. I could have been on benefits with my baby, looking after *him*.

Mum blamed all the stress of my illicit, illegitimate baby as the cause of Dad's stroke. It was all my fault.

For five years we struggled on, five miserable years for all of us. I only went to the shops, that was my three times weekly outing. I'd already lost touch with all my friends when I'd dropped out of school suddenly. There were days, most days, when I felt as old and worn out as my parents. Mum aged dramatically during those years. She was already old, much older than my school friends' parents, but Dad's stroke aged her further.

And where was Keith in all this? In Manchester, living his life, completely unencumbered by our misery. He had long ago moved out and settled himself far away, visiting only at Christmas and occasionally for a few days in the summer. He rarely rang even though Mum and Dad had a phone now, something they hadn't had during his childhood or a lot of mine. At least he didn't know about my pregnancy, my baby. I couldn't have stood his taunts if he had known. For Keith life continued as it had before Dad's stroke. He couldn't possibly move back, his job was based in

Manchester, his life was in Manchester.

None of us ever saw his life there, we were never invited and after Dad had his stroke it was never likely that any of us would visit anyway. I never saw Keith's life until he died and I had to sort out his estate. A laughable word for the mess he left behind. His life, his important life, was no less miserable than ours had been, from what I could see. Just different. And it was just as small as my life is.

♫♫♫

'You look tired,' Carl says at breakfast.

'Couldn't sleep.'

'Oh.' He gets up to go to the buffet. Is he feeling guilty? Does he know that he set me up for a night of mind-churning?

'Was it because of what I said?' he asks when he comes back. So he does know.

I nod slowly. 'Probably.' I offer a faint smile, fold my napkin and get up to go to the buffet myself.

'I'm sorry,' he says when I come back with a bowl of cereal. 'I should mind my own business.'

'It's okay. Maybe it's time I confronted my past.' Wow, I don't know where that came from. I sit and stare at my bowl, watching the milk soak into the cereal.

'You mean you want to see if…'

'Maybe. But I don't want to talk about it, not now, not here.' I grab my spoon and push it into my breakfast, then fill my mouth.

After breakfast Carl takes me to see Fiona and has the sense not to mention finding my son again. The atmosphere between us, while not exactly tense is maybe a little difficult. I'm sorry about that, I suspect he is too.

♫♫♫

Dragging my chair behind me as I enter her room, I find Fiona missing. She's obviously off on one of her exercise walks. I position my chair in its usual spot under the TV and wait for her.

'You forgot to take my washing back with you,' she says as she clomps into the room with her walker.

Charming.

'And hello to you too,' I say, feeling that enough is enough.

'Oh, yes, hello.'

'How are you today? I see you've been off walking around.'

'Yes, good.' She clomps over to her chair and lowers herself into it.

'That's excellent, isn't it. You must be feeling so glad to be so mobile.'

'Mmm.' She picks up her phone and starts scrolling through it. Oh, I see, it's okay for her to do that. Finally, she looks up at me. 'Some good news arrived this morning, well, in the night, but I only saw it this morning. They've booked us on a flight.' She grins from ear to ear waiting for me to congratulate her. Which I do. Why not? When she tells me which day the flight is I realise that I'm going to have to book another night at the hotel. Only one extra night though, maybe my credit card can stand it.

Twenty-three

The pattern of our final days is established, breakfast with Carl, mornings with Fiona, afternoons and evenings with Carl. I collect Fiona's dirty washing and take her clean clothes up when she needs them. I inspect her washing and rinse through anything I think cannot wait until we get back to the UK. Otherwise, it will be going in a proper washing machine. Hers.

'Apparently we'll both be travelling business class,' I tell Carl over breakfast on our last but one day. 'Fiona messaged me this morning. She implied she insisted I went with her but I think the insurance company put us together because she's going to need help on the plane.'

'What time is your flight?' He pulls his phone out and starts looking for his own flight details. When I tell him, his face lights up. 'I'm on that exact same flight. So I won't need to wait around at the airport after all.' Carl had already offered to take me to the airport but as his flight was an evening flight he assumed he'd be hanging around afterwards.

'Shame we can't sit together.'

'Perhaps you could wander down from your superior

seat and come and say hello.'

'Maybe, I'll see if I can fit it in.'

We start to discuss exactly when we should leave for the airport, which is only about a thirty-minute drive. I'm so grateful because it means he will help with the luggage, although he also has to take the rental car back. I'll meet Fiona at the airport when she arrives by hospital ambulance, since there's no room for me to go with her, but it's worked out quite well, I'd much rather go with Carl.

'I need to extend my stay for another night,' I say as we leave the breakfast buffet.

'Okay, shall I meet you back at your room so I can drop you off at the hospital?'

We agree a time and I head for Reception.

As before I have to pay my extras bill, my meals and that bottle of wine I bought for Carl and I to drink, before I can book another night. It's the only wine I've bought since Carl has insisted on buying all the others. I feel guilty. So guilty. I still have a few US dollars and I've decided that once we reach the airport and I know I'm not going to need them for anything, I am giving them to Carl. And he is going to accept them, whether he likes it or not. Not that there are many, but it's a gesture, the thought that counts.

'So if you can just book my room for tonight, that's just the one night.' I grin to myself; I can't believe I'm finally going home. Although, to be fair, it hasn't been all bad, but only because I've met Carl. He's made this into a proper holiday.

'Ah, oh, just a minute please.' The receptionist frowns at her computer screen, taps her keyboard with her talons, then disappears into the back office. When she comes back she smiles at me with her mouth, but not her eyes. I don't like the look of this. 'We have a little problem,' she says.

'Yes.' Please don't let it be my card limit, please, please, please. I cross my fingers behind my back.

'We're full.'

'Full?'

'Yes, we have a new group arriving this evening and your room is already booked.'

'Okay. Well, what about another room. Anything will do. It's just me, just one night.'

'There's nothing. We're full. So sorry.' She looks away and I can see she thinks that's the end of the conversation.

'But what can I do?'

'Try another hotel. There's a phone over there and local calls are free.' She looks to the next person in a queue that has formed behind me.

'What other hotel?'

She shrugs, her eyes wide, her face impassive. 'Try the internet.' This time she bends around me to see the next person properly.

I slump into the chair by the *local-calls-are-free* phone and start scrolling through my phone for hotels in Barbados. It takes me ages to reach the first one that looks suitable and is near here, when I finally get through I'm relieved that they have a room which I can book. I feel my anxiety levels start to reduce as the hotel takes my booking – until we get to the credit card bit.

'Sorry, declined.'

'Declined?'

'Yes, sorry.'

'But why?'

'It doesn't say, madam. You have another card, yes

please?'

'No,' I say, then try to redeem my pride. 'Not on me, I'll ring again later.'

'Thank you.' Her tone suggests she knows as well as I do that I won't be ringing again. What the hell am I going to do? I can't ask Carl to fund a hotel room for me. It's all too much. I stand up and start to slink away.

'Madam, madam,' the receptionist calls.

I glance over at the desk, not thinking that she means me. Have they suddenly found me a room? That would be wonderful, except I now cannot pay for it.

'Madam.'

I approach the desk.

'Madam, you need to vacate your room by noon. Do you need any help with your luggage?'

I'm speechless for a moment or two. Of course I need to go, but where?

'No, thank you.' I breathe in and out and leave, attempting to hold my head up. I'm sure Talons smirks.

Back in my room I get my case out and start to pack. Maybe I could sleep at the hospital with Fiona like I did the first night. Would that be possible? I'm stuffing everything into my case, at least there's more room in my case now that most of Fiona's *things* have gone, not that I need any more room because I don't have any more clothes anyway.

I sit on the bed and put my head in my hands. Then I remember my US dollars and I unlock the safe so I can get them out and count them. I'm excited, if only I had thought of this earlier, I could have asked the other hotel to hold my room until I arrived to pay. But it's no good, there's nowhere near enough money even with my English pounds. Stupid me.

A knock on the door makes me jump. Carl.

'Are you all right, you look very pale. You're not feeling ill, are you?'

'Not really.' I sigh and head back into my room and Carl follows. Maybe I'll just have to bite the bullet and see if he can lend me some extra money, if he's got some cash I could add it to what I already have. So much for giving it to Carl, I'm asking for more and I already feel so much in his debt.

'What's wrong?'

So I tell him, cringing inwardly as I broach the punchline, the part where I beg him to lend me money. But before I get the words out, he interrupts me.

'Stay in my room,' he says.

'I, I couldn't.'

'Why not? It has two beds. It's already booked. There's plenty of space. It's only one night.'

'Oh, I…' I can't even look at him.

'I promise I won't take advantage of you.' He grins then laughs. 'Come on, let's get your bags over there and then we can get on with our last full day.'

'But is it allowed? I mean your room is only booked for you.'

'I don't care if it isn't allowed, but I'm sure it is. It's certainly not a single room and I'm certainly not paying a single room price.'

'Oh, but, what, I…'

Carl picks up the hotel phone and dials Reception. He asks the pertinent questions; gets the answer he needs and puts the phone down.'

'Just as I thought, no problem at all. There, that's settled. Is this case ready to go?'

I nod, close it and put it on the floor. Accepting Carl's offer is the lesser of two evils, my alternative is to beg money from him. He might feel insulted if I turn him down. He might not lend me the money. He might not even have it; he's already spent a lot on *me*.

Seeing the concern on my face Carl grabs the handle of my case. 'Don't worry, I'll treat you with the utmost respect, treat you like the lady you are.'

I laugh out loud. That's funny.

He laughs too, although he looks a little uncertain of himself now. 'I could take you to another hotel if you prefer. I don't want you to feel pressured.'

I imagine myself in another hotel, on my own, eating on my own, travelling to and from the hotel and airport on my own. I can hardly expect Carl to continue being my taxi if I refuse his offer.

'I'll still give you a lift to the hospital and tomorrow to the airport. We could still have dinner together.' Now he looks sad, looks as though he wishes he had never suggested it.

'No, you're all right. Like you say, there are two big beds and plenty of space and there's a lock on the bathroom door.' I smile as brightly as I can but Carl doesn't return my smile.

'I'll take this on ahead, you catch up with me when you're ready,' he says.

Now, we both feel uncomfortable. So, so awkward.

♫♫♫

'You're late,' Fiona says, with her usual charm.

'Sorry. Drama at the hotel.' Since she's sitting up on the bed, I slump into her chair.

'Well, nothing compared to the drama here.' She folds her arms.

'What? Is everything okay? Are you still able to go home tomorrow?'

'Yes, yes, but not in the ambulance.'

'Oh, why not?' At least she can still go home.

'Because, apparently…' Fiona wobbles her head in annoyance. 'If I turn up in an ambulance the airline might think I'm not fit to fly, even though I have a letter from the surgeon to say otherwise. The hospital doesn't think I should chance it.'

'Ah. Right.'

'You've got a taxi booked, haven't you? I'll have to come with you.'

When I don't reply immediately, mainly because I'm thinking about how I'm going to have to impose on Carl even further Fiona feels the need to snap at me again.

'That's if it's not too much trouble for you.'

'Of course. It's no trouble at all.' Is now the time to tell her that we won't actually be travelling in a taxi. Will she be able to get in and out of Carl's rental car? Maybe I'll see what he says and maybe we will be getting a taxi after all. Will I have enough money to pay for a taxi. 'It'll be absolutely fine,' I reassure her and watch her pinched little face relax a little. I remind myself that while all this is a strain on me it's an even bigger strain on Fiona.

I leave the hospital several hours later with Fiona's dirty washing but it's actually less than I arrived with as I had to bring her clothes for travelling in. She's very specific about what she wears and when. I haven't given much thought to what I'll be wearing. I've been rotating and rinsing through the same light dresses while I've been here. It's so hot in Barbados that it's hard to imagine how cold it will be back home. It's still the middle of winter. I did pack my fleece but only because Fiona instructed me to pack hers after Jill suggested it, but I don't have a coat for either of us. I just couldn't fit them in the case.

♫♫♫

I wait until we're lying around our hotel pool making the most of soaking up the sun before I drop the bombshell on Carl.

'It's fine,' he says. 'Why is that such a problem?'

'Fiona can be…' I struggle for the right word. 'Tricky.'

'Tricky?'

'Well, cantankerous and picky.'

'Cantankerous.' He starts to laugh.

'Well, I'm just warning you, that's all.'

'Don't worry. I'm sure we'll be fine.'

Back in Carl's room he lets me use the bathroom first. I could be in my own room because it's exactly the same as Carl's, same pair of double beds, same lamps and drawers, everything the same. Once I'm out he dashes into the bathroom and I hurriedly get dressed while he's in there.

'That wasn't too bad,' he says once we're both dressed and ready. 'Was it?'

'No.' It wasn't but it's a little bit stressful and I'm glad it's only the one night.

We have a leisurely dinner from the buffet – a different crumble and thin custard today, but addictive nonetheless – drink two bottles of wine and we laugh a lot. The subject of my son doesn't come up, I think Carl is wisely not mentioning it and I certainly don't want to think about it, let alone talk about it. We finish with brandy and giggle our way back to Carl's room. Again, he lets me use the bathroom first.

211

I'm snuggled down in my own bed when he finally comes out.

'You comfortable?' he asks.

'Yes, thank you.' I am too, not just because the bed is comfortable, strangely more so than the exact same bed in my own room, but because I'm quite relaxed, although I know a lot of that is due to the alcohol.

Carl climbs into his own bed. 'Sleep tight,' he says. 'We've got a busy day tomorrow.'

'Don't remind me.'

He switches the light off and we both settle down. It's dark in the room apart from the tiny red light of the smoke detector centred on the ceiling. There's no sharp blue light on the TV, which there was in my room, so I suspect he's unplugged it.

I can hear him breathing but I know, like me, he isn't asleep. Finally, he speaks.

'I always imagine that red light up there is a camera,' he says, the sound of a smile in his voice.

'Really?' I laugh softly. I've never stayed in hotels, so it's all new to me. I obviously haven't acquired Carl's paranoia.

'Yes. Silly really. Though I'm not the first person to think that.'

'No? Oh.' I lie there looking at the light, occasionally it blinks. Perhaps he's right.

'Is it infrared then? Can it see in the dark? Like on those TV nature programmes?'

'Oh God, you've made it worse now. I'd never thought of that.' He chuckles, his voice low and deep and really rather nice.

Out of nowhere I hear myself say the words that I hope I won't regret. 'Then let's give them something to watch.' It's too late, they're out there and before the sentence is finished, I'm climbing into his bed.

Twenty-four

'What time is it?' I'm bleary eyed and still half asleep as I mutter the words.

'Um, let me check.' Carl leans over me and grabs his phone from the bedside table.

'Ten-to-ten.'

'What? No.' I sit up in bed, pulling the sheet around me. 'We've missed breakfast. We'll never make it.'

'Never mind, it's not that great, is it?'

I flop back down on the bed. 'No, but…'

'We'll go for an early lunch, or brunch if you like, later, on our way to pick up your friend.' He laughs and wraps his arms around me. 'Let's have a lie in for now.' He chuckles into my ear and I can't help laughing back.

'But don't we have to vacate? What if the cleaner comes in?'

'I've put the sign on the door and put the chain across.' He kisses my neck; I wriggle my delight and snuggle back down into the bed with him.

'Good. That's good.'

'What, this?' He nuzzles my ear.

'Yes, but I meant that you've put the chain on.' I

giggle, like a schoolgirl. I feel like a schoolgirl. 'What time do we have to vacate?'

'Noon. So we have plenty of time.' He squeezes my leg and we giggle together. Silly giggles. I feel silly. And happy.

Later, I say, 'You know you're my first since the last time.'

He looks at me in amused puzzlement. 'I hope so. You're my first since the last time too.' He gets out of bed.

'No, I mean…' Now I feel silly, wished I'd never said it.

He stops, turns and faces me. He's naked and it's hard not to be distracted. He isn't embarrassed or ashamed. I wish I could be like that. I know I won't be; I'll dash around and pull something on while he's in the bathroom.

'You mean…' he says, frowning. 'That this is the first time since *that* time?'

I can't look at him now, I just look down onto my chest where my hands clutch at the sheet.

'Yes,' I mutter.

He's suddenly round by my side of the bed, sits on it and wraps his arms around me. He doesn't say anything, nothing. And I'm glad for that.

♫♫♫

'I thought you'd forgotten about me,' Fiona spits as I enter the room. 'Where have you been? I've been messaging you.'

'Have you?' And I ignored every one of her messages, especially as they were terse and rude right from the off. 'I've been packing and so on,' I say, my tone matching hers. 'We agreed we'd leave for the airport at two, so I'm hardly late.'

'It's gone one,' she snaps.

'Yes, so plenty of time.'

'I suppose you've been out shopping with your new *friend*.'

I could correct her. I could tell her that we've been for a long, leisurely brunch, that we sat overlooking the sea and laughed and giggled like kids. I could, but I don't.

'Right,' I say, picking up her carpet bag, which weighs a tonne. 'What in here can go in my big suitcase and in the hold?'

'Nothing. I need it all with me.'

I weigh the bag in my hands. 'Is your shampoo and stuff in here?'

'Yes.'

'All that will need to go in the hold. No liquids in the cabin, remember?' She must know this, she's travelled a lot, I haven't. Carl pointed it out when he showed me what must go in the hold and what need not.

'It might get lost.'

'Well it definitely will if you insist on taking it on as hand luggage, they'll just bin it. Surely, you know this.'

'I haven't flown in a while.' She narrows her eyes at me, like a sly cat. 'I usually cruise. No silly restrictions.'

'I'm just wondering if I can get this whole bag in the suitcase? There's a bit of space in it now, more than when we came because…' I don't finish the sentence but Fiona gets my meaning and scowls at me. I'm sure she's getting worse. 'You can just carry your handbag then. Or I could.'

She studies me for a moment or two, evidently considering her options.

'Okay,' she says. That bag can go in the case, I'll just take a couple of *things* out of it. But I carry my own handbag. Just so we're clear.'

'Fine with me.'

'Oh, I have that too.' She points into the corner where a brand-new walker is folded up. 'The hospital got it for me. Wasn't that kind?'

'Yes. It was.'

'Course they'll slap it on the insurance bill, probably twice the price.'

I don't answer but instead collect up everything in the room and pack it either into her bag or give it to her for her handbag. She asks me for the passports and when I hand over just hers, she scowls at me again. She's really not in a good mood today.

'Are you in pain? Is everything okay?'

'No. No real pain. Plenty of drugs.' She rattles her handbag.

'Do you think some of those should go in the hold?'

She snaps a no at me so I don't pursue it, not that I get the opportunity because Fiona then proceeds to tell me how we're to pull up at the airport and find the assistance from the airline as arranged by the insurance. We will then be escorted through the departure process and into the waiting lounge. I don't know why she feels the need to tell me this, again, she's already told me in person and via messaging. I nod along and agree with her because it's just easier that way.

'Could I have your passport as well?' she says, as she finishes.

'Why?'

'Because then I can ensure that we get treated the same, you know, together. I don't want us to get separated. It says on the email that they'll allocate our seats on arrival. We want to be together.'

'But I'll be with you. Right next to you. I don't think you need my passport.'

'You had mine,' she snaps.

'And now you've got it back. Do you need help putting your shoes on?' I know she does.

She waits until I'm kneeling on the floor wedging her feet into her shoes before she delivers her next speech.

'Oh, by the way, there's only one taxi at the other end. You'll have to come with me. You probably should anyway, just to get me settled. It seems only right what with everything that's gone on.'

I get up from the floor. 'What do you mean?'

'You'll have to come to my place and then maybe get the train from there.'

'But I assumed I'd go in my own taxi straight home. Isn't that what the insurance company have arranged?'

Fiona looks guilty as she looks away from me.

'No. They said they could only arrange transport to one destination, my home, obviously.'

'Why's that?' But I already know the answer, the cheap insurance that Fiona bought, that's why.

I'm seething as well as disappointed. I suspect she's known for days. Whatever the truth of it she doesn't answer me, just starts rummaging in her handbag.

'I'm going to take this bag down and put it in the suitcase,' I say. 'I'll be back up soon for you.'

'You should have brought your friend up, then she could have helped carry stuff down and saved you an extra trip.'

I turn and smile. She thinks Carl is a woman.

Out in the car I'm still seething about the onward journey from the airport. I tell Carl about it as we rearrange the contents of my suitcase to accommodate Fiona's bag.

'Oh, that's a bit tough.'

'I know. I had imagined I'd go straight home. I've even brought a big carrier bag to put Fiona's extra stuff out of my case so she had everything with her.'

'Mmm, how capable is she of making that journey on her own?'

'Perfectly, she said earlier this week when I asked the same question. Said she had already arranged some help once she got to her own home.' I'm beginning to wonder now if she was lying or if she's realised she's not up to getting home without help. I don't quite know where that leaves me. It's true I have almost two more weeks off work, but I hadn't imagined spending them with Fiona.

'You could come home with me,' Carl says, watching my face for a reaction. 'I mean we'll drop you off at your own place. My son's picking me up from the airport, so it's no trouble, hardly a detour at all.'

'Thank you. I think I might just take you up on that. Thank you.' That makes me feel a lot better. I have options now. Fiona does not call the tune, not entirely. 'By the way, Fiona thinks you're female.'

'Why?' Carl frowns at me and laughs. 'What have you said?'

'Nothing. She's just assumed and I haven't corrected her.'

I go back up to find Fiona sitting in a wheelchair with a nurse ready and waiting to wheel her down. It takes a few minutes in the lift before we arrive at the car. I introduce Fiona and Carl. Fiona's face is a picture as Carl says hello and smiles broadly, but I'm glad to see that she's biting her tongue, though not for long.

'I think I need to sit in the front,' she demands and the nurse agrees it would be a better position for her.

Soon we're heading off to the airport, me in the back and Fiona lording it in the front. I've warned Carl not to waste his breath on small talk with Fiona, but pleasantness and politeness wins out and he can't help himself.

'How long have you lived in London, Fiona,' he asks.

'Always,' she snaps.

'Only you don't have a London accent, particularly,' he adds and in the rear-view mirror I catch the reflection of his sweet smile.

'You mean I'm not a Cockney? Not everyone who lives in London is a Cockney.' There, that's him told. I did warn him.

'No,' he says, keeping his tone pleasant. 'I suppose not.'

'You don't look like you come from Wiltshire, do you? But I'm not commenting on it, am I?'

I have to step in and lean forward in my seat. 'Yes, you are.'

'No, I'm not.'

'You are. You just have. In fact, I think your comment was racist.'

'And calling me a Cockney isn't racist?'

Carl shifts in his seat and catches my eye in the mirror, then he shakes his head.

I lean back and don't respond to Fiona. There's an uncomfortable atmosphere in the car and we've got another thirty minutes before we get to the airport. But at least she's quiet now which is preferable to her speaking. But her silence doesn't last long.

'Are you two having sex?' she asks.

'Not at the moment,' Carl deadpans.

That takes the wind out of Fiona's sails for a moment or two, but not for long enough.

'But you have been, haven't you? I can smell it on you.'

My mouth drops open in shock, but Carl isn't fazed.

'I doubt it, we took a very long hot shower together before we left. Washed all that sin away.'

I lean round so I can see Fiona's face and she looks just as though she's swallowed something nasty, like a wasp.

She doesn't speak for the rest of the journey. Something to be grateful for.

♫♫♫

It's busy at the airport which is much larger than I anticipated. We pull up as close as we can and Carl tells us to wait while he goes off to enquire about the assistance the insurance company has arranged.

'Well, you're a dark horse,' Fiona says, without a hint of shame for her rudeness.

'So's he,' I say, jumping out of the car before she can answer, but I can see the look of horror on her face.

Carl is soon back with the wheelchair and an airport employee pushing it. While Fiona is helped out of the car and into the chair, Carl gets out the suitcase and sets it down. I'm just grateful he has done that and that the case has wheels.

'Can you manage on your own?'

'Of course she can?' Fiona answers. 'She's not the one with the broken leg. Anyway, she's used to humping things around, aren't you? It's her job.'

Carl catches my eye and smiles. We both ignore

Fiona who sits in her wheelchair as though it's a throne with her airport servant waiting patiently behind her.

'We'd better go,' she says. 'We need to check in.'

I turn to Carl and say in a loud voice, 'Thank you for bringing us to the airport. We really appreciate it, don't we Fiona?'

'Yes. Thank you. But you were coming here anyway, weren't you? Pamela said you were on this flight too? So no trouble for you really, was it?'

Carl and I exchange smirks; the woman is incorrigible.

'My offer still stands for the other end,' he whispers in my ear, making the hairs on the back of my neck stand up.

'Thank you. I'll see how it goes, get to the bottom of whether Fiona has arranged help, and message you when we land.'

Then Carl kisses me, full on the lips and with passion. I know it's mostly for Fiona's benefit but I still enjoy it. Then he winks and climbs back into the car so he can return it to the rental company.

'Come on.' And I lead the way, marching on and dragging the case behind me.

At the check-in desk the process is not so very different from boarding the ship except that we don't have our photographs taken. We hand over our passports together – at Fiona's insistence – and when the attendant reads our names out, Fiona sniggers when he calls me Eleanor.

Once we're finished and the suitcase has disappeared down a conveyer belt, we head off to the upper-class lounge.

'Come on, Eleanor Rigby,' Fiona says, with spite in her voice.

I scoot round in front of her and stop dead and the attendant pushing the chair stops just as suddenly to avoid crashing in to me.

'Hey,' Fiona calls.

'It's *Pamela* Rigby actually, thank you very much.'

'Err, sorry,' she mutters, not sounding sorry at all and not looking directly at me.

We're taken to the upper-class lounge where a buffet is laid out and it's all very lovely. The attendant leaves us but says he'll be back when the plane is ready to board.

'Isn't this nice?' Fiona says, swaggering in her chair. 'Take me round to the buffet, I'll see what I fancy.'

I do as I'm told, but, nice as it all looks, I don't fancy any of it because I'm still full from my brunch with Carl.

'Damn it,' I say loud enough that Fiona picks up on it.

'What now?' Her tone screams irritation.

'Nothing. Just forgot to give Carl something.' I meant to give him my few remaining US dollars, at least he could use them to buy refreshments, they won't be free like ours. Because of Fiona's performance earlier, I completely forgot. I'll definitely give them to him when I get a lift home, so it's fine really.

I wheel Fiona and her full plate back to our little seating area and then she despatches me off to get her a glass of wine. I get myself one too, why not? It's going to be a long flight.

I'm sitting happily in my seat – we've both had two glasses of wine now – and staring out of the window at the planes as they taxi towards the runway or refuel when Fiona nudges me. When I don't respond she digs her elbow in deeper.

'What?' I'm as snappy as her now.

'Look, look who's over there.' She points with her head, a movement which is supposed to be subtle but isn't. I turn to look. 'Don't turn round, don't turn round.'

'Then how can I look?' Not that I'm in the least bit interested in who is over there.

'Get up and walk around me as if you're checking something, then you can have a good look.'

Sighing, I get up and do as I'm told. 'Where am I looking?'

She does the thing with her head again and I follow the direction. There's a man in his sixties with a thatch of grey hair and a deep tan, sitting with a woman whom I assume is his wife.

'Who are they?'

'Sit down.' She pulls at my clothes until I do. 'Well?'

'Well what?'

'It's Wayne Marshlands. In the flesh. Aren't we lucky to be on his flight?'

'If you say so.'

'You don't know who Wayne Marshlands is?'

'No.'

'He's the garden designer on TV, got that show, *We Build Your Perfect Garden.* You must have seen it. Or heard of it?'

I shake my head. 'I don't have a garden and I work in a garden centre, so no, I don't really watch gardening shows.'

Fiona sighs and rolls her eyes. 'Go and get his autograph.'

'Who?'

'You. Go on. Get his autograph for me.'

'No. I'll take you over there and you can get it for

yourself.'

'I can't do that.'

'Why not?'

'It's, it's undignified.'

'But okay for me to do it?'

'Well, yes.'

'Well, no.' I pull out my phone because I've just felt it vibrate. It's a message from Carl.

Good Wi-Fi here. He follows it with a lot of laughing emojis. *How's your friend now?*

Yeah, she's fine but annoying. How are you?

Took me ages to get back from dropping the car off, but settled and waiting to board now. What's first class like?

Upper class, actually, I reply. *Very nice.*

Lucky you.

I'm just about to reply when Fiona pokes me in the leg. 'We'll be boarding soon and I need to use the facilities. Now,' she adds when she sees my eyes return to my phone.

I reply to Carl telling him I'll message shortly, then wheel Fiona off in search of a toilet.

We're both a bit red-faced and sweaty when we return to find the attendant waiting for us.

'They're boarding your plane, you have priority.' He grabs the wheelchair and strides off as I scurry along behind him carrying Fiona's walker.

It's hot out on the tarmac where we're waiting to get into the lift that will help Fiona get on the plane without the need to climb the stairs. I can go with her – lucky me. Strictly speaking it's more of a truck than a lift and once we're in it, it lurches forward before juddering as it raises us. I'm gripping on for grim death but Fiona's chair is quite stable and secured to the floor. After several juddering attempts the lift is lined up with the plane door and we are urged, along with several others, onto the plane. It's not easy, even with the walker Fiona is very unsteady on her feet. She glances back longingly at the wheelchair, but it's not coming with us. We're lucky we're in upper class because we don't have far to go and when we are shown to our seats Fiona is thrilled to bits.

'We'll be able to sleep after dinner,' she says with glee.

Suddenly the eight-and-half-hour journey doesn't seem so awful. Poor Carl in the cheap seats.

Twenty-five

My seat never actually gets turned into a bed because I'm up and down all night taking Fiona to the toilet, which, fortunately is right near us. The good thing is that because the toilet is so small she can manage by herself once in there, because there are plenty of things to grab onto and lever herself up. Wish I could say the same about the loos in the airport.

That had been a cringefest. I felt sorry for Fiona but also annoyed, she didn't seem to want to help herself.

We have both slept a bit on the journey home and I'm sure that it's a lot more comfortable than further back in the plane. And the food has been delicious, even though I refused another glass of wine when we had dinner as I'd already had two large ones in the departure lounge. We've now had breakfast and they've cleared away and I'm just wondering if now would be a good time to wander down and see if I can find Carl when we're told to buckle up as we're now approaching Gatwick. I've left it too late.

I feel more apprehensive about landing than I did taking off, but only because I really didn't know what to expect. Taking off was a strange tugging experience, but as we ascended I think I preferred that to this falling sensation. Straining against my seatbelt I peer over at Fiona, she looks white.

'Okay?' I mouth.

She nods at me then looks away.

As we hit the tarmac with a gentle bump I feel relieved, but that feeling doesn't last long, because I don't know what to expect now.

While the plane starts to empty we're asked to wait until everyone else is off. Within ten minutes there's just us and a few others with walking sticks and crutches waiting in the aisles.

'Think they'd have let us off first,' Fiona snaps.

'I suppose it takes the pressure off, knowing there's no one waiting behind you.'

'Huh.'

Finally, we're off, Fiona having stumbled around with her walker is finally united with a wheelchair and another airport attendant. He takes us to a waiting electric cart. There's some debate as to whether I can go with them or have to run alongside, I hope not. Eventually, he decides there is room for me.

As we hurtle along I switch my phone back on and see a message from Carl. It's a simple, *Okay?* I send a smiley face and thumbs up back. I love emojis they say so much more than words sometimes can.

'Is that lover boy?' Her tone is so nasty that I don't even answer, anyway Carl has sent me another message.

I'm in the baggage reclaim, ring me when you get here.

We're heading that way in our little cart and I hope I get the chance to see Carl. However, first we have to go through passport control, I'm not sure what this normally involves, having never been through an airport before, but it seems very fast and efficient. We don't even have to get out of the electric cart.

Baggage reclaim is full of people standing and watching a conveyor belt. The attendant parks the cart and jumps out.

'If you'd like to come and identify your luggage, I can retrieve it for you.'

I cannot say thank you enough because in the few minutes we've been here I've seen a few people hauling their cases off the belt and it looks like a fitness and strength challenge. And I'm so tired now.

'And hurry up,' Fiona yells. 'I need warmer clothes, I'm freezing.'

We've flown in lightweight clothes which was no problem because we had duvets on the plane, but now, we're both cold but all we have in the case is a fleece each. I hope Fiona's going to be warm enough.

I'm about to message Carl when he taps me on the shoulder. I turn and he hugs me. I rest my head on his chest – so nice.

'How was your flight?' he asks. 'How's Fiona?'

I glance over to the cart but fortunately the way it is parked means she can't see us.

'It was okay.' I hear the sigh in my voice.

'That good, eh?'

'Well, to be fair probably better than yours. The food was amazing but we didn't get a lot of sleep, despite the comfort. What about you?'

'I managed a few hours.' He grins before continuing. 'Folded up, cramped in the cheap seats, I was so tired so it was easy to nod off. You wore me out.'

I laugh and he hugs me tighter.

'My son's waiting in the arrivals hall. Are you coming with us?'

'I can't. I thought I could but I can't leave her. She's…' What more can I say? 'She needs a lot of help. I took her to the loo at the airport before we left. She can't even…well, she needs a lot of help.' I don't tell him how I had to yank her knickers down, how she complained how rough I was – I didn't think I was – or that I had to wipe her bum. 'I can't let her go home alone. She did say earlier this week that she'd arranged help, but she hasn't mentioned it since and when I tried to bring it up, she cut me dead...'

'Oh.'

The attendant coughs to get my attention.

'Better find my case,' I say, pulling away from Carl. As I say these words I watch it pass us and I decide to let it go around again. Two more minutes with Carl.

'Where does she live?'

'London.' I laugh. 'I don't remember the address but I expect it's some lovely leafy area, a big house in a Victorian terrace, that's the impression I have, though she's never said. She did say she'd lived there for years so it must have been the family home, before her children grew up and her husband died, so I'm sure there'll be plenty of room for me.'

'How long will you have to stay with her?'

'We haven't discussed it.'

'Don't you think you should?'

'Yes. Yes.' The sense of this hits me in face. 'I will, now. I was thinking a day or two.' I spot my case coming around again and point it out to the attendant.

'She might have made other arrangements,' Carl says. 'You need to check with her. Then message me. We'll wait until you do, in case you are coming with me.'

My heart lifts, of course she's made other

arrangements. Her family are coming over or a friend is staying. Just because she hasn't discussed it with me doesn't mean she hasn't done it. She's so secretive that she wouldn't tell me. She won't want me, it's obvious to us both that we're friends by circumstance not choice. And yet she told me I'd have to go with her to settle her in.

'I don't think I'll be able to come with you, Carl.'

'I'll wait for your text.'

Carl gives me a kiss and leaves, dragging his case behind him. I scurry back to Fiona suddenly feeling happy and optimistic and probably fooling myself.

'What do you want to do now?' I ask Fiona as I yank out our fleeces before zipping up the case again.

She gives me a look, that same narrow-eyed look that implies I'm stupid. 'Get in the taxi and go home.' She shifts in her seat as she pulls on her fleece, wincing, and I don't think it's just for my benefit.

'Yes. Have you made arrangements for when you get home?'

'What?'

'Is one of your sons coming over to help you? Or do you have a friend staying?'

'What?'

'Well, you need help. I don't think you can manage on your own.'

'Of course I can't,' she snaps at me. 'You're coming with me.'

That's settled then.

While the electric cart takes us through to the arrivals hall I message Carl to tell him to carry on without me. I'm feeling quite despondent, and cold. It's also just as well that I didn't give Carl the dollars because I'm going to need them to fund my journey home. I've no idea how much a train ticket will cost. Too much, I suspect.

There's a fat, old man waiting with Fiona's name scribbled on a piece of card. This doesn't fill me with confidence.

I approach him while the attendant helps Fiona out of the cart and into another wheelchair.

'You Fiona?'

'No, but I'm with her.'

'Good. I had to park a bit away, but not too far.'

'Okay.'

Fiona and the attendant join us and I grab my suitcase and Fiona's walker.

'You want me to carry that?' the taxi driver asks, eyeing the walker. I'm tempted to unfold it so he can use it properly because he looks like he needs it. He's as dicky on his feet as Fiona. Actually, worse.

He sees me studying him. 'Got a bad back,' he says.

'Of course.'

When we reach his car, Fiona gasps. 'I can't get in that.'

The car, a big, low slung Mercedes, looks okay to me.

'Sorry, love. It's all I got.' He opens the passenger rear and front doors while we all peer in.

'But I told the insurance company I needed something decent, something firm. It's too low. Look at it.' She turns to me. 'That car your lover had was much better than this.'

The taxi driver looks affronted. 'This is always happening. Often I get here and it's someone on crutches from a skiing accident.'

'How do *they* manage?' I ask, thinking if they can, surely Fiona can.

'They just lie in the back seat.'

'I'm not doing that.'

'What's the alternative?'

'You could ring the company, tell 'em what you want.' The driver shrugs. He really doesn't care.

'Ring them, ring them. Pamela, ring them.'

So I do and when we find out it will be at least a two hour wait, we both groan. After a debate we agree that we'll try to get Fiona in the car. The airport attendant is keen to get back to the terminal as he has another assignment soon and the taxi driver just wants to get on with it. We decide it would be better if Fiona was sitting in the front seat, carefully strapped in she should be better there than rolling around in the back. The fact that she's so small is a blessing and a curse.

We need to bank the seat up a bit, short as Fiona is her legs would still not be at the required angle. We don't have a cushion and, in the end, the only logical thing to do is the fold up my fleece and use that. Fiona needs to keep hers on as she is so cold.

'You work outside, you're tough,' she says to me.

'I wear a coat in the winter,' I say, but more to myself than her, as I shrug off my fleece and fold it up. I wish I'd stuffed my cagoule into the case, I could at least have worn that, but I didn't. Oh well, when I do get home, I have coats there. I wonder when that will be?

With the aid of the walker Fiona stands up and shuffles towards the car. The attendant whisks the wheelchair away and says he has to go now. The taxi driver hovers by the boot and so it's left up to me to manoeuvre her into the car.

We manage it, but not without several howls from Fiona and I think we're both worried that we might have done her new hip some damage.

'You managed, see,' the taxi driver says, getting in and starting up the car while I clamber into the back.

'No thanks to you,' I snap.

'Told you, I have a bad back.' He swings the car round and out towards the car park exit. When we reach the exit machine he produces a ticket from his pocket and presents it to a machine which beeps its disapproval.

'Damn,' he says, glancing at the cars queuing behind us.

'What's wrong?' I really don't want to know.

'I've only got cash. It only accepts cards. I'm going to have to back up, which means getting the two cars behind us to back up first, then I'll have to find an exit that takes cash.'

'Is there one?' spits Fiona.

'Yeah, on the far side. That's the one I usually use.'

'Why didn't you today then?'

He doesn't answer but attempts to back up, much to the annoyance of the car behind whose driver toots his horn angrily.

'How much is it? I ask.

'Eight pounds.'

'Try my credit card,' I say, fumbling in my handbag and hoping and praying there's enough to cover eight pounds, surely there is.

'It's contactless and your card isn't,' he says with disdain.

Bloody cheek. 'Okay, try this.' And I hand over my debit card, confident I can afford eight pounds. Probably. I almost cleared out my bank account before I came on holiday, leaving enough to cover my direct debits, and I haven't been paid again yet.

He flashes the card over the reader and it beeps through and the barrier lifts.

'Get a receipt,' Fiona snips. 'We'll be claiming that back.'

I'm glad she had the foresight to say that, but the debt is mine and I hope I get all the cash back. Apart from her bill on the ship she hasn't paid for anything else, I have.

Finally, we're on our way. Even this early in the morning London is alive with traffic and people and Gatwick isn't in central London. I have no idea where we're going but after what seems like hours, though isn't, we pull into a lovely, leafy street. This is just what I imagined, just how I described it to Carl. Large three and four storey Victorian houses line both sides of the street, their bay windows smug with affluence. This is where she lives, now I see the street name I remember it from the insurance forms.

'Nice road,' I say without thinking.

Fiona doesn't answer.

'Which one, love?'

Without speaking Fiona indicates that he should keep going. And we keep going, on and on, past the splendid Victorian terraces all the way to the end and finally pull up outside a flat, grey building that could be a 1960s police station, or an office block. It's quite hideous.

And this is where Fiona lives.

Twenty-six

We stagger into the building, no mean feat given that the main door, which Fiona has a key fob for, weighs a tonne and I have to hold it for Fiona without hitting her with the suitcase. My heart sinks when I see a flight of concrete stairs in front of us and no sign of a lift. How the hell is Fiona going to manage those. She can do stairs, apparently, the physio taught her how to, but these are not like the stairs inside a house, nor like the ones she learnt on in the hospital.

'It's that way,' Fiona says, stumbling forward. She points to a door and I hope there's a lift behind it.

It's only when she uses a key to open the door that I realise it's her front door. Thank the lord for small mercies, she lives on the ground floor.

We find ourselves in a narrow corridor with doors leading off. It's dim as the only natural light comes from the glass above the door at the very end. Fiona flicks a light on. Everything is beige. Carpet, walls and even the doors. And bare, nothing on the walls.

'Straight on,' she says, leading the way with her walker. She stops in front of the far door and opens it. I leave the suitcase in the corridor and follow her into the room. Her lounge. Everything beige again. Even the sofa and two chairs. There's a teak type dining table in the corner and an odd teak sideboard that might have belonged to her parents, against the wall. At least the window is large and the morning light, a weak winter sun, floods into the room.

'Could you go back and get my post?' Fiona asks and I do as she says.

There are three letters on the mat by the front door. Three. For over two weeks away, just three. She doesn't get the junk mail that I do. Having picked them up I take them back and hand them to her. She gives them a cursory glance then lays them neatly and squarely on the sideboard. There's nothing else on the sideboard. Or the table. Or the walls. Apart from a large TV and a small computer on one of those desks where the keyboard is tucked away on a sliding shelf. This place is as though no one actually lives here, except for the sofa where there are two cushions, quaint little cottages. Fiona notices me noticing the cushions.

'Tapestry,' she says. 'My hobby.'

'Wow. They're…' I search for the words thinking that old-fashioned and odd isn't what she's expecting. '…so detailed,' I add. This pleases her and she smiles brightly, probably the brightest smile I've seen on her, ever.

When my mum died and I discovered that I was homeless because no one – including me – had ever thought to add me to the council tenancy, I looked at private flats to rent before I was lucky enough to get a social housing flat. Some were unfurnished but some were ready furnished with the basics, somewhere to sit, to eat, to sleep. That is exactly how Fiona's flat looks, like a furnished place waiting for a tenant to love it. I compare it to my own place, I like to think it's full of personality, even if it sometimes looks a bit cluttered, but this place has no personality whatsoever, or clutter. The polite person in me wants to tell her she has a lovely place but the realist knows I'll be lying and I don't think my face will be able to hide it.

'I'll show you around,' says Fiona. 'Then you'll know where everything is.' She smiles a smile of pride.

'Okay,' I say, smiling back at her.

She clomps back out to the corridor and opens the first door on the right.

'Kitchen.'

'Oh yeah. Neat.' I mean it too, the work surfaces are completely bare, not a toaster or bread bin in sight. The room is small so maybe that's what works. It's also beige. Worktops and cupboard doors are beige, so are the floor tiles. The only non-beige items are the sink and washing machine, though, incredibly, even the cooker and fridge are beige. Who knew such things existed?

'I pride myself on my organisation and tidiness,' she says as we shuffle out of the kitchen and along to the next door which she doesn't open. 'My room. You don't need to go in there.'

'No.'

She turns across to the other side of the corridor. 'Bathroom.' She nods to me to open the door and I prepare myself for another onslaught of beige. I'm not disappointed, and it is very neat and tidy. 'You can have this shelf,' she says, opening a cupboard door and showing me an empty shelf. Who the hell has an empty shelf in their bathroom cabinet?

'Thank you.'

'And finally, your room.' We shuffle along and open the door to *my* room. A single bed covered in a beige bedspread sits in another sea of beige. There's an ancient wardrobe-dressing table combo in one corner, another relic from her parents' house by the look of it. 'You can put your case in here for now.'

She watches as I wheel it the few feet into the room. It almost fills the space not occupied by the bed and wardrobe. I'm not complaining though, at least I have my own room here and don't have to share with Fiona and it's only for a night or two until we get her sorted out. No doubt she's pleased about not sharing with me too. If it was the other way round it would be trickier as I only have a one-bed flat.

'You can unpack when you come back,' she says to me.

'Come back?'

'You need to go shopping, obviously there's no food here. I'll give you a list.'

'And you need to tell me where to go.' I really can't be bothered but it's obvious there won't be any milk or bread, just as there wouldn't be at my place.

'I usually take a taxi to the big Sainsbury's a few miles away but I'm going to let you go to the Tesco local, it's just at the end of the road and down a bit.'

While Fiona makes her list, I use the bathroom and take the opportunity to have a sly look through her cabinet. Apart from the empty shelf there are three others, almost bare, though once we put her ship purchases into them, they'll be full. Maybe that was what the empty shelf was for.

When I come back Fiona is waiting with the list in her hand. She's also sitting down on an armchair with a thick rug over her legs. She looks comfortable, probably more comfortable that she's looked, or been, since falling off the toilet. When I say so, she tells me that the chair is exactly the right height and firmness for her and it reclines. She also tells me – a bit too gleefully – that the matching sofa and the other chair don't recline, which is fine by me. She hands over the list. It has the usual milk and bread and a few other items and, almost inevitably, her *things*. She's actually written '*things*'.

'Okay, I'm going to need some money.'

Fiona frowns at me.

'Or a debit card, or something.'

'Can't you pay for it and we'll split the bill later?'

'No. I've pretty much run out of money, and credit limit.'

'Have you? You obviously spent far too much enjoying yourself in Barbados.' Her head does a little self-righteous wobble. 'There's a money exchange office near to Tesco's, you can change some of those US dollars you must have left. That should cover it.'

That's it. That's the final straw.

I slump onto her sofa and sink almost to the ground before bouncing back up. I don't want the speech which I know is going to come out of my mouth to sound like a bad-tempered rant, which it will if I'm standing up and towering over her, even though I'm hardly tall.

'Fiona,' I say as sweetly as I can. 'I need what's left of those dollars to pay for my train fare home. I just hope I have enough to cover it. I have no idea if it will. Also, I really didn't spend much money enjoying myself, as you put it, in Barbados, because I couldn't afford to. I used my credit card to pay for your hospital deposit and my hotel bill and it is now officially maxed out. It was declined the last time I tried to use it.' I'm not going to tell her that I had to stay with Carl for our last night. She doesn't need to know that. 'I have a few pounds in my purse and I can't use my debit card again until I get paid, which isn't for another week. Frankly I was worried about using it to pay for the parking. I scrimped and saved for that cruise and used every spare penny I had to pay for it. I have nothing left and even when I get paid, I won't have a lot of spare because I need it to pay my bills. I'm almost penniless because of everything I've had to pay out on your behalf.'

Fiona studies me for a moment or two before speaking. 'You'll get it all back from the insurance company.'

'I hope so. But when?'

'We'll submit the claim immediately, once you're back from shopping.'

'Which brings us back to paying for the shopping. Unless you have any cash, I won't be going.' I force myself to lean back on the sofa because during my non-rant, I've edged forward and am in danger of falling onto the floor.

Fiona looks at me with disgust, as though I've squandered money left, right and centre. I have. On her.

She reaches down by the side of her chair and grabs her handbag, finding her purse inside and opening it. She goes to the part where the notes and her cards are. I can see it's bulging and I have to fight myself not to say something really nasty. She pulls out a twenty-pound note and offers it to me in such a way you'd think she was giving me her kidney.

'I don't think that will be enough?' I say. 'You want two packets of your things. How much are they?'

Fiona twitches, says nothing and pulls out another

twenty-pound note. 'I want the change,' she says.

'Let's hope there is some. There's nothing on here to make a proper meal with, do you have something in your freezer we could have for dinner tonight?'

'Huh. Dinner? You're not in a hotel now.'

'We still need to eat properly. You more than me. You need to recover from that major op.' I nod towards her hip.

'I don't know what's in the freezer, I can't remember now.'

'No problem. I'll look.' And before she can object or tell me it's a secret I zip off out of the lounge, close the door behind me and go into her kitchen. The freezer is stuffed full and it doesn't take me long to decide we'll be having fish, chips and peas tonight.

Fiona has reclined her chair and has her feet up and the TV on when I go back in. I've brought her a glass of squash since there's no milk to make tea and I put it down on the side table next to her chair.

'I'll need your front door key and that fob to get into the building,' I tell her. I can see the look of reluctance on her face. She really does not want to give me her key. I don't know what she thinks I'm going to do with it, get it copied and hand it out to everyone I pass. Finally, she relents and hands her keyring over, once she's extracted it from her handbag.

In Tesco's I get the items on her list and add one or two of my own, including a bottle of wine. White, which will go nicely with our fish and chips.

♫♫♫

'You've been a long time,' she says in her usual accusatory tone when I return.

'Well, I've been out enjoying myself.'

'There's no need to be sarcastic.' She turns the volume on the TV up.

'Isn't there?' I say as I take the bags into the kitchen and start to unload. I put the kettle on, once I've hunted it down and found it in the cupboard under the sink, and make us both a cup of tea. When I take hers in, she's sitting with a pinched look on her face. I put the tea on her table and then rummage in my pockets for the receipt and change.

'I did wonder if you were ever going to give me that,' she moans as she picks up the receipt and scrutinises it. 'Wine? That wasn't on the list.'

'No, I thought it would be nice with our dinner.'

'I'm on a lot of painkillers, I can't drink wine.'

'Okay, well I can.'

'There are other things on here that I didn't ask for. You can pay me back for everything when you get paid.'

'Can I?' I mutter, not believing the gall of the woman. 'Shall we put the heating on? It's so cold in here.' I'm still wearing my fleece and I won't be taking it off.

'No, it's on a timer. Anyway, I find it quite warm, quite cosy.' Of course she does snuggled under her blanket. I cannot be bothered to argue with her. 'I've put your things in the bathroom.'

'Oh no, I don't keep them in there. I can't have them cluttering up the bathroom.'

'Okay. I'm going to go and unpack my case. There's a lot of your stuff needs washing, so I'll put your machine on later.' I don't wait for her to answer because I don't want to hear her answer, instead I dash out of the room, close the door behind me and go straight into the bathroom. I pick up her *things* and then open her bedroom door; I'm sure she won't mind if I just pop them on her bed.

It's as beige as the rest of the house, the bed is also a single – I suppose she *is* small, but even so. Other than a lamp there is nothing on her bedside table, not a book, not a picture, nothing. I cannot understand how she has no photos of her sons, her grandchildren, anywhere. She's a strange one.

In my room I ring Carl and we have a good long chat. I tell him about my shopping trip, not that there's much to tell and he asks me when I think I can leave and go home. I tell him I really don't know.

Once I've unpacked, I sort out the washing, my own included and load up Fiona's machine. I'm glad I had the foresight to bring a pair of jeggings with me and pull them on, I wish I had put them on before I went shopping, but I need them just as much in here. I wonder what time the damn heating comes on.

It's almost three when I finally go back into the lounge to find Fiona dozing in her chair. I've come to ask her what to do with the washing once it's finished. There's no tumble dryer and I can't find a clothes horse in any of the obvious places.

She doesn't wake even when my stomach rumbles like thunder, so while she sleeps on, I decide to make us a very early dinner. It takes me the best part of an hour before it's ready mainly because I have to hunt for even the simplest thing, even something to cook in. I do find the toaster in a cupboard though, so that's good.

I take another cup of tea into her just before our meal is ready; I've been drinking wine in the kitchen.

'Ah, there you are. I wondered where you'd been.'

'I haven't been anywhere and you've been asleep,' I

say, echoing her tone.

'I haven't.'

'Doesn't matter. I've made you another cup of tea.'

'Does it have sugar?'

'No. Do you want sugar?' I dutifully trot off to the kitchen to get some when she tells me she does. 'Dinner is nearly ready.'

'Bit early.'

'I know, but we're all over the place what with flying overnight.' I try a smile, not that it's easy.

'You'll need to set the table.'

'Can't we just eat off our laps?'

'Certainly not.'

So I hunt around in her sideboard to find the mats and lay the table. Then we spend quite a time manoeuvring Fiona from her comfortable seat onto a dining chair, she winces and I don't think she's comfortable at all. When, finally I bring in our meal, I've almost lost the will to live never mind eat.

I also bring in the wine and my glass. I intend to drink the entire bottle whether Fiona approves or not.

'Where's my glass?'

'I thought you weren't drinking?'

'I've changed my mind. I'll take my painkillers later.'

So I fetch another glass, pour her some wine and sit down to eat. I wish I'd bought two bottles now.

'Did you speak to your family while I was out?' I ask, innocently.

'No, and before you ask, they are not coming. They are far too busy to be troubled by this nonsense.' She waves at her hip with a chip on a fork.

'Good for them,' I say, taking a very, very large glug of wine.

Twenty-seven

'That was quite a passable meal,' Fiona says once we've finished, I've cleared up and she is sitting back in her armchair.

'Thanks. I think.'

'Obviously you've been enjoying a la carte dinners every evening but I've been eating simple home cooked meals in the hospital, albeit a bit too spicy for me at times, so fish and chips was a welcome change.' Fiona's rambling suggests that the glass and half of wine she's had – which should have been mine – has gone straight to her head.

'Dinner in the hotel was definitely not a la carte, more pick and mix buffet. Don't suppose you have any wine hidden away anywhere?'

Fiona studies me and tilts her head in a way that suggests she does and she's just deciding whether I'm worth it. 'Only red,' she finally says.

'Perfect. Shall I fetch it?'

'Yes. All right. It's in the cupboard in the hall, on the floor behind the vacuum cleaner and the mop bucket.'

I'm suitably shocked when I find not one but six

bottles hiding behind the mop bucket. What a dark horse. I bring clean wine glasses and set them down on Fiona's side table while I open the bottle.

'Just a small one for me,' Fiona says as I pour. 'Not that small,' she says when I stop. In the end her large glass is full. 'You prefer white,' she says.

'No. I like either.'

'Ah. I prefer a full-bodied red, not that I drink very often. Rarely really.'

There's no answer to that, because I've no idea what her drinking habits are.

'I need this because I'm winding myself up to go to the toilet. I haven't been since the plane.'

'What? No?' It really hadn't occurred to me that she would need to go. What kind of help am I? Useless. Although she went so many times on the plane I doubt she's had much need since then. 'Do you need help?' I hope she doesn't.

'Yes, I think I might. Perhaps I'll just have a little more wine before we go.'

I top up her glass because she's already drunk over half of it. She drinks faster than I do. She empties her glass before finally hauling herself up off the chair and leaning on her walker.

'Lesh go then,' she slurs.

We shuffle along to her bathroom and I open the door to let her in. She looks at the toilet seat, it's a lot lower than the one in the hospital and on the plane, but Fiona is short so it should be okay. She's not supposed to bend further than ninety degrees, or something, I think that's what she said. Given how this happened in the first place I suppose her mistrust of toilets is justified. I'd be nervous too. In fact, I am nervous on her behalf.

She joggles around, pulls up her skirt, yanks down her knickers and freefalls onto the toilet. I don't know where to look and I can't forget her comment about seeing her *fanny* when she made me wash her. I let my eyes roam all over the bathroom, corners, walls, ceiling.

'Ah, that's where you hang the washing,' I say, spotting a pull-out line over the bath, it's one of those four-line affairs.

'Well, of course. Where else?'

I turn to answer her and see that she is straining on the toilet and going a bit puce. Oh please, can't I leave now?

'It's no good,' she says, snatching a piece of loo roll and reaching under herself. 'Help me up.'

Between us we get her up and her clothes sorted out and we both wash our hands and I help her back to her chair then excuse myself to hang up the washing. I'm really not cut out to care for someone, I'm far too selfish and inept. Then it hits me, like a punch, maybe that's why I never fought to keep my baby. I knew I'd be useless. 'But you helped look after your parents,' a kind little voice in my head says.

When I return Fiona has a full glass again and a silly look on her face.

'You haven't taken painkillers with that, have you?'

'No. Don't need them now. This is far better. Cheers.' She takes a big swig. 'I've filled yours up, so don't waste it.' There's a mischievous glint in her eyes.

'We'll have to try and get you some proper help.' I sip my wine.

'What do you mean?'

'Well, I can't stay here indefinitely. I have a life of my own. And a job.'

'Yes, but you would have been away for a few more

weeks anyway, wouldn't you? They're not expecting you back at work yet.'

She's right, but even though my holiday has been cut short I don't want to waste my time off work being her carer. It's not as if we're even good friends, or friends at all really, more companions of circumstance.

'Yes, but this really isn't for me. It's a shame your family can't come over. I thought you said you had arranged for a friend to help.'

'Did I?'

'I thought so. I suppose you'll be having longer off work. How long?'

'Months,' she says, her tone dismissive. 'Sit down and chat to me. I feel as though we've hardly had a proper conversation. It was difficult in the hospital.'

I plonk myself on the bouncy sofa, grab my glass and notice that Fiona is grinning inanely. She's drunk.

'It's such a shame our holiday was cut short by all this nonsense. I'm so annoyed. We need to get on and do that insurance claim so we can get our money back. Do you have all the paper stuff and receipty things?'

Receipty things? Fiona is definitely drunk.

'Yes. I do. But I don't think we should do it now.'

'No time like the present, thash what I say. Strike while the iron's hot, onwards and upwards.'

'I think we've drunk too much to concentrate on it properly.' *You* definitely have.

'Tomorrow then, first thing.' She grins again and raises her glass. 'Will you be seeing your lover when you get back home? Is that why you're so desperate to leave?'

I laugh. I am not going to answer that.

'You'll have to help me have a shower tomorrow. I can't climb into that bath on my own. Shame it's not a walk-in shower. I've been telling the housing association for years that I need one, now I definitely do.'

'Oh, I live in a housing association flat too. Mine has only the one bedroom. Did you move here after your sons left home?'

'Mmm. I think you might have to get another bottle out. Your glass is nearly empty.'

My glass is half full, but hers isn't.

'I don't think we should have any more. Not if we're starting the insurance claim in the morning.' I hope it doesn't take long; I hope I get my money back quickly.

'Maybe you're right.'

'When the taxi turned into your street I imagined you lived in one of those big Victorian houses we passed. They look nice, don't they?'

'Would be far too big for me now.'

'I wonder how big their gardens are?'

'I've got a garden,' Fiona snaps.

'Wow. Have you?' I glance over at the big window and notice, for the first time, that there's a door in it. It's pitch black outside now, so I can't see anything outside. I get up to close the curtains over the window. Fiona watches me with suspicious eyes but doesn't speak. I feel compelled to carry on the conversation, God knows why. 'I live on the first floor, so no garden for me. I've lived there for years and my place is full of clutter, not like yours, so neat and tidy.' I want to say sparse and without any personality but of course I don't. 'Have you lived here long?' I vaguely remember her saying she had, but she wasn't specific.

'A while.' She doesn't look at me.

'I expected to see photos of your family everywhere.' I laugh. 'I still have photos of my cat on display and he died five years ago.' I laugh again, not that it's funny, I still miss my cat.

'No pets allowed here.'

'No, nor where I live, but… you know…'

'No. I don't.'

'What are your neighbours like?'

'Nosy.'

'What about your friend who might come and help you?' I'm not letting it drop, I'm sure she told me there was someone.

'Too busy, as it turns out.'

'Maybe we could ring social services or something.' I'm really clutching at straws now.

'Certainly not. I think I'd better go to bed now.' She starts to haul herself up and I have to jump up to help her. I have to help her into her bedroom, help her change into her nighty and virtually lift her into the bed. It's a good job she's small and I am strong. We don't bother with cleaning our teeth or anything else, apart from changing her incontinence pad. It's so embarrassing.

'Did this happen after you had babies?' I ask.

'What?'

'You know, this… weeing thing.'

She narrows her eyes at me. I wish I'd never mentioned it; I'm probably as drunk as she is and my tongue is loose. 'Only it happened to me after I gave birth. For a while.' My tongue is definitely loose.

She pounces. What did I expect? 'You don't have any children. You told me you had no family.' There's a nasty tone to her voice.

'I don't. Not anymore.'

'What happened to it?'

I can't tempt fate; I can't say he died. Oh me and my

big mouth. 'I had to give him up for adoption. So I don't have any children.'

She looks me up and down, her lips pursed, judging me, deciding how weak I really am.

'Me neither,' she says, her voice tiny. She flicks off her bedside light and plunges us into darkness.

I want to ask what she means. What *me neither* means. But I've already opened a can of worms, do I want to poke a stick in it too? I creep out of her room and close the door behind me.

♫♫♫

I don't know whether it's the effects of the wine or sheer exhaustion but I sleep so deeply that when I wake up, I don't know where I am. Then I remember.

'Pamela, Pamela.'

I haul myself out of bed and head towards Fiona's room. Her voice sounds croaky as she's calling my name, over and over.

'Morning,' I say, wincing at my own rasping voice. Definitely too much wine. 'How did you sleep?'

'Better than in the hospital,' she says.

'That's good.'

'Get me up now, I need the toilet.'

'Okay.' I need the loo too; I don't suppose I could just nip in before her. Better not.

I manhandle her out of bed and position her frame in front of her. Together we proceed to the bathroom and once she's settled on the toilet, I leave.

In the kitchen I fill the kettle – the running water making me cross my legs – and put away last night's washing-up from the draining board.

'Pamela, Pamela.'

'You okay?'

'Help me off here. It's pointless. You're going to have to go and get me some stuff for this.'

'Stuff?'

'I'll tell you what it is. There's a chemist not far.'

Another trip out for me then.

Fiona stumbles over to the sink and washes her hands. I suppress a groan when she runs the taps.

'Now for a shower,' she says.

'Oh, I've made a lovely cup of tea. Why don't we have breakfast first. Give us some strength.'

She considers this for a moment or two and I get the feeling that she thinks I have an ulterior motive, which I do. I just want to use the toilet.

'All right.' She clomps out of the bathroom and I tell her I'm just going to use the loo and will be along in a minute while pushing the door closed behind her.

She's sitting in her chair with her cup of tea untouched and still on the side table where I left it. She has breakfast TV on. Loud.

'Tea okay?'

'No, I like sugar, I told you that yesterday. Two sugars.'

'Okay.' I take the tea away and add two sugars to it.

'I'll have cereal and toast with jam,' she says when I take her tea back.

I don't need to ask which cereal as there is only one here, the one I bought yesterday and it's not one I like. Honey Monster Puffs are super sickly. I make her a bowl and take it in to her. Her eyes light up like a little child's. My brother liked these when he was a kid, though I'm sure they used to be called Sugar Puffs. I always preferred Weetabix and should have bought some yesterday. I just wasn't thinking. Maybe I can get some when I go out again.

After two more cups of tea, and toast and jam we're ready for the shower. I'm dreading it and I suspect Fiona is too. What if she falls?

It's a struggle in the bathroom but in the end, once she's standing there naked as a baby, her body so small she could pass for a child, I lift her into the bath. She has one of those smooth bodies that despite having two babies, doesn't have any saggy skin or stretch marks. This whole thing is so undignified for us both. Now what?

She can't sit down because she's not supposed to sit so low but she's struggling to stay standing up. I'm afraid that if I put the shower on the force will knock her over.

Fiona sighs and gripping the walls, she looks at the shower head, looks at me and her eyes light up. She's had an idea. Good, because I'm woefully short of them.

'Take your clothes off and get in with me. You can have a shower at the same time and you can stop me from falling over. Come on it'll save you time too, you've got a lot to do today.'

Have I? Oh God.

'Come on. Don't be shy. In boarding school we all piled into the showers together.'

Boarding school. How long ago was that? Even in my rough old school we didn't quite do that and so, I, like most of my friends then, hated the communal school showers. I never expected to be revisiting *that* experience at my age.

I have my swimming costume in my case and I consider putting it on. It would, at least, save my modesty even if Fiona doesn't care.

'Come on, you'd better hurry because the heating

goes off soon and I might use all the hot water then there'll be none for you.' She's playing her trump card.

'How long is it on for?'

'Hour in the morning, hour in the evening. Takes the chill off a treat.'

'Yes. Perhaps we could have it on longer now.'

'Oh no,' she says. 'It's on a timer. Can't be changed. Come on, get in. You're wasting time.'

I do as I'm told and I cringe throughout the entire experience which is as short as I can possibly make it, even though Fiona insists on having her hair washed. When we're finished I grab a towel for myself then realise I really ought to sort out Fiona first, so I wrap it around her and jump out of the bath before lifting her out. Then I grab my own towel but not before she makes a comment about my body.

'What's wrong with your stomach? Have you had a disease?'

'Where? What?'

'Those white lines?' She points to my stretch marks, the ones from my teenage pregnancy.

'Stretch marks.' I pull my towel around me.

'How have you got those?' She's frowning at me. Is she for real?

'Teenage pregnancy,' I snap.

'Ahh. Yes. The one you gave away.'

Cruel bitch. I had hoped that she was so drunk she hadn't heard me or wouldn't remember.

'You're lucky, you don't have any after having two babies.'

'Aren't I?' she says, gripping her walker with one hand while attempting to dry herself with the other.

♫♫♫

Half an hour later and we're both dried and dressed, I've even dried Fiona's fluffy, old lady hair. I wonder if I'll bring up her age and how she lied to me. She's constantly brought up my real name, but I haven't age shamed her back.

Yet.

'You'd better get your coat on if you're going out,' she says.

'I'm already wearing it.' I'm wearing my fleece; I need it indoors now that the heating has gone off. Fiona has settled herself in her chair and has a blanket over her, so she's all right.

She fumbles around in her handbag, pulls out a pen, writes me a note and gives me a ten-pound note. I wonder if there'll be enough to buy myself some Weetabix?

'What is this stuff?'

She narrows her eyes at me before replying. 'Shitting medicine,' she says and I'm so shocked to hear her swear that I laugh really loudly.

'Sorry,' I say.

'I'm glad you're so amused. Believe me, being constipated is no laughing matter.'

'No. Of course not. I'm sorry.' I don't think I am though.

She instructs me to get all the insurance stuff out and she'll have a look through it while I'm out. Then she tells me where the chemist is and I leave her flat yet again, ringing Carl's number before I'm even out of the building.

When he answers I download onto him immediately and when I've finished he laughs his head off.

'It's not funny,' I say, but even I'm laughing now. 'I want to go home.'

Twenty-eight

I wait in line at the pharmacy and when I get to the counter, I hand over the note to the assistant.

'Is this for you?'

'No? A friend.'

'Does your friend have this on prescription?'

'I don't know. She didn't say. I don't think so.'

'What's her name and address. I'll check.'

I give Fiona's name and my guess at her address as discreetly as I can and the pharmacy assistant's eyes light up with recognition.

'Isn't she on a cruise?'

So I have to explain the situation, quickly and quietly so that everyone in the queue doesn't hear me and the assistant nods and frowns accordingly. She gives me the shitting medicine in a plain bag, takes my money, there's not much change but it might be enough for Weetabix, then tells me to wait. She comes back with three stuffed carrier bags; they're taped closed so I can't see what's in them.

'These are Fiona's,' she says, smiling and handing them over. 'Her special order, they came in last week.'

'Oh, but I don't have any more money…' God knows how much these must cost.

'Don't worry, they're already paid for.'

I stagger out of the pharmacy, the bags aren't heavy, just bulky. I can't see anywhere to buy Weetabix – I was going to walk back to the Tesco Local, but I can't take these with me, far too bulky and the plastic handles are already cutting into my hands – so I go back to Fiona's flat. Maybe I'll go out again later.

As I approach the building front door I try to get the key fob out of my pocket without dropping the bags, but it's no good, I'll have to put them down to find it.

'Let me help,' a friendly voice says.

I turn and am greeted by a smiling woman.

'Thank you,' I say as she opens the door and I puff my way in.

'Just moved in?' she asks.

'No, no. Staying with a friend.' I smile and head off to Fiona's flat. The woman walks alongside me.

When I stop at Fiona's door she's still there, and opening the door to the flat next door.

'You're staying with Fiona?'

'Yes.'

'I thought she was on a cruise.'

'She was. Bit of an accident. So we're back early.'

'Accident?' the woman says, her face creased with concern. 'I'm Fran, by the way.'

I tell her my name and a short version of Fiona's mishaps. She's genuinely concerned, or I think so anyway, and asks lots of questions. She finishes up with a very pertinent one, to me, anyway.

'How are you managing with the personal things? Showering, and so on?'

I shudder at the memory of this morning's shower

fiasco, our skin on skin and Fiona's scathing comment about my stretch marks. 'Not too well.' Tomorrow I'll be wearing my swimming costume.

'I have all the paraphernalia,' she says, laughing. 'My husband broke his leg a few years ago so I have a bath seat and all sorts of aids. Happy to lend it all to Fiona.'

I almost bite Fran's hand off. I can't say yes please fast enough or loud enough.

'I'll bring them round later.' She smiles and lets herself into her own flat.

'What's that?' Fiona snaps when I burst into her living room with the bags.

'Don't know, they're yours. The pharmacy had them for you.'

'Ah, yes. Bit late now, I wanted them for my holiday. Put them in my bedroom please.'

I take them through and attempt a sneaky look at the contents but without ripping a bag open it's impossible to see anything. I've a pretty good idea what they are. *Things*.

'I met Fran, your next-door neighbour,' I tell Fiona when I return and give her the shitting medicine, and watch while she immediately takes a large swig from the bottle. 'She's going to bring some aids round. Should make life easier.'

'You didn't tell her, did you? About me?'

'Yes. She asked after you.'

'Of course she did. She's nosy. And now she knows all my business, thanks to you. Where's my change.'

I hand over the change, counting it into Fiona's hand.

'Don't worry about saying thank you,' I say with no attempt to hide my sarcasm.

'Thank you, I'm sure. And you can thank me

because I've made a good start on our claim and have even spoken to the insurance company. They've sent the claim forms through, but stupid idiots insist that we fill them in by hand and I don't have a printer. How archaic.' This from the woman who didn't know how to get email on her smart phone until recently. 'I've emailed them to you, so you can deal with that, since I've done everything else,' she adds.

'What can we do if we can't print the forms?'

Fiona shrugs her answer and I can't think of anything either.

There's a sudden, loud knock on the door.

Fiona jumps, almost out of her seat.

'If that's her next door you can tell her to push off. I don't want her *aids.*'

I answer the door and accept Fran's offerings of a framed toilet seat, and a bath seat with the immense gratitude I feel.

'The loo seat is adjustable,' she says, smiling. 'It was in the box, because it hasn't been used for a few years, but I've reassembled it and guessed at the right height. You might need to alter it. Is Fiona in?'

I want to reply that of course she is because she can't really go anywhere yet but just nod instead.

'Can I come in and say hello?'

'Yes,' I say, the smile on my face so big it makes my ears ache. Naughty really, I know.

As we're passing the bathroom Fran comes in with me and sets up the toilet seat. She lowers it a little more once she sees it in place. The bath seat, she plonks in the bath. Then we both go through to see Fiona whose pinched face and narrowed eyes speak volumes.

Fran greets Fiona like an old friend, Fiona only manages the barest of greetings.

'What *have* you done to yourself?' Fran asks, sitting down on the bouncy sofa.

'Broken my leg,' Fiona mutters, scowling.

'If you need any help at all, both of you,' Fran glances over at me, 'Just let me know, I'm a qualified nurse, you know. Retired, but still capable. And I know all the tricks. What's this?' She picks up the bottle of shitting medicine from Fiona's side table. 'Lactulose. Bit constipated? It's all the painkillers. I can give you a bit of dietary advice on that.'

Fiona scowls but I want to punch the air with joy.

'I'm making a cup of tea. Would you like one, Fran?'

Another scowl from Fiona.

Twenty minutes later, after Fran has lectured Fiona on the wisdom of drinking plenty of fluids, how incontinence can be often be cured – depending on what's caused it, not that Fiona is forthcoming on that and I don't even know how we got onto the subject – and how she recommends oil for the scar once the dressing is off, Fiona is twitching in her chair. When she starts to get up, it's Fran who jumps up as though it's an automatic reaction, puts the walking frame in position and helps Fiona to the bathroom. I don't get involved at all. When they return, Fran is smiling, and Fiona has a look of definite relief on her face, though she's not exactly smiling.

'Well, that's a start,' Fran says. 'Keep taking the lactulose but don't overdose.' She laughs, Fiona doesn't.

'I bet you found that easier with the proper toilet seat,' I say.

Fiona mutters something that sounds like agreement.

I offer another cup of tea and go off to make it while Fran settles down with Fiona, not that Fiona looks particularly happy about it.

When I come back Fran is just ending a call on her phone. Apparently, she has made an appointment with Fiona's GP and has even offered to take Fiona in her car. I feel so relaxed with Fran, who is evidently one of those super organised, capable yet easy-breezy people, that I sit down and start chatting with her. I feel as though I'm catching up with an old friend, it's the oddest and yet best feeling.

I'm soon telling her about my life and my job, meeting Carl and how keen I am to get back home. I tell her about our ordeal on the ship and in Barbados, the flight home, everything. It feels good for me to just to let off a bit of steam about it, just like I do with Carl. Fiona doesn't say much during this exchange, and I can sense her irritation at times, but I don't care. Fran is friendly and fun, telling us about her grown up son and her new granddaughter.

'You remember my Ben,' she says, turning to Fiona. 'He was a proper little handful, wasn't he, Fiona? Hard to believe he's in his thirties and a responsible father himself now.'

'Yes, he stole the milk from my doorstep.' Fiona sucks in her cheeks and sneers.

'Such a long time since they delivered milk,' Fran says. 'Those were the days, eh.'

When I ask Fran how long she's lived next door she says it's over thirty years, because she was pregnant with Ben when she moved in.

'How long have you lived here?' I ask Fiona.

'I don't know,' she snaps. 'Do you mind if we end this little gossip nest, I'm feeling very tired.

'Of course.' Fran jumps up. 'You know where I live if you need anything.'

As I see her out I casually ask if she has a printer, and she does. So on the doorstep I email her the insurance claim forms and she promises to pop the printouts round later.

Fiona is livid when I tell her.

'She'll know all our business now, not that there was much left to know after you'd told her everything.'

'So what? She seems very nice. A good neighbour.'

Fiona doesn't answer, just turns up the volume on the TV even louder.

After I've made us both a sandwich for lunch, and cleared up, there's a knock at the door. Fortunately, Fiona has nodded off in her chair. It's Fran, with the printouts.

'I've got this too,' she says, offering me a small contraption that looks a bit like a drainpipe. 'Fiona should be able to put her own socks on with it.'

'Oh brilliant,' I say, remembering this morning's nastiness when I put her socks on and didn't get the pattern on them lined up perfectly.

'All helps with her independence. Not as if you can stay here for ever.'

'Fiona thinks I can.'

'It must be hard for her; she's always been very self-reliant. And you hardly know each other really, do you?'

'Not really. We are just friends of convenience, not that I'm finding it very convenient now. Sorry, I don't mean to sound so... mean.' I half wince and half grin and Fran smirks at me before I continue. 'Shame her sons are too busy to fly over and help. You'd think one of them could find the time, wouldn't you?'

'Sons?' Fran frowns. 'Fly over from where?'

'Canada. They both live there with their families.

Fran's eyebrows knit together in an expression of

bemusement.

'I think you've got that wrong.'

'I'm sure Fiona said Canada, I'm sure she did. Anyway, wherever they are, you'd think, what with her being a widow, that one of them would make the effort.' I'm talking in a loud whisper now, fully aware that Fiona could wake up and hear and be annoyed with me for discussing her business with her 'nosy neighbour.' I'm also aware that we're chatting on the doorstep and anyone could walk through the building door and hear us. I'm also aware that I'm sounding very bitter.

'Widow?' Fran says, shaking her head. 'Fiona isn't a widow.'

'Yes. I've definitely got that right. Her husband died about ten years ago.'

'No, he didn't.'

'Maybe eleven years ago then.'

'No.' Fran shakes her head. 'Ian definitely isn't dead. I saw him in Sainsbury's only a few weeks ago. Had quite a chat and catch up with him, actually. He's a granddad too, had one of his little grandsons with him.'

'Oh, I thought they lived in Canada,' I say, confused.

'No. Not Fiona's grandson. Fiona and Ian moved here as newlyweds just after we moved in and Ian left after eighteen months. They divorced. She's not a widow. She doesn't have any grandchildren because Fiona doesn't have any children.'

Twenty-nine

Fiona's still asleep when I check on her after the revelation from Fran. She's reclined her chair, has her rug over her and the TV is playing a game show extremely loudly. She couldn't possibly have heard our conversation over that row even if she had woken up. I don't know how she can sleep through it.

I go back along the hall to my bedroom and, because it's so damn cold in this flat, I climb in under the duvet. I ring Carl.

He's as shocked as I am when I relay the story.

'Are you sure it's true?' he asks.

'Yes. Even though I've only just met Fran I believe her more than I do Fiona. They can't come and help because they don't exist.'

'You're right. Either one of my sons would drop what they were doing and help if I was in the position Fiona is. Although, it helps that they don't live in Canada.'

'Neither do Fiona's sons,' I say. 'Because they don't exist.' Carl laughs. I have to admit it is laughable. I don't really know why she's lied so much about it. 'And she led me to believe that she had lived in one of those great big houses that I imagined she would.'

'What did she say?'

'It wasn't so much what she said but what she didn't… or maybe I just assumed and she didn't correct me. I suppose you could accuse *me* of that, not telling people stuff.' I sigh, thinking about my big secret, my lifetime secret that has followed me around and made me feel guilty and sad my entire life.

'Hardly the same,' Carl says. 'You didn't actively tell people lies; you just didn't tell them anything. Really not the same at all.'

'Well, she knows about that too. I blurted it out when we'd had a few too many wines and she judged me for it. Bitch.' I'm shocked at my own description of her. Shocked but justified. 'She lied about her age too, said she was my age but she's ten years older.'

Carl laughs. 'She looks far older than you, far older than her real age actually. I thought she was a little old lady when I met her. Are you going to say anything to her, about her sons I mean?'

'She hasn't got any sons.' I snigger.

'Hey, I was thinking,' Carl starts.

'Yeah?'

'Only a few days to the weekend, why don't I come up and stay with you and we could go to the theatre or something. I usually go to a London show a couple of times a year. It would be great to go with you.'

'Stay where? Here?' Now I laugh loud.

'Yes. Why not?'

'Single bed,' I say.

'O-k-a-y, so it'll be cosy.'

I laugh again. 'Well, quite apart from that, Fiona would never, ever allow it. I can say that without a shadow of a doubt and without even asking her.'

'Ask her anyway.'

'I can't. I really can't. Anyway, I don't want to be in her debt.'

'In *her* debt. Listen to yourself. She's in *your* debt. Thousands of pounds as I recall.'

'Yes, and we're supposed to be submitting our claim today.'

'Are you going to ask her about her imaginary family?'

'I don't know.' I think for a while. 'Probably not. What's the point?'

'I'd ask, if it was me, but you must do what's best for you. I can still come up even if I can't stay with you. Text me her address and I'll see if I can get a hotel near, we can still go to the theatre together. I'll see what's on. Any preference?

♫♫♫

When Fiona wakes up we sit for an hour and a half and fill in the forms. I feel both relieved and horrified by the total amount once we're finished.

'You can take them to the post office and get us a copy each,' she says, 'Before you post them. And send them so they have to be signed for. I don't trust that insurance company.'

'Trust? Mmm. I'll go tomorrow. It's cold and dark out there now. You'll have to tell me where it is and you'll have to give me the money to pay for the postage, and the copying.'

She tuts. She actually tuts. The damn cheek of the woman.

'Okay. But I'm adding it to what you owe me. We'll

go half each.'

I let out a long sigh, mutter something about seeing what I can find for our dinner and disappear into the kitchen where, after much rummaging in the freezer, I decide on pie and chips, with tinned carrots. I'm not into all this cooking malarkey, not that this is proper cooking. I usually have my lunch at work in the garden centre restaurant. The prices are reasonable, the food is cooked fresh every day, and I get a staff discount, so it would be stupid not to. I usually just have a sandwich for tea and on the days when I don't work I usually have pasta. Fiona doesn't have any pasta, I've looked. Not one solitary bow-tie or shell anywhere. Who doesn't have pasta in their kitchen cupboards?

When it's ready I help Fiona to the dining table and bring our plates in without saying much. I then retrieve a bottle of her red wine from its hidey hole under the mop and bring in two glasses.

'Oh,' she says. 'Is that my wine?'

'Yes. Since I have NO money, I can't afford to buy any. Do you want some?' I open the bottle before she replies and pour myself a glass.

'Since you've opened it, I might as well.'

We eat and drink in silence. I'm not a big lover of meat pies, especially flaky pastry ones, but I eat it anyway. Fiona manages about half of hers, but given her size I think that's probably normal for her. I can't be bothered to do pudding so coax Fiona back to her comfy chair while I clear up. I take the wine bottle into the kitchen with me and pour myself another glass. I'm hiding out in the kitchen, it's warmer in here although I've noticed that the heating has now come on, obviously it's its time. I don't feel very charitable towards Fiona at the moment, her lies are weighing on my mind and I feel manipulated into being here, being her servant. But what else can I do? I can hardly leave her alone. Not yet. She needs help. My help.

'Carl is coming to stay at the weekend,' I say, going back into the living room with the bottle of wine which is now less than a third full. I'm tipsy and brave.

'Stay where?'

'Here. With me. In my room.'

'Oh no. NO. It's a single bed.' She smiles and waves her head about in triumph.

'I know, it'll be a squeeze. But it's only one night. More wine?'

'I'd better before you drink it all.' She holds her glass out.

'Plenty more in the cupboard.'

'No. NO. And no, your lover cannot come to stay.'

'We're going to the theatre. He's going to see what tickets he can get. I've never been to the theatre in London. Ever. I'm looking forward to it.'

'My husband and I used to go all the time.' She lets a smug smile play across her lips. 'But your lover *isn't* staying here.'

'Fine. I'll go and stay with him. He can find us hotel.'

'But you can't. I need you here. How will I get ready for bed? How will I have a shower in the morning? Who will make my meals? You can't just leave me. You're just too selfish. Too, too selfish.'

I don't answer. The truth is I'm almost enjoying this. I tell myself it's the effect of the wine that's making me so mean. I drain my glass, get up, go and get another bottle from the mop cupboard. I open it in the kitchen and refill my glass. I hold the bottle behind my back when I go into the living room.

'More wine?' I pull the new bottle out like a

magician.

'Another bottle.' Her neck wobbles with indignation. 'I'll add the cost to the list of what you owe me.'

'Okay, do. I'll subtract your list from my list of what *you* owe *me*.' I smile. I am enjoying myself too much. Naughty me. Naughty wine.

'The insurance company will pay you back for everything. You know that. We've just done the claim.' There's the indignation again.

'Not that,' I say. 'I mean the cost for my time being here, looking after you, running all your errands, your cooking, your washing. All that, you know. And the personal stuff.'

I watch her mouth drop. She blinks several times. Takes another swig of her wine and doesn't say anything.

I plonk myself on the bouncy sofa and take yet another mouthful of my wine. Even though I've eaten pie and chips and tinned carrots I can feel the wine bypassing my stomach and going straight to my brain. I hiccup loudly, then burp. Oops.

Fiona frowns. 'Oh, Eleanor,' she says. 'That's disgusting.'

'It's Pamela. How many times do I have to tell you?'

'Says Eleanor on your passport.' She grins at me in a point scoring way. Fiona is obviously suffering from wine brain, too.

'It says you're sixty on your passport.' Two can play that game.

'No, it doesn't. There's no age on passports. You're lying.'

'Your date of birth is on your passport and your age works out to sixty. At least my name is actually Pamela, even if it's my second name. So who's lying now?'

'At least I never abandoned my baby.' We both gasp after the words are out of Fiona's mouth. I can tell by the look on her face she wishes she'd never said it. I wish she'd never said it, because now, all bets are off.

'You couldn't abandon your baby, could you? Because you've never had any, have you?'

Fiona takes in such a long breath that I worry her lungs might explode. I wish I hadn't said that too, but it's too late now. Anyway, she started it. And, I think, justifying my actions to myself, accusing me of abandoning my real baby is far worse than talking about her imaginary ones. Far worse.

Fiona finally stops breathing in only then to start wailing.

'Who told you? Her next door? Nosy gossip. I told you not to get involved with her. No good ever comes from mixing with people.' She blubs and cries and I sit and watch. I do feel a little bit sorry, sorry for saying it, sorry for her, but I don't feel as sorry as she should.

Finally she stops, pulling a tissue from up her sleeve and wiping her nose.

'I'm sorry,' I say. 'That was cruel of me.'

She looks at me but doesn't answer, except her face gives her away. There's utter contempt written all over it.

'You can apologise to me now,' I say. 'Then we can move on.'

'Me apologise?'

'Yes, for your cruel remark about my baby, about abandoning him.'

'But it's true.' She looks shocked that I might find her remark upsetting.

'No, it's not. I didn't abandon him. He was taken away from me to be adopted. I was sixteen. I had no

271

say in it.' I can feel the tears coming now but I'm not going to wail like Fiona did. I have more dignity than that.

Except I don't.

Fiona sits and watches me just as I watched her.

When I'm done, she says she's sorry. I can hardly believe my ears.

We've both finished our wine but the bottle is still half full. I put the lid back on and take it, with our glasses back into the kitchen where I make us a cup of tea each and I remember to put two sugars in Fiona's.

'Thank you,' Fiona says, stiffly when I come back.

'You're welcome,' I reply, equally stiffly.

'I'm not a widow either.' Her voice is tiny, so tiny I have to ask her to repeat it because I can't believe what I've just heard.

'Oh?'

'No, my husband left me. We didn't really get on. He was far too messy for my liking.' Well, that fits.

'Oh,' is all I can manage again.

'And I've never been on a cruise before. Not been on any holidays abroad on my own. Went to Spain with Ian, my ex, once. But it was a disaster.' She offers me a weak smile.

'Really? But you knew how everything worked.' She did, she told me what we had to do, muster stations springs quickly to my mind.

'I read about it all on cruise forums, there are hundreds of them. And, although I did work for the Civil Service, I was just a clerk, filing nonsense and counting the years until I could get out of there and get my Civil Service pension.' She's staring off into the distance, remembering how she felt then, I suspect. 'I used the tax-free lump sum to pay for my cruise.'

I can't quite believe Fiona's sudden burst of honesty. It's so out of character, or maybe she's relieved to drop her façade now.

'Are you leaving off your painkillers again tonight?' I ask, trying to subtly remind her how much wine she's had.

'No, I've already taken them.'

That probably explains the loose tongue.

'Would you like some pudding now. Ice cream and fruit?'

When I come back from the kitchen Fiona nods at me.

'I've been thinking,' she says. 'On this one occasion your lover can stay. Just the one night though and I'd prefer it if you kept him in your room. I don't want to see him or him to see me, like this.' She waves her arm up and down her body.

'He's seen you already. Remember. He drove us to the airport. You sat next to him in the front seat.'

Fiona purses her lips. 'Even so…' she says, turning away. 'And don't let him leave his things in the bathroom, you know, shavers and man hair and stuff. And don't let him pee on my toilet seat.' She shudders. No wonder her marriage didn't last long.

'Okay.'

♫♫♫

Carl arrives at noon on Saturday. He's carrying a big bouquet of flowers.

'Oh, they're lovely,' I say, holding out my hand to take them.

'They're not for you. They're for the lady of the house.'

'She doesn't want to see you. I've told you this.' I

can't help laughing. 'You've got to stay in my room out of sight.'

'Like hell,' he says and steps around me, kissing me softly on the cheek as he passes. 'Straight ahead, is it?'

'Nooo.'

'Hello, Fiona,' he says, laying the bouquet across her lap.

I watch her simper and grin and smile like a baby. She loves the attention.

Maybe that's all she wanted all along.

Thirty

Six months later...

It seems a long time ago and yet it seems like yesterday since we became friends, me and Fiona.

Carl helped. Charmed her, smarmed her even. Now they too are good friends, though not as good friends as Fiona and Fran.

The events of the weekend when Carl came to stay are still vivid in my memory. After he had charmed Fiona he asked me why it was so cold in the flat. I told him the heating wasn't on, wasn't allowed to be on. He hunted out the boiler controls, adjusted the timer and before long we were toasty warm. When I said that she probably kept it cold because of the cost, he offered to subsidise her gas bill while I was staying there. Of course Fiona accepted; a leopard never quite changes its spots.

We went to a show in the West End that evening, a play Carl had picked out and I loved, though I'm hard pushed now, even six months later to remember the exact plot. All I do know is that I enjoyed it, and the dinner we had beforehand. Later, when we were cuddled up at night in the single bed, we giggled ourselves to sleep.

Fran saved us that weekend too. She cooked Fiona's evening meal so we could leave early for dinner, she stayed and ate with Fiona – I hadn't realised at that point that Fran was a widow – a real one, and fairly recently too. The next morning, while we slept on after our late night, it was Fran who came in early, showered Fiona without any fuss or getting soaked to the skin – unlike me she didn't have to get in with her – and made Fiona's favourite sickly sweet breakfast. It was also Fran who moved in less than a week later when I finally went home with Carl, who drove up to collect me. Although I've come back and stayed several times now, sometimes just me, but often with Carl too. As I said, we're all good friends. So good in fact that Fran persuaded Fiona to seek medical help for her bladder problem, it's early days yet but Fiona is hopeful, more, she says, than she's ever been.

So here we are again, me and Carl, having spent the night in Fiona's spare bedroom, again. We have a double bed here now; it didn't take too much juggling of the furniture to fit it in. And we've redecorated the room to our taste, at Fiona's insistence, gone is the beige drabness of before. That also is true of the whole flat, though not by our doing. Once Fiona had unburdened herself of her lies – she'd been telling the *family* story for so long she almost believed it herself – she started to fill her home with treasures and knick-knacks. Pride of place among them is a photo of the four of us, Fiona, Fran, Carl and me, riding the London Eye. Of course it was the first time I'd been on it, but Carl and Fran had been before, and it was Fiona's first time as well – she even admitted it. She was as excited as a kid, so was I and I have that same photo framed on my wall at home too.

Fiona is almost back to normal physically and last night we took the momentous step of booking another cruise – Caribbean, the same itinerary as before. The four of us. It's taken this long for the insurance company to pay up, but they came good in the end and paid the whole claim, apart from the few taxi rides I couldn't get receipts for. Thank God Carl stepped in and became my driver or I would have been greatly out of pocket. I've been able to pay Carl back – he loaned me the money to pay off my credit card, I could never have done it myself and would have incurred excessive interest. I'm looking forward to seeing all the islands I never got the chance to see last time. Carl is going to hire a car when we stop off in Barbados – we're there for two days – and he's going to take me to meet what's left of his family over there.

I'm still at Jolliffe's, so is Derek, still on till number four, still getting his hair pudding-basined once a year, but everything else has changed. Tim and Cherry finally accepted an offer from a big chain – 'Too good to turn down, Pam,' Tim had said – and now I'm working in the office. Me, the girl who didn't even finish her schooling. It seems I've got quite a flair for paperwork. Who knew? It also means I'm no longer out in all weathers humping sacks and pots around, and to my surprise I don't mind at all. I've taken quite a liking to a regular manicure, and getting soil under my nails everyday no longer appeals.

So now I come to the elephant in the room, no not my name – you're singing that song again, aren't you? Never mind. I don't.

No, the elephant is my baby boy, the one that was

taken away from me. The one I couldn't keep.

I got on that website eventually, registered my details and crossed my fingers that I'd be matched up with my son whilst also hoping nothing would come of it. Well, it didn't take long for a match to be made. We were put in touch and talked first via email and then on the phone. He had a lovely childhood, so maybe it was for the best. He has a wife and two children – so I'm a granny. But I'm jumping ahead of myself, I haven't met my grandchildren; I haven't even met my son in person yet. That's why we're here, because he lives near London and today's the day. We're meeting for lunch and I'm petrified – even though he's been looking for me for years, since he was eighteen.

I've answered a hundred or more questions, he knows the truth about his conception, how I cannot tell him who his father is, either skinny little Alan Wilson or hunky footballer David Woodward. Ironically, his name is David too, though he prefers Davy. He knows why I couldn't keep him, how I had no say in it. Over the phone and via video calls we've cried together and we've laughed together.

♫♫♫

'Good luck, Pam,' Fiona says. Yes, she calls me Pam, that's how good our friendship is now. 'It'll go great. And if it doesn't,' she whispers into my ear as she hugs me, 'You know we're just around the corner.'

Carl gives me a hug and a kiss. He doesn't say anything, just grips my hand before they walk away, Carl, Fiona and Fran. They're having lunch in a pub just around the corner and if things don't work out here or he doesn't turn up I can just walk round and join them.

I glance up at the entrance of the restaurant Davy's suggested, take a deep breath and climb the couple of steps before pushing on the door. It's plush and expensive and I feel underdressed in my best summer dress, new shoes which are already rubbing my heels, and my matching handbag. I'm early, so I've set myself up for looking a fool if he's a no show.

I give his name to the waiter and am shown to a table. He's already there, Davy. He jumps up and we just stare at each other, taking everything in, yet hardly seeing each other through the tears. I'm trembling and so is he. He's tall, much taller than me, not that that is difficult. His hair is short and wavy and fair like mine. His build is hunky, not weedy like Alan Wilson. His eyes are like mine and so is his nose. I can even see a little of Keith in his mannerisms, fortunately he doesn't seem to have Keith's mean streak.

We sit down and we're still staring. I cannot believe I made this person, this grown man. I see the similarities between us and I see the similarities between him and the man I think is his father. Carl has done some research, discreetly asked some old friends, checked online, and he's discovered that David Woodward is dead – sadly only recently. And I wonder when would be a good time to tell Davy this.

'I've wondered about you my whole life,' Davy says, after we've ordered, though it was a struggle to concentrate on the menu. His adoptive parents were always honest with him, telling him how they chose him especially because his birth mother couldn't keep him.

'Me too.' I dab at my eyes again. I cannot believe I am here; he is here, we are together. 'You're my only blood relative, all my family are gone now.'

'No,' he says, reaching over and holding my hand.

'You have a whole new family now. My children are your blood relatives too.

'Of course. Of course.' I feel silly now, but he smiles and makes me feel better.

He pulls out his phone and flicks to the photos.

'I took this one this morning.' He shows me a golden-haired child, waving a fairy wand. 'That's Lula and here's Alex. They can't wait to meet you.'

I've seen a hundred photos of them already, but I'm looking forward to seeing them in real life.

'I thought you and Carl could come and visit next weekend?' His voice is tentative.

'Yes. I'm sure we can arrange it.' Carl doesn't work weekends and since moving into the office at Jolliffe's, neither do I.

Then we talk, and we talk and we talk and it's all trivia and nonsense really, but we've got a lifetime of catching up do to, his lifetime. And mine.

THE END.

From the author, CJ Morrow:

Dear Reader

Thank you so much for reading **It's Pamela Rigby Actually**. I hope you enjoyed reading it as much as I enjoyed writing it.

I was on a Caribbean cruise when I started to write this book. It was always going to be about Pamela and her attempt to not live down to her namesake. However, the story changed dramatically when my husband broke his leg – he slipped on a door mat just as the ship lurched, he certainly didn't do what Fiona did!

We were, just like Pam and Fiona, disembarked from the ship in Barbados and my husband went to hospital. Some, though obviously not all, of the details are based on our experiences. When you are a writer – almost no experience is wasted. Writing this book has also been cathartic for me; my husband was always my top priority but we both found being stranded very stressful. Fortunately, he is young enough and fit enough to be fully recovered as I write this (June 2020).

Happy reading and I hope you never break a leg in the middle of the Atlantic, or anywhere else for that matter.

CJ

Other books by CJ Morrow

Printed in Great Britain
by Amazon

44213853R00162